Homer's Odyssey: A Retelling in Prose

David Bruce

Published by David Bruce, 2022.

This is a work of fiction. Similarities to real people, places, or events are entirely coincidental.

HOMER'S ODYSSEY: A RETELLING IN PROSE

First edition. July 7, 2022.

ISBN: 979-8201165970

Written by David Bruce.

Table of Contents

Homer's
Odyssey:
A Retelling in Prose

Cover Image:
Ulysses Recognised by his Dog Argos. Robert Brown. English School. Active between 1836-1859. Engraving.

***

Educate Yourself
Read Like A Wolf Eats
Be Excellent to Each Other
Books Then, Books Now, Books Forever

***

Do you know a language other than English? If you do, I give you permission to translate this book, copyright your translation, publish or self-publish it, and keep all the royalties for yourself. (Do give me credit, of course, for the original retelling.)

I would like to see my retellings of classic literature used in schools, so I give permission to the country of Finland (and all other countries) to buy one copy of this eBook and give copies to all students forever. I also give permission to the state of Texas (and all other states) to buy one copy of this eBook and give copies to all students forever. I also give permission to all teachers to buy one copy of this eBook and give copies to all students forever.

Teachers need not actually teach my retellings. Teachers are welcome to give students copies of my eBooks as background material. For example, if they are teaching Homer's *Iliad* and *Odyssey*, teachers are welcome to give students copies of my *Virgil's* Aeneid: *A Retelling in Prose* and tell students, "Here's another ancient epic you may want to read in your spare time."

***

Note

If you are unfamiliar with the Trojan War and such concepts as *xenia*, read the "Background Information" appendix first.

Xenia

The guest-host relationship. Civilized people of the ancient world followed rules of hospitality. Uncivilized people (and other beings) did not.

Chapter 1: Athena and Telemachus

Muse, goddess of inspiration, please help me. I have an important story to tell, and I need help to tell it. Please use me to tell the story.

Help me to tell the story of a man of twists and turns. His mind twists and turns to seek solutions to problems. His journey twists and turns in the Mediterranean — and beyond. His strategy conquered Troy. He is a man who tried mightily — but failed — to bring his companions home, fools though they sometimes were.

Help me to tell the story of Odysseus, the great individualist and mastermind and man who feels pain deeply.

All other heroes of the Trojan War were home by now — or dead. Only Odysseus remained away from his home. Odysseus was kept captive by Calypso the sea-goddess.

Still, most gods and goddesses pitied Odysseus now, so long absent from his island kingdom: Ithaca. But Poseidon, the great ruler of the seas, did not pity Odysseus. No, Poseidon was still angry. Poseidon still wanted Odysseus to suffer, to stay away from home, to long to see his day of homecoming. But Poseidon was now absent, away on a visit to the Ethiopians.

Zeus, the king of gods and men, at home on Olympus among the gods and goddesses, spoke his mind about another homecoming: "Mortals have no shame, blaming the gods as they so often do for their own problems. Look at Aegisthus. Paris, Prince of Troy, visited Menelaus, King of Lacedaemon, and then ran away with his lawful wife, Helen, taking her to Troy. Angry, Menelaus and his older brother, Agamemnon, took hundreds of ships loaded with soldiers and fought a ten-year war to get Helen back. Clearly, pursuing another man's wife is destructive, and Aegisthus should have realized that. But he didn't, and he looked with desire at Clytemnestra, the lawful wife of Agamemnon. I even sent the messenger-god Hermes to tell him to leave Clytemnestra alone. Did he listen? No. Did he pay the penalty? Yes. Aegisthus killed Agamemnon when he returned home, and Agamemnon's son, Orestes, kept anger in his heart. When Orestes became a young man, he exacted proper revenge and killed Aegisthus and avenged his father, exactly as a man ought to do."

Athena, goddess of wisdom, sensing an opportunity to act and to help her favorite mortal, spoke to her father, Zeus, "Father, all you say is true. Aegisthus deserved what he got. He did the wrong thing, and he paid the proper penalty.

"But what about Odysseus? He has been cursed by fate. He is far from home, held captive on an island by Calypso. He longs to see his day of homecoming. He longs to see even the smoke of cooking fires rising from Ithaca. Is Odysseus your enemy? Has Odysseus shown you disrespect?"

Zeus replied to his favorite daughter, "No, Athena. Odysseus is not my enemy. Odysseus has never shown me disrespect. But Poseidon, the earth-shaking god of earthquakes and of the sea, hates Odysseus, who hurt his son, the one-eyed Cyclops Polyphemus. Poseidon knows that he cannot kill Odysseus — Odysseus is not fated to die just yet — but Poseidon knows that he can cause Odysseus great trouble and delay his day of homecoming.

"Still, Poseidon is gone now. So let us think together how we can help Odysseus to return home."

"If you mean what you say," Athena replied, "then send Hermes to Calypso to tell her that she must let Odysseus go free so he can attempt to return to Ithaca. I, meanwhile, will go to Ithaca, to see his son, Telemachus, and help him to grow up.

"I will put courage in Prince Telemachus' heart. I will advise him to call an assembly and speak out against the suitors who are courting his mother — Odysseus' wife, Penelope — even though Odysseus is still alive. I will advise him to speak out against the suitors who are treating him and his household badly, slaughtering his sheep, pigs, cows, and goats, partying on his property while showing him disrespect. I will also advise him to visit the mainland, to go to Pylos and Lacedaemon to seek news of his father.

"The son of a hero should also be a hero. It is time for Telemachus to stop being a boy and start being a man. Perhaps he will do a deed that will be remembered."

Zeus agreed with her plan.

Athena armed herself with a spear and disguised herself as a mortal man: Mentes, lord of the Taphians. Then she flew — the gods and goddesses have that power — down to Odysseus' palace on Ithaca to see Telemachus and the swaggering suitors for herself.

The suitors were behaving exactly as she had known they would. They were playing dice and drinking wine while servants heaped tables in Odysseus' Great Hall with huge platters of meat — meat butchered from Telemachus' own animals. Athena stood in the doorway, waiting to be noticed and hoping to be welcomed.

As all know, although not all act on their knowledge, strangers ought to be noticed and welcomed. What is the difference between a civilized society and an uncivilized society? A civilized society feeds the hungry. A civilized society takes care of the needs of guests. A civilized society treats strangers as guests. An uncivilized society does not do these things.

Of course, both host and guest must be civilized. The host must not rob or murder his guest. A guest must not rob or murder his host. A host must feed his guest, give the guest water to wash with, and give the guest a place to sleep. A guest must not run away with his host's wife, as Paris, prince of Troy, did, and a guest must not stay too long, must not waste the property of his host, and must not treat his host with disrespect, as the suitors were doing to Telemachus.

The proper relationship between guest and host has a name: *xenia*. A civilized society is a society that observes *xenia*. An uncivilized society is a society that does not observe *xenia*.

Telemachus saw Athena, disguised as Mentes, first. She, of course, appeared as a mortal man and not as a goddess to him. Having been raised correctly, he went immediately to her, horrified that perhaps that she had been waiting a long time at the doorway for someone to notice her and to greet her. He shook her right hand, and then he took her spear, both to relieve her of her burden and to disarm her. Always, it is a good idea to disarm a guest until you are sure that the guest knows and observes *xenia* properly.

He led Athena into the Great Hall, put her spear on a rack filled with other spears, and then led her to a high seat of honor among the tables laden with platters piled high with meat. They sat together, a servant brought them water so they could wash their hands, and they ate. Only after they had eaten did Telemachus, who had been raised properly, ask her who she was. He hoped to learn, if he could, news of his father. The suitors, having feasted while ignoring Telemachus' guest, danced to the music of the bard Phemius, a man who, like many of the other servants in the palace, was forced to serve the suitors. Unfortunately, some servants were loyal to the suitors, not to Telemachus.

Telemachus unburdened himself to Athena: "Look at these young men! They party every day, eating food that does not belong to them and drinking wine that does not belong to them. Their days are filled with games and feasts and music. They take and take, and they give nothing in return. If only my father, Odysseus, were alive, they would run away from the palace as fast as they can. But my father is dead. He will never return to Ithaca. But tell me about yourself. What is your story?"

"My name is Mentes," Athena said. "I had heard that my friend of long ago, Odysseus, had returned to Ithaca, but I see that I was wrong. The gods must be preventing his return. I will tell you that you are wrong about the death of your father. I know that Odysseus is alive. No, I am not a prophet, but the gods sometimes speak to people who are not prophets. Your father will return to Ithaca soon. But tell me about yourself. What is your story? You certainly resemble your father."

"Odysseus is said to be my father," Telemachus said, "but sometimes I wonder if that is true. We can know for certain who our mother is, but does anyone truly know who is his father? I wish that my father were here, and yes, people say that Odysseus is my father."

"All will be well in the end," Athena said. "Penelope has given birth to a fine son. But what is going on in the palace? Anyone would think from all the food and wine that this is a wedding-feast, but the young men are not acting like guests at a wedding. Anyone would think that they are uncivilized delinquents rather than guests."

"They are courting my mother — against her will! She is the wife of a man whose white bones lie unburied somewhere," Telemachus replied. "I wish my father had died among friends. If he had died at Troy, his friends would have raised a burial-mound for him and have properly mourned his death. If he had returned home to Ithaca and died, we would have raised a burial-mound for him and have properly mourned his death. But no, he died friendless and alone, far from home.

"The suitors are uncivilized. They waste all my possessions. They party all day. My mother does not know what to do. She does not know whether her husband is alive or dead, and therefore she does not know whether to remain faithful to a living husband or to seek a new husband because she is a widow. If Odysseus is alive, Penelope has a duty to remain faithful to him. If Odysseus is dead, Penelope ought to remarry. In the meantime, as we wait for reliable news about whether Odysseus is alive or dead, the suitors run wild. Someday, they will try to kill me to get me out of the way. There are over a hundred suitors. What can I do against so many?"

"The suitors are behaving shamefully," Athena said, "but if they knew Odysseus, they would leave the palace quickly. I know Odysseus, and he would not allow the suitors to run wild. The last time I saw Odysseus, he was on a mission to get poison to put on the heads of his arrows. If that Odysseus were to return to Ithaca, the suitors would soon be dead.

"But Odysseus is not here. You, Telemachus, are here. Think. What can you do to rid your palace of the suitors? You are your father's son, and you know your father would not permit such outrageous actions in his own palace.

"Listen to me. In the morning, call an assembly of the men on Ithaca. Speak out against the suitors. Let the other men know what the suitors are doing. They are running wild. They are uncivilized. They do not respect *xenia*. They take and take, and they give nothing in return. They produce nothing of value. They live only to eat and to produce human excrement.

"In the assembly, tell the suitors to leave your palace and to return to their own homes. Tell them that with the lords of Ithaca and the gods as your witnesses.

"As for your mother, let her act as she thinks best. If she thinks that she ought to remarry, let her return to the house of her father so that he can arrange a suitable marriage for her. A marriage with one of the suitors is not a suitable marriage — not when they act like this!

"Also, Telemachus, get a ship ready and journey to the mainland to seek news of your father. Perhaps you will hear something of value. First go to Pylos to consult Nestor, the wise old man of the Greek forces during the Trojan War. Then visit Lacedaemon, where Menelaus is king. See what, if anything, they know of your father.

"If you hear that Odysseus is still alive, then wait one more year for him to return.

"But if you hear definitively that he is dead, then return home, raise a burial-mound for him, and mourn him. Find a husband for your mother. And then take thought of how to kill the suitors. They will not leave willingly — not when they can party at no cost to themselves here. You are not a boy any longer, so it is time for you to grow up. A beard is on your face, yet you are clinging to the ways of boyhood.

"Think of Orestes, a young man of your own age. Aegisthus killed Orestes' father, so Orestes killed Aegisthus. For this righteous killing, Orestes has achieved renown throughout the world. If you succeed in killing the suitors, you also will achieve renown throughout the world.

"Telemachus, you are tall and handsome. Be brave, too. I must leave now and return to my ship, but think about and remember everything that I have advised you."

A proper host, Telemachus replied, "I will. You have advised me the way a father would advise a son. But stay a while. Bathe, and then return to your ship bearing a gift from me to you. This is the way that *xenia* works."

Athena, pleased with Telemachus, replied, "No, I must be going now. But I will return. Keep the gift until I return."

Then Athena, shape-shifter extraordinaire, turned herself into a bird and flew away, letting Telemachus know that he had been honored with a visit from the goddess Athena.

Meanwhile, in the Great Hall, Phemius the bard sang of the Homecomings of Heroes from the Trojan War, a song that did not include the homecoming of Odysseus, whom Calypso was holding captive on an island.

In her quarters, Penelope heard the song of the bard and wondered whether she was a widow or a wife. If she was a widow, her society demanded that she remarry and go to live with her new husband, turning over the palace to Telemachus. But if she was a wife with a living husband, her society demanded that she remain faithful to Odysseus and stay on Ithaca to preserve his property as much as she was able to.

Upset by the bard's song, Penelope went to the Great Hall, accompanied by two serving-women. Ever-prudent Penelope would never appear before men she was not related to without serving-women to accompany her.

"Phemius!" she cried. "Stop singing that song! It breaks my heart, knowing that Odysseus has not returned home although twenty years have passed. I need my husband here — now."

Telemachus spoke up, "Don't blame the bard for Odysseus' absence. So many warriors failed to return home from Troy. Let the bard sing. Go back to your quarters and attend to your work. I will look after things here."

Telemachus disliked his mother's appearing before the suitors, although she never appeared before them alone. Wild young men who drink and party are dangerous.

Penelope obeyed her son. She wanted him to grow up, become a man, and take command. In ancient Greece, women obeyed men. She left the Great Hall, and in her quarters, she wept for Odysseus.

In the Great Hall, the suitors spoke — loudly — about Penelope's beauty, and about how they wanted to go to bed with her.

Telemachus spoke to the suitors, "In the morning, I will call a council of all the men of Ithaca. You suitors who wish to marry my mother — although she is unwilling to remarry — must leave my palace and return to your own homes. You take and take, but you never give. Go to your own homes and devour your own possessions! Enough! I pray to Zeus that all of you will receive justice — justice of a kind that will make you regret what you have done to my possessions."

The suitors were shocked. Telemachus had never spoken to them with such daring before.

Antinous, one of the leaders of the suitors, spoke up: "Telemachus, you must have received encouragement from a god, if such a thing were possible. Otherwise, you would not dare to talk to us in such a way. Still, I doubt that you will ever be crowned King of Ithaca."

"If the crown ever comes to me, so be it," Telemachus replied. "Father Zeus can award the crown to whomever he desires. Still, many princes are on Ithaca, and one of them may hold the crown, now that Odysseus is dead. But whether I ever become King of Ithaca, I intend to be king of my own palace. Odysseus won this property for me, and I intend to keep it."

Eurymachus, the other leader of the suitors, countered, "All of this lies in the hands of the gods, but yes, of course, by all means you are the ruler here. I would be a hypocrite if I were to say anything but the truth. But who was your guest just now, the one who left so quickly? Did he bring news of your father?"

"My father will never return to Ithaca," Telemachus said. "I no longer listen to the rumors that are spread by strangers, although my mother insists on questioning them. But the guest was Mentes, a man who is a friend to my family from long ago." However, Telemachus knew that his guest had been the goddess Athena, not a mortal man.

The suitors resumed their partying, and then, late at night, they left the palace until the following morning.

Telemachus prepared for bed. An aged servant named Eurycleia, whom Laertes, Telemachus' grandfather, had bought when she was young and pretty, but had never bedded because he did not want to upset his wife, lit his way with a torch. That night, Telemachus did not sleep, but lay awake, thinking over everything that Athena had said to him.

Chapter 2: Telemachus Calls a Council and Sets Sail

In the morning, Telemachus arose and sent out heralds to summon the men of Ithaca to a council — the first called since Odysseus had left to fight at Troy twenty years ago.

The men arrived quickly — and so did the suitors.

The people at the council could easily be divided into two groups. One group consisted of the aged: men who had been too old to fight in the Trojan War twenty years ago, and who were very old now. The other group consisted of young men: Telemachus, and the suitors, many of whom were a few years older than he.

No middle-aged men were here. The men who would have been middle-aged now had gone to Troy with Odysseus, and they had perished either fighting there or trying to return home after the war. In addition, few fathers were present. Mostly, sons and grandfathers were present. Most of the fathers had left Ithaca to go with Odysseus to Troy and had died.

A generation of very old men, and a generation of very young men who had grown up without fathers to teach them the correct way to behave, attended the council.

Telemachus looked like a magnificent young man. Even now, Athena was looking after him. In the guise of a mature father figure named Mentes, she had encouraged Telemachus to take steps to grow up. He had taken the first step and called the council, so Athena, shape-shifter extraordinaire, rewarded him by making him taller, stronger, and more handsome.

But first to speak was an old man named Aegyptius. Old men should always be respected and listened to. He had four sons. One had gone to Troy with Odysseus and had died, two worked hard on their father's farm, and one, despite his father's best efforts, ran wild with the other suitors.

Aegyptius spoke up: "Who has called the council, and for what purpose? Is an attack imminent? Is a crisis underway? Let the man speak, and may Zeus be with him."

May Zeus be with him — these are lucky words, Telemachus thought.

Telemachus spoke up, addressing his first words to Aegyptius to show respect: "I called the council. No attack is imminent. No public crisis is underway. Instead, the crisis is in my palace. My father — my protector — is dead. And now my palace is besieged with suitors who take and take and never give. They claim to woo my mother, but they do it against her will, and not in the proper way. They should go to her father and talk to him, making a case for being a good husband and a good son-in-law. They should give gifts to Penelope. Penelope's father should choose the best man for her to marry. But the suitors don't do that. Instead, they infest my palace. They drink my wine, and they slaughter my sheep, pigs, cows, and goats to fuel their feasts. Tell the suitors to leave my palace. They are not respecting *xenia*, and they are not respecting the gods who wish *xenia* to be properly observed. I am just a boy, and my father is dead. I have never been a warrior, and I cannot fight off over one hundred suitors."

Telemachus was so angry that he started crying. Heroes of the ancient world sometimes cried. Even Achilles, the greatest warrior of the Trojan War, cried. The old men of the council pitied Telemachus, but Antinous, one of the leaders of the suitors, spoke up first:

"Don't blame the suitors for your problems, Telemachus. Instead, blame your mother. For nearly four years, I and the other suitors have been courting her, and she has been lying to us, leading us on. Her most recent trick was to set up a loom and say that she intended to weave a shroud for her father-in-law, old Laertes, in preparation for the day he dies. For three years, she led us on, promising to marry one of us once the weaving was done. By day, she would weave the shroud. By night, she would unweave what she had woven. Finally, one of her serving-women told us what she was doing. We caught her in the act of unweaving the shroud. We forced her to finish it.

"So, Telemachus, let us give *you* advice. Tell her to marry one of us, whomever she chooses. Until she does, we will continue to court her, to drink your wine, and to slaughter your animals to fuel the feasts we eat in your palace. If she refuses to marry us, her good reputation for remaining faithful to Odysseus will grow, but your possessions will diminish. We suitors have no intention of leaving your palace until Penelope remarries."

"What you ask is unreasonable," Telemachus replied. "I will not make my mother remarry. To do that I would have to force her out of the palace and give her back to her father. I am not going to do that to the mother who raised me. Instead, you and the other suitors must leave my palace. Find somewhere else to feast! Devour your own animals! Respect the gods who decree that *xenia* should be followed! I pray to Zeus that you be punished for all you have done!"

Zeus, the god of *xenia*, heard Telemachus, and sent him a bird-sign: Two eagles glided down to just above the council, they fought, and they flew away to the right — the lucky side.

A bird-sign is an omen, yes, but a seer must interpret omens.

Just such a seer was present in the council. Halitherses, old warrior and reliable seer, spoke up, "Men of Ithaca, listen to me. Suitors of Penelope, this especially concerns you. Odysseus is not dead. He is somewhere near, and he is plotting bloody vengeance against the suitors. It's best for us old men to find a way to stop the suitors from besieging Odysseus' palace — or for the suitors to stop on their own. When Odysseus left for Troy, I prophesized that twenty years would pass before he returned home. The twenty years are over, and now, just as I predicted, he is returning home."

Now Eurymachus, the other leader of the suitors, spoke up, making clear his intentions and the intentions of all the suitors: "Shut up, old man, old seer, old prophet. Birds are common, and not every bird bears a message from Zeus. I know more than you do. What do I know? I know that Odysseus is dead and that he will never return to Ithaca — and I wish that you were dead, too. Unless you keep your 'prophecies' to yourself and stop trying to incite the boy against us, we suitors will force you to pay for your actions with a heavy fine.

"And let me say this in public to Telemachus. Force your mother to return to her father so that he can marry her off. Unless she does, we will continue to act as we have always acted, taking and taking and never giving. And why shouldn't we? Is there anyone for us suitors to be afraid of? We certainly are not afraid of Telemachus, a whiny little mama's boy! We also are not afraid of prophecies, of seers, and dare I say it — I do! — of the gods who put prophecies in the seers' mouths. We will continue to woo Penelope and to feast in Odysseus' palace."

Telemachus said to Eurymachus, "The gods and the men of Ithaca know how you and the other suitors are acting. Now I intend to sail to the mainland with a ship and twenty crewmembers. I sail in search of news of my father. If I hear that Odysseus is still alive, then I will wait for one more year for him to return. If I hear definitively that he is dead, then I will return home, build a burial-mound for him, and mourn him. I will also find a husband for my mother."

Mentor, another old man of Ithaca, spoke up against the suitors: "Men of Ithaca, we remember Odysseus as a good and a wise king. His son and his possessions should be treated with respect. I do not envy the suitors with all their partying. They do not think that Odysseus will ever return home. They do not think that they will ever have to face justice and pay for the crimes they have committed. But can't we do something? We are old, and we are few. The suitors are young, and they are many. Still, must we old men be silent?"

A third suitor, Leocritus, spoke out: "Mentor and you other old men of Ithaca, don't try to fight us. You would lose. Even if Odysseus with all of his armed men were to return to Ithaca, Penelope would get no joy from him. Instead, we suitors would quickly kill Odysseus and all of his armed men. Let the council end now. You can do nothing to stop us."

The council ended. The old men went to their homes, and the suitors went to Telemachus' palace.

Calling the council had failed to remove the suitors from the palace. The mature men of Ithaca were too old to help Telemachus remove them.

Still, Telemachus had succeeded in making known his objections to how the suitors were acting. No one could now say that he had never objected to the suitors' actions. The old men of Ithaca now knew how bad things were in Odysseus' palace. They had heard rumors, yes, but rumors can be false. Now they knew that the worst rumors were true.

Telemachus walked along the beach and prayed, "Athena, thank you for appearing to me and giving me advice, but look at what is happening! The suitors ignore my wishes!"

Athena heard the prayer and appeared. This time she assumed the shape of wise old Mentor, and again she advised Telemachus: "You have good blood in you, and I think you have your father's spirit. Your father was a brave man, and you can be a brave man as well. The suitors are running wild, and they will pay with their blood for what they have done and are doing. But you have a journey to make. Go back to the palace and keep an eye on the suitors.

But quietly get ready provisions for your journey: wine and barley-meal. I will arrange for you to use a ship with twenty crewmembers."

Telemachus returned to the palace, and the suitors, as usual, were slaughtering his sheep, pigs, cows, and goats, preparing to feast and to party.

Antinous, hoping that Telemachus was now the boy of old after his brief rebellion of calling and speaking out at the council, grabbed his hand and did not let go, saying to him, "Telemachus, young person, feast with us and drink with us. We will give you whatever you need. You say that you want a ship with twenty crewmembers? We'll arrange that for you."

Indeed we will, Antinous thought. *That way, the twenty crewmembers can keep an eye on you so that you don't become a danger to us.*

"How can I enjoy the feast now that I have grown up?" Telemachus asked. "When I was young, you moved into the palace. I was too young to realize what you were doing and how badly you were acting. But now I have grown up. How can I enjoy you wasting my possessions and giving nothing in return? But yes, I will go in a ship to the mainland — as a passenger. Obviously, you are not going to allow me to be the master of the ship."

Let him think that I will allow the suitors to provide me with a ship, Telemachus thought. *I will be gone before they discover that they have been deceived.*

Telemachus withdrew his hand from Antinous' grasp and walked away.

The suitors began to talk about him.

One suitor said, "He's starting to think deep, dark thoughts about us. Why does he want to go to the mainland? Perhaps he wants to hire mercenaries to kill us. Or maybe he wants to get poison to slip into the wine we drink."

"This can work to our advantage," another suitor said. "His father drowned while on a voyage, so why can't Telemachus drown while he is on his voyage? That way, when one of us marries Penelope, we can also divide Telemachus' goods — he won't be needing them!"

Meanwhile, Telemachus and Eurycleia, an aged and loyal servant, went to Odysseus' storeroom, and Telemachus told her his plan to visit the mainland and ordered her to prepare wine and barley-meal for him to take on his journey.

His plan shocked Eurycleia: "Why must you go to the mainland to seek news of your father? Won't the suitors seize their opportunity and kill you? Shouldn't you stay here to guard your possessions?"

"I have the help of the gods," Telemachus replied, "but promise me that you won't tell my mother that I am gone — at least not until ten or twelve days have passed. She won't miss me. She will think that I have gone to visit one of the farms. Perhaps she will think that I have gone to visit old Laertes, my grandfather."

Eurycleia promised, making a vow to the gods that she would not tell Penelope. The provisions having been prepared, Telemachus returned to the Great Hall and the suitors.

Meanwhile, Athena — disguised this time as Telemachus himself — arranged for twenty crewmembers, and she borrowed the use of a ship from Noëmon. Telling all the crewmembers to go to the ship at nightfall, she made sure that all was prepared. She then went to Odysseus' palace and — as the gods can do — made the suitors sleepy. The suitors left the palace to find their beds, and Athena, who now appeared in the form of Mentor, told Telemachus, "The ship is ready."

They went to the ship, and Telemachus assumed command, giving orders to his friends, "Let's load the ship with provisions from my storeroom. No one except for one servant knows of the journey we will make. Not even my mother knows."

They loaded up the ship and set sail. With the sails filled with wind, they drank wine, but first they poured out an offering to honor Athena. All night the ship sailed.

Chapter 3: Telemachus and King Nestor

At dawn, the ship pulled into the harbor of Pylos.

On shore, King Nestor and his people were sacrificing bulls to the gods and preparing a feast. One time that people in ancient Greece could legitimately enjoy a feast was during a sacrifice to the gods. King Nestor, who was both old and wise, understood the rules of feasting and of *xenia*.

The men on the ship got onto shore, Telemachus last of all. This displeased Athena, who was still disguised as Mentor: "Telemachus, you are the leader of this expedition. Act like it! Don't bring up the rear! Lead! You undertook this expedition in order to discover news of your father, so now go to King Nestor and seek the information you desire."

King Nestor was a good person to ask about Odysseus. He had served in the Trojan War with Odysseus and knew him well. Even then, King Nestor was too old to fight, but he shared his wisdom with Agamemnon, leader of the Greek forces.

Telemachus, still timid, still hung back.

"How can I approach King Nestor? I am so young, and he is so worthy of respect."

"Speak, and the gods will give you the right words," Athena answered.

Athena led the way to King Nestor, while Telemachus followed her.

King Nestor saw them — strangers — approaching, and so did Pisistratus, his young son. Both King Nestor and his son understood the rules of *xenia*. Pisistratus reached the strangers first. Having been raised correctly, he welcomed them. He held their hands and led them to the feast and asked them to sit down and refresh themselves. He also gave them wine to pour as a sacrifice to Poseidon, being careful to give wine to the older man first.

"Say a prayer to the sea-god Poseidon," Pisistratus invited them. "The feast you see is in honor of him. And pour an offering of wine to honor the god."

Athena was pleased with the actions of Pisistratus. He knew how to treat an older man such as Mentor, and he knew how to welcome strangers and how to respect the gods. Athena also knew how to act correctly. She prayed to Poseidon, "Great sea-god, please grant our prayers. First reward

King Nestor and the Pylians for the sacrifice that they have made to you. Then allow Telemachus and myself safe passage home again."

Telemachus also poured an offering of wine to Poseidon, and then everyone feasted. After everyone had eaten and drunk their fill, King Nestor knew that it was the proper time for conversation, so he asked, "Friends, who are you and why are you travelling?"

Telemachus remembered the encouragement that Athena had given him to speak to King Nestor, so he answered, "We come from Ithaca, and we seek information about my father, Odysseus, with whom you fought at Troy. No one knows where he is buried. Can you tell me how and where he died?"

"Troy was a hardship for all of us," King Nestor said. "So many people fought and died there. Great Ajax is buried there. So is Achilles. So is Patroclus. So is my own son Antilochus.

"Your father and I never quarreled, never disagreed. Your way of speaking is just like his. Your father, cunning mastermind, conquered Troy, but Zeus and the gods prepared hardships for many Greeks as they attempted to return home. Agamemnon and his brother, Menelaus, quarreled about what to do. Menelaus wished to return home right away, but Agamemnon wished to first offer a sacrifice to Athena. Half of the Greeks followed the advice of Menelaus and left at dawn; half of the Greeks followed the advice of Agamemnon and stayed to offer a sacrifice to Athena.

"Menelaus, Diomedes, and I left at dawn, eager to return home. Diomedes and I made the journey safely, but many of the others did not, as I have learned from the news of travelers to Pylos. True, the Myrmidons of Achilles made it home safely, as did Philoctetes the master archer. So did King Idomeneus of Crete. But Agamemnon was killed by his wife's lover, Aegisthus, when he left Troy and returned to Mycenae. But Agamemnon's son, Orestes, won renown throughout the world by killing the murderer of his father."

"How true," Telemachus said. "Orestes will always be remembered. I wish that the gods would help me to earn such renown. I wish that the gods would help me to get rid of the suitors who besiege my palace."

"I have heard news of the suitors," Nestor replied. "Why is this happening? Do you willingly allow yourself to be bullied? Or are the gods against you? Do they cause the people of Ithaca to despise you?"

Nestor thought, *Orestes won renown by killing the murderer of his father. You, Telemachus, can also win great renown by ridding your palace of the suitors, killing them all if necessary.*

Nestor continued, "Odysseus may perhaps return someday, either alone or with an army. Let's hope that Athena is on your side. She helped Odysseus immensely throughout the Trojan War. Goddesses seldom show such favoritism toward a mortal. With her on your side, you could rid your palace of the suitors."

"I would love for those things to happen," said Telemachus, "but Odysseus will never return, and I cannot rid my palace of the suitors, even if the gods should help me."

Insulted, Athena, who was still disguised as Mentor, said sharply, "The gods are much more powerful than you think, Telemachus. Don't be a fool! It is better for Odysseus to return home years late than to be like Agamemnon, who quickly returned home and quickly was murdered. The gods are very powerful, but even the gods cannot stop a mortal's fated day of death."

"Mentor," Telemachus said, "let us not speak of Odysseus. He has been dead for a long time. But I wish to ask King Nestor, who is so wise, something else: What are the details of Agamemnon's death? Was Menelaus present? How did Aegisthus manage to murder Agamemnon?"

"Menelaus was not present," King Nestor replied. "If Menelaus had found Aegisthus alive in the palace of Agamemnon, he — not Orestes — would killed him. He also would have fed Aegisthus' corpse to the dogs and the birds, not allowing Aegisthus' soul to travel to the Land of the Dead until a hundred years had passed.

"Aegisthus wooed Agamemnon's wife, Clytemnestra, and he succeeded in seducing her, even though Agamemnon had left behind a bard to guard her. Aegisthus got rid of the bard, marooning him on an island, and Clytemnestra moved into Aegisthus' palace.

"Menelaus was delayed during his journey when his pilot, Phrontus, died. He stayed behind at Sounion to bury him, and when he resumed his journey home, he was driven off course. A hurricane split his fleet in two, and Menelaus and five ships landed on Egypt. Away from home he stayed, amassing wealth.

"Aegisthus killed Agamemnon, and then he ruled — badly — as King of Mycenae for seven years before Orestes, having grown up, killed him, avenging the murder of his father. Orestes then buried both Aegisthus and his mother on the same day that Menelaus sailed into the port of Mycenae.

"Telemachus, learn from this story. Don't stay away from your home too long. Be present so that you can protect your possessions. However, I advise you to visit Menelaus and ask him for news of your father. If you wish, I can lend you a chariot and horses to visit him, and I can send my son with you as a guide."

Athena praised the old king: "Thank you for a well-told story. Now let us pour wine for Poseidon and then think of sleep."

They poured the wine, and Nestor, a good host, wanted them to stay with him, not return to their ship: "Stay here with me. It is not right for Telemachus to sleep on the deck of a ship, not when I have plenty of rugs and blankets with which to make beds."

Athena replied, "That's a good idea. Let Telemachus stay here, but I will return to the ship and sleep there and make sure that things are OK. I'm the oldest — all the crewmembers are the same age as Telemachus. At dawn, I'll visit the Cauconians while Telemachus pays a visit to Menelaus, with the loan of your chariot and with your son as his guide."

Athena then changed herself into a bird and flew away, amazing all who saw her. Gladdened, King Nestor told Telemachus, "The gods are protecting you. This was Athena, the bright-eyed goddess."

He then prayed to Athena, "Please bless us. Please bless me, my children, and my wife. I will sacrifice to you a heifer whose horns have been wrapped with gold."

They shared a drink and went to their beds to sleep.

Nestor thought about Telemachus, *He has the protection of the gods, but his situation with the suitors is still very bad. I wish I could help him fight the suitors and drive them from his palace. But I am too old, and Pisistratus, my son, is too young and inexperienced to help him. Antilochus, my one son who would be of the proper age and who would have the proper experience to help him, lies buried on the plain before Troy.*

The next morning, King Nestor issued orders. He had promised Athena a sacrifice of a heifer whose horns had been wrapped with gold, and he kept his word, ordering the sacrifice, and he requested that most of Telemachus' crewmembers attend the sacrifice — but two crewmembers needed to stay behind to guard the ship. Athena also attended the sacrifice.

As the heifer was being sacrificed, Polycaste, the youngest daughter of King Nestor, bathed Telemachus in accordance with the ancient custom, making the guest comfortable and showing him proper *xenia*.

Following the feast, King Nestor ordered that a chariot and a team of horses be brought to them. He also ordered that provisions for the journey of Telemachus and Pisistratus be stowed away in the chariot.

Telemachus and Pisistratus rode all day, stayed with the good host Diocles that night, and rode again in the morning and reached Lacedaemon, home of King Menelaus and of Helen, at dusk.

Chapter 4: Telemachus, King Menelaus, and Helen

In Lacedaemon, King Menelaus and his people were celebrating a double wedding. One of the times that people in ancient Greece could legitimately enjoy a feast was during the celebration of a wedding.

Menelaus and Helen's daughter, Hermione, was being sent to Neoptolemus, the son of Achilles. They would be man and wife in the land of the Myrmidons. Menelaus' son, Megapenthes, whose mother was one of Menelaus' slaves, was marrying the daughter of Alector of Sparta.

All were enjoying the feast and the music and the dance when Pisistratus and Telemachus drove up in the chariot, then stopped and looked at the palace in awe.

Eteoneus, aide-in-arms to Menelaus, reported to the king, "Strangers are in the courtyard. Should I offer them hospitality, or should I send them on to someone who has leisure to attend to them?"

"Don't be a fool, Eteoneus," Menelaus said. "You and I have enjoyed hospitality as we traveled the Mediterranean. Now it is our turn — and our civilized duty — to offer hospitality to other people. Invite the strangers in, make them comfortable, and let them enjoy the feast."

Eteoneus and servants attended to the strangers, and to the strangers' team of horses. Telemachus and Pisistratus entered the palace, marveling at all they saw. Women bathed them in accordance with the ancient custom, and Telemachus and Pisistratus sat by Menelaus, who said to them, "Enjoy the feast, and then tell me who you are. No doubt you are the sons of kings. Anyone could tell that by looking at you."

Menelaus then gave them good cuts of tender meat, the cuts that he himself had been served. As they ate, Telemachus whispered to Pisistratus, "Just look at the palace — lots of gold, amber, silver, ivory, and bronze. The halls of Zeus on Mount Olympus must look like this."

Menelaus overheard him, and he said, "The palace of no mortal man can rival that of Zeus, but the palaces of few mortal men can rival my palace. I have wandered for eight years around the Mediterranean, visiting Cyprus, Phoenicia, Egypt, Ethiopia, and Libya.

"While traveling, I made a fortune, but at home someone killed Agamemnon, my brother. I have undergone hardships, as have those who fought for me in the Trojan War. I wish that I had stayed here — even after Paris had stolen two-thirds of my wealth — and never had gone to Troy. That way, those who died fighting for me during the Trojan War would still be alive, as would my brother.

"I mourn for many men who died for me, but for no one as much as I do Odysseus. No one labored more mightily for me, and his days ended in suffering. And how much must others suffer who mourn him: Laertes, his father; Penelope, his wife; and Telemachus, who was just an infant when his father left to fight at Troy."

Hearing this, Telemachus wept, and Menelaus recognized who his visitor must be. He hesitated, not knowing whether to call the prince by name or to let him introduce himself.

Helen entered the room, immediately recognized who Telemachus must be, and did not hesitate, but said, "I have never seen anyone resemble Odysseus more. This young man must be Telemachus, son of the man who fought at Troy to return me, whore that I was then, to you."

Menelaus replied, "I think you are correct, dear. I too see the resemblance, and just now when I mentioned Odysseus, this young man started crying."

Pisistratus said, "You are right. He is Telemachus, the son of Odysseus. We are delighted to speak to you, a man who is like a god. Nestor sent me with him to be his escort as he consulted you about his father. With Odysseus gone, he has no man to defend him and his possessions."

"It's wonderful to have the son of my friend as a guest," Menelaus replied. "Odysseus and I spent years fighting together at Troy. We have a bond, and I would give him a city. Unfortunately, the gods have denied him his day of homecoming."

All grieved. Telemachus grieved for his father. Menelaus grieved for the men who had suffered for him. Helen wept. Pisistratus wept, thinking of Antilochus, his brother who lay buried on the plain of Troy.

Thinking of Antilochus, Pisistratus said, "My father, Nestor, has always spoken highly of you, Menelaus. So now, can we please speak of something else? I prefer not to cry while eating a meal. It's not that I think we should not grieve over the warriors who fell at Troy. I myself lost a brother there: Antilochus, a fast runner and a mighty warrior."

"Well spoken," Menelaus said. "You speak with the wisdom that is normally given only to the old. You are like your father — you have his wisdom in words. Zeus has blessed Nestor, who grows old in comfort at home, surrounded by family. Come, let us finish eating, and let us drink. Tomorrow, Telemachus can talk about his father."

So much sorrow was in the house. To dispel the sorrow, Helen mixed a drug in the wine. The drug was called heart's-ease, and she had learned about it in Egypt. Anyone who drank wine in which the drug had been mixed would feel no sorrow — not even if his family died, not even if an enemy murdered his family in front of him.

It's good that I know about this drug, Helen thought to herself. *It will make this meeting happier. And, of course, it comes in handy to keep my husband under control when he grieves for all the men lost at Troy and wonders if all that suffering and death was worthwhile just to get me back.*

Helen brought the wine, they drank, and Helen said, "Menelaus, guests, let us dine and drink and tell old stories to each other. I remember when Odysseus disguised himself and snuck into Troy to spy. He had disguised himself in rags, and he even whipped his own body to make the blood run and make it seem like he had led a hard, abused life. Wearing rags, he came into Troy, and everybody thought that he was just another beggar. He no longer resembled the king and warrior who camped before Troy with all the other Greeks. I was the only one who recognized him. I took him to my apartment, I gave him a bath, and I gave him good clothing to wear and took away the filthy rags that he had used to disguise himself. I also made him tell me the plot of the Greeks. He left my apartment, and he made his way to the gate of Troy, killing Trojans as he went. The Trojan women grieved, but I was glad. By then, I was on the side of the Greeks, and I regretted leaving my husband and infant daughter and coming to Troy with Paris."

Did you really? Menelaus thought, even though he was under the influence of the drug. *Did you take Odysseus to your apartment to keep him from spying among the Trojans? And why did Odysseus kill so many Trojans as he made his way to the gate of Troy? Was he forced to kill them because you bathed him and gave him fine clothing and totally destroyed his disguise?*

Was he forced to fight for his life because now the Trojan warriors were able to recognize him? Were you trying to get him killed? And what did you do with the information that you say Odysseus told you about the Greeks' plan?

"Your story is well told, Helen," Menelaus said. "I also have a story to tell. What a mastermind Odysseus was! What courage he had! He came up with the idea of the Trojan Horse, and he and I were among the warriors who hid in the horse when the Greek army left the horse behind and pretended to sail back home. That night, with the horse inside Troy, you and your newest husband, Deiphobus, whom you married after Paris died, visited the horse. You circled the horse three times, mimicking the voices of the wives of the men inside the horse, trying to get them to call out and reveal themselves to the Trojan warriors. Odysseus is the man who saved us. Odysseus is the man who told us that our wives were not outside, that they were not in Troy. All listened to Odysseus and kept quiet except for Anticlus. When you mimicked his wife's name, he started to cry out, but Odysseus put his hands over Anticlus' mouth and saved our lives."

Menelaus thought, *Yes, Helen, you told a good story in which you want us to believe that you helped Odysseus, but I know better. I remember when you tried to get us all killed.*

Telemachus was aware of the tension between Menelaus and Helen. Hoping to prevent a fight between husband and wife, he said, "Thank you for the story about my father, Menelaus, but even his great courage could not prevent his death. It's time for bed. It's time to enjoy sleep."

Telemachus' tactic worked. Helen ordered her serving-women to make up beds for Telemachus and Pisistratus, and all slept.

The next morning, Menelaus asked Telemachus, "How may I help you? Why have you journeyed to see me?"

"I came to seek information about my father," Telemachus replied. "My palace is overrun by suitors who court my mother against her will and who slaughter my sheep, pigs, cows, and goats, feasting every day while giving nothing in return. I hope that you can give me definitive news about my father, whether the news is good or bad. If you know that he is dead, tell me. Perhaps you even saw him die. Tell me the truth."

"The suitors don't know what they are doing," Menelaus said. "They want to crawl into Odysseus' bed, but they don't realize what kind of man he was. Should he return home, he will slaughter them all.

"But let me tell you what I know. I was on an island off the coast of Egypt, still eager to return home but having little luck. The winds were not blowing, and we could not sail. Twenty days had passed, and we were running out of food. Fortunately, Eidothea, the immortal daughter of the Old Man of the Sea, pitied me, and she told me how I could get home, and how I could get information.

"She said to me, 'My father always takes a nap among the seals each day. He counts each seal, and then he lies down and sleeps. You and three men grab him while he is asleep and hold on to him. He is a shape-shifter extraordinaire and will transform himself into many shapes, but hold on to him. When he stops shape-shifting and has assumed his own true shape, then he will answer any questions you have.'

"We did as she advised. That morning, three trusted men and I went to the place where the seals gathered. Eidothea was waiting for us with four sealskins. The stench was overwhelming, but she daubed sweet-smelling ambrosia — the food of the gods — under our noses, and so we did not smell the stench. Just as she said, the Old Man of the Sea came on shore, counted the seals, and lay down for a nap.

"We grabbed him, and we hung on although he turned himself into a snake, a panther, a boar, and even moving water. Tired, the Old Man of the Sea resumed his real shape and asked me, 'What do you want, Menelaus?'

"I replied, 'I want to know how to return home. Apparently, one of the gods is against me and prevents my homecoming. Tell me what I have to do to return home again.'

"The Old Man of the Sea told me, 'You left Egypt without first making a sacrifice to Zeus and the other gods. You will never make it home until you return to Egypt and make a sacrifice.'

"Bad news for me: another delay before I returned home. But at least I would return home. I then asked him, 'What about the other Greeks? Did they make it home safely? Or have some of them died — did any drown on their way home, or did any die after reaching home?'

"The Old Man of the Sea replied, 'Do you really want to know such bad news? You know who died while fighting at Troy. Two more died while returning home or after reaching home. And one more has not returned home, but is being held captive.

"'Little Ajax died while journeying home. A storm arose, his ship broke into pieces, but he made it to a rock, hanging onto it and boasting that he had survived despite the fury of the gods that had been directed against him. Poseidon heard that boast, and he used his trident to split the rock that Little Ajax was clinging to. Little Ajax fell into the sea and drowned.

"'And what about your brother? Agamemnon did not drown on his way home, but he met his death nevertheless. Agamemnon reached home and rejoiced, but a watchman saw him and sent news of his return to Aegisthus. Aegisthus had planned ahead. Knowing that Agamemnon would return home, he gave a watchman two bars of gold to look for Agamemnon. Now, after an entire year of staying alert, the watchman saw Agamemnon's day of homecoming.

"'Alerted by the watchman, Aegisthus set a trap for Agamemnon. Aegisthus hid twenty armed men in his palace and he ordered a feast to be prepared for the returning king. Agamemnon sat down to eat, and Aegisthus and his twenty armed men slaughtered him and all of Agamemnon's men.'

"So the Old Man of the Sea told me how my brother had died. I wept," Menelaus said. "The Old Man of the Sea then said, 'No more weeping, Menelaus. Go to Egypt, make the sacrifice, and then hurry home! You may be able to avenge Agamemnon's murder — if his son, Orestes, has not already done that. At the least, you will be able to attend the funeral of Aegisthus.'

"I then asked the Old Man of the Sea about the hero who was being held captive, unable to see his day of homecoming.

"'That man is Odysseus,' the Old Man of the Sea told me. 'I saw him on the island of the sea-nymph Calypso, crying and longing for his day of homecoming. Calypso keeps him captive and will not allow him to leave. He has no ships, no men. He has no way to return home.

"'But you, Menelaus, have no such fate. You will return home, and when it is time for you to cease living in your country, you will go to the Elysium Fields, where life after death is easy. You are married to Helen, and so you are Zeus' son-in-law; therefore, ease awaits you.'

"I followed the advice of the Old Man of the Sea," Menelaus said. "I returned to Egypt, and I sacrificed to the gods. There I made a burial-mound for Agamemnon. After stopping at Mycenae and seeing Orestes, I returned home with Helen.

"But, Telemachus, stay here for ten or twelve days. When you leave, I will give you gifts: three stallions, a chariot, and a precious cup for you to use in pouring offerings to the gods."

Tactfully, Telemachus replied, "I would be willing to stay with you — even an entire year! — to hear your stories, but I must return home. I left my crewmembers in Pylos, and they will wonder about me. As for the gifts, simply give me a keepsake to remember you by. I can't use those horses. Here the land is level, but Ithaca is hilly. It's much better land for goats than for horses."

Menelaus thought, *Yes, I can understand why you wish to leave early. The suitors are ruining your possessions, and you need to return to keep an eye on them. I wish I could help you, but I have not been home long after years of warfare and of wandering, and there is no way in Hell that I am leaving Helen alone.*

"You speak well," Menelaus said. "I can understand that horses are of no use on Ithaca, so I will change the gifts. I will give you a mixing-bowl that is a work of art. It is silver with a rim of gold, and Hephaestus, the blacksmith god, created it himself."

As they talked, Menelaus' servants prepared dinner, and back at Odysseus' palace on Ithaca, the suitors played games, throwing spears and a discus, and enjoyed themselves. But the ringleaders of the suitors, Eurymachus and Antinous, strongest of the bunch, sat by themselves and did not participate in the games.

Noëmon, one of the young men on Ithaca, walked up to Eurymachus and Antinous and asked, "Do you know when Telemachus will return? I lent him my ship, but now I want to go to the mainland, where I have some horses suckling young mules. I want to bring a mule home and break him for work on the farm."

Eurymachus and Antinous were shocked. True, Telemachus had not been around for a few days, but they had assumed that he was visiting his grandfather or one of his farms. They had not dreamed that Telemachus would have enough initiative to go to the mainland.

Antinous asked Noëmon, "When did Telemachus go, and who went with him?"

Noëmon replied, "He left days ago, and the best young men of Ithaca went with him as his crew. Mentor also went with him. At least he looked like Mentor. But I saw Mentor recently, so he can't have gone to the mainland. A god must have gone with Telemachus."

Noëmon left, and the suitors gathered together. Antinous, furious, said, "Telemachus is becoming a danger to us. Why did he go to the mainland? Is he trying to gather armed men to force us out of his palace? We must kill him before he kills us. Give me a ship and twenty armed men, and when he returns home, we will sail out to meet him and kill him and his crew. His father is dead, and soon he will be dead."

All of the suitors — no exceptions — approved the plan.

Medon the herald overheard the plot. Loyal to Penelope and Telemachus, he hurried to tell Penelope what he had heard.

Seeing him come toward her, Penelope said to him, "Why are you coming to see me? Have the suitors ordered you to tell me to order the serving-women to prepare their feast? How I hate the suitors! I wish that this would be the last meal that they will ever eat!"

Medon replied, "My news is worse than that. The suitors are plotting to murder Telemachus, who sailed to the mainland to seek news of his father."

"Why did he feel that he had to go to the mainland?" Penelope asked. "Is he trying to get himself killed?"

"Perhaps a god encouraged him, or perhaps it was his own idea," Medon replied, "but he wanted to discover news of his father. He wanted to learn whether his father is alive or dead."

Penelope sank to the floor, cried, and said to her serving-women, "Zeus has given me more torment than I can bear. My beloved husband is dead, and my son may soon be dead. If only I had known that he was planning to travel to the mainland, I would have kept him here. Send someone to Dolius, my old servant, who can tell Laertes about Telemachus. Maybe Laertes will know what to do."

Her old servant Eurycleia told her, "I knew that Telemachus went to the mainland, but he ordered me not to tell you until at least ten or twelve days had passed. He didn't want you to worry about him. Right now, bathe and put on fresh clothing, and then you may pray to Athena to protect your son. But please don't make Laertes, an old man, worry about his grandson. He already has too much grief to bear."

Penelope took her advice. Refreshed, she prayed to Athena, "Hear my prayer, bright-eyed goddess. If Odysseus has ever favored you, has ever sacrificed to you, save his and my son, Telemachus, from these suitors." She then cried out in grief.

One of the suitors in the Great Hall heard the cry of sorrow and said, "Penelope is preparing for her day of marriage. She knows that it is inevitable, and she does not know that we are going to kill her son."

Antinous told him, "Shut up! Keep your mouth closed so that no one can learn about our ambush!"

Antinous then chose twenty men. They armed themselves, boarded ship, and sailed out to set an ambush for Telemachus.

In her rooms, Penelope mourned and then slept. Athena saw her, and she thought of a way to help her. She created a phantom in the form of Iphthime, Penelope's sister, to appear to Penelope in a dream.

The phantom said in the dream, "You need not mourn, Penelope. The gods have heard your prayer. Your son will return safe from his journey. The suitors' ambush will not succeed. Telemachus has never offended the gods."

In the dream, Penelope replied, "My life is troubled. My husband has been absent for twenty years, and now my son is in danger. The suitors plot to kill him."

"Be strong and have courage," the phantom replied. "Nothing will happen to Telemachus. He has a protector. The goddess Athena sails with him. She will take care of him. Athena knows what you are going through, and she sent me here to reassure you."

"Can you tell me whether Odysseus is alive or dead?" Penelope asked.

"The gods do not tell all," the phantom said and then departed.

Penelope felt much better after the dream, but Antinous and twenty armed men sailed to set up an ambush to kill Telemachus. They landed on a rocky island, and they waited for Telemachus to sail near so they could kill him.

So ends the Telemachy: *a mini-epic starring Telemachus.*

Chapter 5: Odysseus and Calypso

The next morning, Dawn rose from the bed of her lover, Tithonus, who is both old and immortal. When he, a mortal man, first became her lover, Dawn gave him immortality, but she was unable to make him ageless. Now he grows older and older, and he grows feebler and feebler, but he always sleeps — sleep was a gift that Dawn could give him, a welcome gift to an aged and continually aging man whose every waking moment is filled with pain.

That morning, Athena addressed the Olympian gods in council (all except Poseidon, who was visiting the Ethiopians), saying, "Father Zeus, and all other gods on Olympus, remember Odysseus, held captive on an island by the sea-nymph Calypso. He is unable to leave her; he is unable to see his day of homecoming. And now the suitors who infest his palace and plague his wife plot to murder his son, Telemachus, who has sailed to the mainland to seek news of his father."

Zeus replied, "You know that Telemachus will not be murdered. You know that you yourself will protect him. You know that the suitors will be unsuccessful. As for Odysseus, we shall help him."

Zeus turned to the messenger-god Hermes and ordered, "Go to Calypso and order her to release Odysseus. He will build a raft and sail to the island of the Phaeacians, who will shower gifts on him and sail him home. Odysseus shall return home, and he shall see his loved ones."

Hermes set off at once, flying through the sky — the gods and goddesses have that power — to the sea and then skimming over its surface until he reached Calypso's island. She was in her home, a cavern, pleasantly furnished and very comfortable. Odysseus was not present. As usual, he was on the shore closest to Ithaca, grieving because he so longed to be home.

Calypso was surprised to see Hermes, and she immediately said, "Why are you here?" But then she remembered her duty as hostess and added, "Your visits are so infrequent. You should visit more often. I am very happy to give you any assistance you need."

She set the table with ambrosia and nectar, the food and drink of the immortal gods, and Hermes ate and drank. Then it was time for business. Such is the way of *xenia*.

"You ask why I have come," Hermes said. "Zeus sent me. Zeus says that you are keeping captive a hero of the Trojan War, that you are preventing his day of homecoming. Zeus commands you to release the hero. He is not fated to die here; he is fated to see his loved ones again. You cannot go against fate."

Zeus' command was not pleasing to Calypso: "You gods are angry when a goddess sleeps with a mortal. The goddess Dawn slept with Orion, and so the goddess Artemis shot him with one of her arrows and killed him. Demeter slept with Iasion, and so the god Zeus hurled a thunderbolt at him and killed him. Now you gods are angry at me because I am sleeping with a mortal man. I saved this man's life. His ship was wrecked, and his men all died, but I welcomed him to my island. I am even willing to make him immortal — and to make him ageless. But no one can withstand Zeus, the most powerful of the gods. Since he orders me to release the man, I will release him and I will give him advice as to how he can best reach his home."

"Good decision," Hermes said. "Anyone who disobeys the command of Zeus will regret it." Hermes left and returned to Olympus.

Calypso walked to the beach and found Odysseus grieving as usual. The two slept together because Calypso made him sleep with her. It is not wise for a mortal to go against the wishes of an immortal — the immortal gods and goddesses can do terrible things to mortals. But Odysseus longed to be with Penelope, his wife.

Calypso told Odysseus, "You don't need to grieve any longer. You may leave my island. Build yourself a raft, and I will stock it with wine and water and food. You will see your home again, just as you wish — provided the gods don't interfere."

A chance to leave Calypso's island? This was what Odysseus had long wanted, but he was a cautious man. He thought, *Is this a trick? Has Calypso tired of me and now wants me dead? I am not going to leave this island unless I know that I have a reasonable chance of reaching land safely again.*

Odysseus said to Calypso, "I won't build a raft and leave, goddess, unless you swear a binding oath that this is not a trick to get me killed."

This made Calypso smile. One of the things that she liked about Odysseus was his shrewdness. He was a brave man, but he liked to have the odds in his favor. He was willing to take necessary risks, but not unnecessary risks.

Calypso said to Odysseus, "I swear on the River Styx that I am not trying to trick you, that I am not trying to kill you or to get you killed. Swearing on the River Styx is the inviolable oath of the gods — does that satisfy you?"

It did satisfy Odysseus. No god or goddess can go against an oath sworn on the River Styx.

The two returned to Calypso's cavern, and there they ate and drank. Calypso ate ambrosia and drank nectar, the food and drink of the immortal gods; Odysseus ate food and drank wine for mortals.

Calypso then said to Odysseus, "Are you really so eager to leave me? If you knew the hardships that lie before you if you leave my island, you would not be so eager to leave. I know that you long to see your wife, but why? Is she as beautiful as I am? Does she have a better figure? Why not stay with me and be immortal?"

Be careful, Odysseus thought. *Do not make Calypso angry. The gods and goddesses can do terrible things to mortal men they are angry at. Remember what Artemis did to Orion. Remember what Zeus did to Iasion. Do not say anything to Calypso that will make her angry. I must not say that I prefer Penelope to her. Instead, I must give a reason for wanting to leave her island that will not make Calypso angry. As for immortality, it doesn't work for mortal men. Remember what happened to Tithonus. And if I become immortal and stay here, I will never see my wife and my son and my home again.*

Odysseus said to Calypso, "Don't be angry with me, please. I know that you speak the truth. My wife is not as beautiful as you. My wife's figure is not better than yours. How can a mortal woman compare to an immortal goddess? The immortal goddess will always be more beautiful.

"But I want to see my home again. I want to see Ithaca again. That is what I have been longing for every day. I have faced many troubles before, and I am willing to face more troubles if only I can see my home again."

Calypso thought, *I can understand that Odysseus wants to see his home again. That is reasonable. I need not be angry at him.*

The sun set, and they slept together.

The next day, Odysseus built his raft. Calypso brought him cloth, and he made a sail. It took him four days to build his raft, and on the fifth day he set off, with his raft well provisioned by Calypso.

He sailed for seventeen days, but on the eighteenth day he ran into trouble. All that Zeus and Athena and Hermes had done for him had been done without the knowledge of the sea-god Poseidon. They had acted behind his back while he was away from Mount Olympus, attending a sacrifice held in his honor by the Ethiopians.

But now, returning from Ethiopia to Olympus, Poseidon saw Odysseus on his raft. Poseidon knew that the other gods had acted without consulting him, and he was angry: "Look at Odysseus. He is near the island of the Phaeacians, who are fated to help him return home. I cannot prevent his day of homecoming and I cannot go against fate, but I can still make Odysseus' life difficult."

Poseidon then created a storm, and Odysseus knew he was in trouble. Alone on a raft, and with a big storm coming, Odysseus knew that death by drowning could very well await him. He said to himself, "My friends who died at Troy are more fortunate than I am. They were mourned. Burial-mounds were raised for them. Their souls entered the Land of the Dead. I may drown alone, with no one to mourn me and to give my corpse a proper burial. My soul may be prevented from entering the Land of the Dead until a hundred years have passed."

The storm struck him and his raft. He was washed overboard, and the mast broke. He was underwater for a long time, but finally he surfaced and then clung to his raft.

Help arrived. Ino, the daughter of Cadmus, a mortal woman who had been made an immortal sea-nymph and had changed her name to Leucothea, saw him and knew his fate. She boarded Odysseus' raft and said to him, "Poor man. Poseidon hates you, but even he cannot alter your fate. You will not drown here. Take my advice. Strip off your clothes so they don't weigh you down, then swim for shore with my scarf tied around your waist. As long as you have my scarf, you need not fear death. But when you reach land safely, give my scarf back to me."

Odysseus listened and took her scarf, then Leucothea dived into the sea again. Ever cautious, Odysseus considered his options: *Should I jump into the sea right away and begin swimming? No. Better to wait and stay on the raft until it floats closer to land. That will improve my odds of reaching land safely.*

As Odysseus thought about what he should do, Poseidon sent a huge wave over the raft that tore it to pieces and plunged Odysseus into the sea. He grabbed a piece of floating wood, tore off his clothing, and tied the scarf of the immortal sea-nymph around his waist.

Poseidon saw him and knew that Odysseus was fated to reach land, but Poseidon was happy that he had made Odysseus' journey difficult and dangerous. "Go," Poseidon said. "You will reach a land filled with helpful people, but I do not think that you will have found your journey easy."

Poseidon headed toward his palace at the port of Aegae. Athena took advantage of his absence and calmed the storm and the sea. She allowed the North wind to blow Odysseus toward land.

For two days, Odysseus stayed afloat by clinging to the wrecked raft. On the morning of the third day, he saw land — a sight that made him joyful, as joyful as children are when their father recovers from an illness that could have killed him.

Land there was, but the water was filled with pounding surf and jagged rocks, a place where swimmers could die. "More danger," Odysseus said to himself, "and the alternative to this danger is a different danger. If I try to reach land here, I will be cut to pieces on the rocks. If I cling to the wreckage and try to make my way along the island, a storm will spring up and kill me. Or I will die, devoured by sharks."

A wave washed him toward the rocks, and he grabbed one and hung on to it, although it tore the skin from his hands. When a fisherman grabs an octopus and tears it from its lair, the suckers on its tentacles will cling to pebbles and carry them away. Bits of skin from Odysseus' hands clung to the rock as a wave carried Odysseus away from it.

Odysseus started swimming — and he saw a river flowing to the sea, a good spot to make landfall. He prayed to the river-god, "Help me, please. I am your suppliant. The gods will give help to mortals when mortals request it."

The river-god listened to Odysseus' prayer, and granted his request. Odysseus did not have to fight a strong current. He reached land, and he rested until he could breathe normally and not have to gulp air. Then he remembered the scarf of the immortal sea-nymph Leucothea. If Odysseus had been a different kind of man, he would have been tempted to keep it. It was a treasure — wear it and never fear death! Odysseus was not tempted. He untied the scarf and threw it into the river. It floated downstream to the sea, and Leucothea recovered it. She had shown respect to Odysseus, and now Odysseus had shown respect to her.

Odysseus climbed up the banks of the river, and thought about what he should do: "Man of misery and son of pain. What next? Do I stay here, naked and alone, by the river? Would it be better to leave the river and find a place to sleep? What if a wild beast finds me, naked and defenseless?"

Odysseus walked away from the river, and he found some woods in which two olive trees — which were sacred to Athena — were standing. One olive tree was wild, and the other was cultivated. Odysseus looked at the two olive trees, and he thought, *What kind of people will I find here? Will they be wild and not follow the rules of* xenia? *Will they be civilized and respect* xenia? *Tomorrow I will find out.*

He then piled up dry leaves to make a bed for himself. He lay on the leaves and piled more leaves over himself, and he slept. The leaves kept alive the one small spark of life left in Odysseus the way that a farmer will pour ashes over a fire to keep the embers alive until it is time to build the fire again. No one lives near the farmer, so he cannot easily get a fire again if the embers should die.

Odysseus slept.

Chapter 6: Odysseus and Nausicaa

Odysseus slept, and Athena made her way to the city of the Phaeacians, who used to live near the Cyclopes, savage creatures that were not civilized and did not show *xenia* to strangers. Therefore, the King of the Phaeacians, Nausithous, led his people to another home, the island of Scheria. There they built homes and temples and plowed fields and built a wall around the city and formed a civilization. Nausithous died, but he had raised his son, Alcinous, well, and the gods respected them both and gave Alcinous wisdom. Such things happen in a society that has good fathers.

Athena went to the palace of Alcinous and into the bedroom of Nausicaa, the young Phaeacian princess. The goddess appeared in Nausicaa's dream in the form of the daughter of Dymas, a Phaeacian noble. The goddess appeared to be Nausicaa's age.

The disguised Athena said to Nausicaa, "Haven't you things to do, Nausicaa? Look at your clothing, lying here, neglected. Shouldn't you prepare for your wedding? You are old enough to be married soon, and when you are married, all of your family should be wearing fresh, clean clothing. So tomorrow, go to the river and wash your family's clothing. Prepare for marriage. The eligible Phaeacian men all want to marry you."

Her job finished, Athena flew to Olympus.

Morning came, Nausicaa awoke and dressed, and then she went to her parents to tell them what she wanted to do. She said, "Father, will you arrange for me to use a wagon and mules to carry our clothing to the washing-pools? You should have fresh, clean clothing to wear in council, and I have five brothers, three of whom are still unmarried and are always wanting fresh, clean clothing to wear while courting." So Nausicaa said, neglecting to mention her hoped-for marriage.

But her father, King Alcinous, guessed her real reason for wanting to wash the clothing. He said to her, "Yes, of course. By all means. You will have everything you need." He ordered men to prepare the wagon and mules. Nausicaa gathered the dirty clothing, and her mother packed a lunch and wine for Nausicaa and for the girls who would help her wash the clothing. King Alcinous did not send men to guard the girls. The Phaeacians were at peace, and they were so remote from the rest of the world that they did not fear pirates who elsewhere would kidnap children and young women and sell them into slavery.

Nausicaa and the other girls reached the washing-pools at the river, unloaded the wagon, washed the clothing, and then spread it out in the sun to dry. They bathed in the river, enjoyed their lunch, and then played ball.

As she played ball, Nausicaa resembled Artemis, the virgin huntress-goddess. Nausicaa was more beautiful than the other girls.

It was almost time for Nausicaa to fold the clothing and load the wagon and return home, but Athena formed a plan. Odysseus must awake and meet Nausicaa, and she must give him *xenia*. But how to arrange their meeting? Athena came up with the answer: Nausicaa threw the ball to a girl, but it fell into the river with a splash — a splash that woke up Odysseus.

Suddenly awake, Odysseus wondered, *Man of misery and son of pain. Where are you? Who lives here? Are they wild and do not follow the rules of* xenia? *Are they civilized and follow the rules of* xenia?

I hear voices, the voices of young women. Be careful. You may be hearing the voices of the immortals. Perhaps you hear the voices of Artemis and her attendants. Artemis can be dangerous to mortal men who offend her. Actaeon went hunting one day, and he had the misfortune to see Artemis naked, bathing in a pool of water. He did not mean to see Artemis naked; he was not spying on her. But that meant nothing to Artemis, who fiercely protects her virginity. She turned his body into that of a stag, but he kept his human mind. His own hunting dogs pursued him, caught him, and tore him to pieces. A mortal man would be insane to offend Artemis.

Odysseus was cautious, but he needed help, and to get help he had to be a suppliant, although he was completely naked and covered with seaweed and dried sea-salt. He tore a branch from a tree, held it in front of him to hide his private parts, and stepped out into the open and thought about what he should do.

Odysseus thought, *These are human girls, not immortal goddesses and nymphs, but I am still in danger. I am naked, I look like a wild man, and these girls have no men whom I can ask for help. Instead, I have to be a suppliant before them. What is best for me to do? Should I fall to the ground before the young girl in charge here and grab her knees in the typical suppliant position?*

No! Definitely not! If I were to do that, she would run away screaming and her father and brothers would come and kill me. I need to stay far from these young girls and speak to them and convince them that I am not a danger to them.

Odysseus stood before the young girls with only a leafy branch to hide his nakedness. Seaweed clung to his body, and sea-salt had dried on him. He looked like a wild man who had never known civilization or followed the rules of *xenia*.

Seeing him, the girls scattered, putting distance between him and them, all except Nausicaa — Athena gave her courage.

Odysseus spoke to her, "Princess, show me mercy. Are you a mortal, or are you a goddess? If you are a goddess, you must be Artemis, the huntress-goddess who uses weapons well. In you, I see her beauty, her grace. But if you are a mortal, your father and your brothers must rejoice to have you in their family — you are so beautiful. But one man will rejoice even more than these — the man you will marry. I have never seen anyone as beautiful as you."

Odysseus thought, *I have let this young mortal girl know that she has the power here and that she is in no danger from me. Because I have called her Artemis, she knows that she is safe. After all, a mortal man would have to be insane to do anything that would offend Artemis — remember what she did to Actaeon! I have also mentioned that I know that she has male protectors: a father, brothers, and possibly a fiancé. With so many male protectors who wish to take care of her, I would have to be insane to try to harm her. In addition, I have thrown in some pretty good flattery.*

Odysseus continued, "Wait, once I saw something beautiful like you — a palm-tree on the island Delos, home of a temple to Apollo. To Delos I had sailed at the head of an army during a campaign that led to my misfortune. I marveled at the Delian palm-tree just like I marvel at you."

Odysseus thought, *I have let this young girl know that I am civilized — I know about gods such as Apollo and about temples such as the one on Delos. I have also let her know that I used to be a man of enough importance that I led an army even though now I am naked and alone.*

Odysseus continued, "Yesterday, princess, after many days at sea, I washed ashore. I have suffered misfortune, and I have no doubt that I will suffer more misfortune. Please show me mercy; please give me *xenia*. You are the first person I have met here. Show me how to get to town, and give me something to hide my nakedness. And may the gods give you everything you desire: a good husband and a happy marriage."

Odysseus thought, *Of course, I know that this young girl is not a goddess. She is simply a young mortal girl who will be married soon. But I have let her know that she is not in danger from me. I have managed to let her know that she is in no danger of being raped by me, something that a man much different from me might attempt. And I have done that without mentioning the word "rape," a word that might cause these young girls to panic and to run home and to gather their male protectors. Now I will see if my speech has been successful. Will this young girl offer me hospitality, or will she run home and tell her father and brothers that a wild man in the woods tried to attack her? Either I will immediately receive the help I need, or I will soon be killed.*

"Stranger," Nausicaa said, "friend, Zeus has given you troubles, but now that you have reached the island of the Phaeacians, you will receive what you need: clothing and food. I am the daughter of King Alcinous, and he will take care of you."

Nausicaa called to her serving-girls, "Come closer. Zeus sends strangers and suppliants, and it is our duty — the duty of civilized people — to help them. Bring this guest wine and food and olive oil and clothing, and bathe him in the river."

Odysseus replied, "Thank you, but allow me to bathe myself in the river. All of you girls stand back a long way from me. I am embarrassed to be naked in front of you girls."

All is going well, but stay cautious, Odysseus thought. *It's best not to be bathed by these young girls. What would happen if a man were to ride by and see these young girls bathing me and then report what he saw to the king? It's best to completely avoid anything that might make someone think that I have had any kind of sexual contact with these girls.*

Odysseus bathed himself in the river, washing away the seaweed and the sea-salt. He rubbed himself with the olive oil, and then he put on the clothing the girls had laid out for him. Athena transformed him, making him taller and stronger and more handsome, with curly hair.

Nausicaa noticed the transformation in Odysseus, and she said to her serving-girls, "At first this man looked wild and uncivilized, but now he looks like a god. In fact, he looks like a potential husband for me. Give him something to eat and to drink."

Odysseus ate, and Nausicaa and the other girls folded the clothing and put it in the wagon, and then after Odysseus had finished eating, she said to him, "Let's go to the town now, but when we reach the town, let me and the others go on ahead while you wait a while before entering town. I don't want people to talk about us. Someone might see us together and say, 'Who is the stranger with Nausicaa? He is tall and strong and handsome. Is he a shipwrecked sailor? Is he a god come down from Olympus? Has he come to answer her prayers and to marry her? That's OK by us. All the eligible Phaeacian men have been courting her, but she has shown little interest in them. Let her marry this stranger.' So they might say, as they criticize a girl who has made friends with a man her parents do not know — something that I would never do."

Nausicaa thought, *I've flattered the stranger by saying that the Phaeacians are likely to think that he is a god. I've told him that I am unmarried and that Phaeacian men are courting me but that I have shown little interest in them. I have fairly strongly hinted that I consider him a potential husband for me. I have also said that I know what a good girl should not do — make friends with a man her parents do not know — even though I am doing exactly that. In short, I have hinted that I would like to marry this stranger.*

Odysseus thought, *Interesting. This princess has shown an interest in me, even hinting that a marriage with me is possible, but she has done it so subtly that I need not reject her outright and embarrass her. I can simply ignore her interest in me. This girl is intelligent.*

Nausicaa continued, "We will reach a grove of poplars with a spring. That is part of my father's estate. Stay there and give us time to walk to my father's palace, then you may go into town and ask for directions to my father's palace. Anyone can tell you how to get there. When you gain entrance to the palace, go past my father and go to my mother and supplicate her. If the queen pities and respects you, she will give you a voyage home."

Nausicaa, the serving-girls, and Odysseus all headed toward town. When they reached the grove of poplars and the stream, Odysseus stayed behind and prayed to Athena, "Help me now, Athena. You did not help me when

Poseidon wrecked my raft. Bring it to pass that the Phaeacians give me *xenia* — that they treat me the way that civilized people should treat a stranger!"

Athena heard his prayer, but she did not appear before him openly. She feared Poseidon, the sea-god, whose anger toward Odysseus still burned.

Chapter 7: Odysseus and the Phaeacians

Nausicaa reached her father's palace, and her brothers carried the clothing inside and took care of the mules and the wagon. She went to her bedroom, and an aged servant, Eurymedusa, made her a meal. Nausicaa was well cared for, with a loving family and household.

Judging that enough time had passed, Odysseus began walking toward the city. Athena created a heavy fog so that no common Phaeacian would see and question him — the common Phaeacians were not as friendly as their king. Disguising herself as a young girl holding a pitcher of water, Athena appeared before him.

Odysseus asked her, "Little girl, please tell me how to reach the palace of King Alcinous. I am a traveler who has met much hardship, and I need help. I know no one in this country."

"Yes, sir," the disguised Athena replied. "King Alcinous is a neighbor of my royal father. I will lead you to the king's palace. Follow me, and avoid the common Phaeacians. They are not friendly toward strangers. They are fine sailors, with quick ships, but they are not hospitable."

Odysseus followed her lead, and as he walked behind her he looked and he marveled. He saw ships and meeting-grounds, and everything was well ordered. All he saw was admirable. The Phaeacians had a society that worked.

They reached the palace of King Alcinous, and Athena said, "Go inside the palace and be bold. You will see the queen. Ask her for help. Her name is Arete, and she is known and respected for her excellence. She is so respected here that she can make peace between arguing men. King Alcinous honors and respects her, as do all the people on this island, even the common Phaeacians. If you appeal to the queen and ask her for help, you will see your home again."

Athena left, and Odysseus walked toward the palace, which was magnificent. Friezes showed that the Phaeacians respected art, and the palace was rich with metal. The walls were bronze, and the doors were gold. The threshold was bronze, and the doorposts were silver. Hephaestus, the god of fire, had made golden and silver statues of dogs. No, they were more than statues — they were guard dogs to keep the king and queen safe. The king and queen's thrones were decorated with weavings created by women — fine works of art. Boys made of gold held torches to make the feast room bright with light. Fifty serving-women worked in the palace, grinding grain or weaving. The Phaeacian sailors were famous for their art on the ocean, and the Phaeacian women were famous for their art with a loom.

Outside the courtyard was an orchard filled with trees that bore fruit all year round: pomegranates, pears, apples, figs, olives, and grapes. Also present were vegetable gardens, and two springs provided water for all: people and plants.

Odysseus looked, marveled, and thought, *Here is a fine society with a fine king who looks after his people. The gods have blessed this place. Why? When the rulers are good, the people will be good. I have heard that the common Phaeacians are not hospitable to strangers, but I have also heard that I will receive hospitality from the king and the queen. When the king and the queen observe* xenia, *they can make the common people be hospitable, too. And a good society is one in which the queen is respected. All of these things lead to blessings from the gods.*

Odysseus entered the palace, where he saw the Phaeacian lords drinking in honor of Hermes the messenger-god. Odysseus walked to King Alcinous and Queen Arete, and he sank at the feet of Queen Arete and beseeched her, "Queen! I ask for mercy! I pray to the gods to make you and your people prosperous. Please give me passage back to my home!"

All were shocked by Odysseus' sudden appearance in their midst. Echeneus, a wise and aged advisor to the king, said, "Alcinous, this is not the way to act. Your people are waiting for you to lead them. Give the stranger *xenia*. Raise him by the hand and give him a seat. Tell everyone to drink to Zeus, and tell a housekeeper to give a meal to the stranger."

King Alcinous knew that the advice was good — he had not acted sooner simply out of shock at the stranger's sudden appearance. He raised Odysseus from the floor and gave him a place to sit, telling his own favorite son to move from a chair so that the stranger might sit down. A housekeeper brought water so that the stranger could wash his hands, and then she brought him food. As Odysseus ate and drank, King Alcinous ordered wine so that all could pour offerings to Zeus, the god of *xenia*, the god who wishes humans to respect suppliants.

After all had poured and then drank, King Alcinous said, "Go home and sleep. Tomorrow morning we will hold a council with the elders, host the stranger, sacrifice to the gods, and arrange an easy voyage home for our guest. At home he must bear whatever the gods send him. But perhaps he is one of the gods, who sometimes come to test mortals to see if we are civilized, if we observe *xenia*."

Odysseus replied, "No, I am nothing like a god. I am a mortal man. I have suffered more than anyone you know. But let me finish my supper. An empty stomach is a misery, always insisting on being fed like a greedy dog. But please give me a safe passage home. Once I have seen my home again, I can die happy."

The other nobles left, leaving Alcinous, Arete, and Odysseus in the palace. Queen Arete recognized the clothing that Odysseus was wearing. She and her women had made the clothing, clothing that Nausicaa had just washed at the river.

Seeking necessary information, she asked, "Stranger, who are you, and from where did you come? Where did you get the clothing you are wearing now?"

"I have suffered much," Odysseus replied. "Far away is an island called Ogygia, where the sea-nymph Calypso lives. When Zeus crushed my ship and all my crewmembers died, I clung to the wreckage and floated to her island. She took care of me and even wanted to make me immortal and ageless, but I never loved her. She kept me captive on her island for seven years. Then she allowed me to build a raft, and she stocked it with provisions. I sailed in the raft for many days, and then I saw your island. Poseidon sent a storm against me and shattered my raft. I swam to shore, reaching a river that was free of rocks to cut me. I covered my body with leaves and slept all night and until the afternoon. When I awoke, I saw your daughter and her serving-maids — your daughter looked like a goddess! I asked her for help. She gave it to me, without ever making a misstep or doing anything that would discredit either her or you. She acted with much more tact and wisdom than most girls her age. She gave me food and wine, allowed me to bathe by myself in the river, and let me wear this clothing. Your daughter has been well raised."

King Alcinous replied, "My daughter, however, did one thing wrong. She did not escort you to our palace; instead, she let you find the palace by yourself."

Be careful, Odysseus thought. *Nausicaa has given you help when you needed help. You don't want the king and the queen to think that she has done anything at all wrong. If a lie will help, then tell a lie.*

"Don't find fault with your daughter," Odysseus said. "She has done everything right. She asked me to follow her, but I chose not to. I didn't want to cause any gossip."

Odysseus thought, *That isn't quite a lie. I simply left some information out. Nausicaa did ask me to follow her, but only to a point outside the city. I need not add any information that will make her parents think that she has done something wrong.*

"I try not to find fault without reason," Alcinous replied. "That is the way of wisdom. But you are intelligent and a good man. If you were to marry my daughter, I would give you a house and wealth. But I would never make you stay against your will. Zeus would not approve of such conduct. If you wish, we will give you transportation to your home. Our ships are magic. They can go anywhere across the sea and return home in just one day. The Phaeacian ships and sailors are magnificent!"

Odysseus prayed aloud to Zeus, "May King Alcinous fulfill his promises. Then his fame will never die, and I will reach my home again!"

The queen ordered a bed to be made for Odysseus, and all slept that night.

Chapter 8: Entertainment Among the Phaeacians

The next morning, King Alcinous led Odysseus to the meeting-grounds, and Athena, disguised as King Alcinous' herald, called the mature men to the council: "Come to the meeting-grounds and meet the new arrival, a stranger who has come here after roving the sea — a stranger like a god!" Athena also made Odysseus taller, stronger, and more handsome.

King Alcinous addressed his people: "Hear me! This stranger has come to us to ask us for aid. I don't know his name, but he is our guest. We are renowned for our hospitality. We show good *xenia* to all who come to our island. Let us show good *xenia* to this stranger also. No one who asks me for a journey home will be long gone from home.

"Come, obey my orders. Ready a ship for a voyage. Pick 52 young men of proven strength — the best of the Phaeacians — to row the ship. When the ship is ready, then the young men can come to the palace for a feast."

I can see why this society works so well, Odysseus thought. *First, the king gives clear orders. Perhaps the common Phaeacians would not themselves be kind to strangers, but the king makes it clear that strangers will be respected. Second, the king praises those who respect* xenia. *The young men who will row me home are, the king says, "the best of the Phaeacians." Finally, the king rewards those who respect* xenia. *These young men who will row me home are invited to a feast in the palace.*

The king continued, "Now let us entertain our guest. Call the bard Demodocus to sing for us. The gods have given him the gift of song — he can entertain all who listen to him."

The 52 picked young men of Phaeacia made the ship ready, then went to the king's palace. There a feast of a dozen sheep, eight boars, and two oxen was prepared for them. The bard arrived. He had the gift of song, but not the gift of sight. The gods don't give all their gifts to one person. The bard's lyre was hung within his easy reach, and he enjoyed wine and food.

Then the Muse inspired the bard — now is the time to sing of heroes. He sang of the Quarrel Between Odysseus and Achilles. Normally, a quarrel between heroes is a bad thing, but Agamemnon rejoiced when this quarrel occurred. He recalled a prophecy that when the two best Greeks quarreled, then Troy would soon fall.

Odysseus heard the song and wept, but he covered his face with his clothing so that the Phaeacians would not see him crying. Only King Alcinous noticed that he was crying.

When the song was over, King Alcinous said, "Now that we have enjoyed food and song, let us go to the meeting-ground so that the young men can participate in athletic contests: boxing, wrestling, running, and jumping."

All, including Demodocus, whom the herald led by the hand, went to the meeting-ground. The young athletes ran a race — Clytoneus won easily. In wrestling, Broadsea distinguished himself with victory. Seagirt out-jumped all the other athletes. Rowhard hurled the discus farther than anyone else. Laodamas, the son of King Alcinous, achieved victory in boxing.

Thrilled with victory, Laodamas said, "Come, let's ask our guest if he wishes to participate in our games. He's built strong like an athlete: big arms, broad chest, strong legs. And he's not so old that he must be a spectator, although his many hardships have taken a toll on him."

Broadsea agreed, "By all means, invite the guest to compete."

Laodamas went to Odysseus and said, "Come, guest, join our games. Win victory in the contests. All the world loves a winner."

Odysseus declined the invitation: "No contests for me. I am a suppliant, beaten down by hardship, hoping for a journey home."

"I knew that you weren't an athlete," Broadsea mocked Odysseus. "You don't know the skills that athletes and warriors know. Rather, you must be a pirate, trying to steal cargo and gold."

Odysseus, warrior that he was and had been, was insulted. Many of the skills used in athletic games are the same as the skills used in combat. "You speak nonsense, Broadsea. You are handsome, but you don't know how to properly speak to a guest and you don't know how to properly treat a guest. You look impressive, but your brain is lacking. I am an athlete, and I am a warrior, not a pirate. I have been at sea, I have been shipwrecked, and I am beaten down by hardship. But you have insulted me, so I will show you what I am capable of doing."

Odysseus picked up a discus, whirled, and hurled it far into the distance. Athena, disguised as a man, measured the distance and called out, "You're the winner. You threw the discus much farther than any of the Phaeacians. No one here can beat you."

Odysseus laughed with pleasure, and then he said, "I can equal that distance again — or beat it. Anyone who wants to can challenge me in contests — but not Laodamas. He is my host and the son of my host, and I must show respect to him. I would be foolish to challenge him. All the other athletes I challenge. Well I know how to shoot arrows — only Philoctetes was a better archer than me at Troy. Still, the old masters of archery are better than I am: Heracles and Eurytus. I must not over-praise myself and think that I am better than I am. That leads to trouble. Eurytus foolishly challenged Apollo, the god of archery, to a contest and Apollo shot him dead because of his boasting. I am also an expert spear-thrower. But at running I think that you can out-distance me. I have been on board a raft for so long that my legs don't have the power they used to have."

All the young men listened to Odysseus, and Odysseus thought, *I have taught the young men a lesson today: Don't insult a guest. I hope that they learn the lesson and that King Antinous will teach them well.*

King Antinous said, "Guest, everything you have said here is correct. You spoke well, and you behaved properly. You were insulted, and your response to the insult was admirable. The adolescent who insulted you should not have spoken that way to you. But let's continue with the entertainment. The Phaeacians are renowned dancers. So, Phaeacians, begin the dance!"

The herald fetched Demodocus' lyre, Demodocus played, and the young Phaeacian men competed in the dance. Odysseus watched with pleasure.

Then it was time for another song. Demodocus sang a comic song of Aphrodite's affair with Ares, the god of war. The two had fallen in lust although Aphrodite, the goddess of sexual passion, was married to Hephaestus, the gifted blacksmith god. Hephaestus learned of the affair, so he set a trap for the illicit lovers. He created fine chains that bound tightly, he placed the chains above his bed, and then he pretended to leave his mansion to journey abroad. Ares ran to Aphrodite and invited her to join him in Hephaestus' bed, and together they ran to the bed. Ares and Aphrodite lay down in bed together, and then the fine chains snared them, locked in lust.

Hephaestus returned home, knowing what and whom he would see in his bed. He invited all the gods and the goddesses to look, also. He complained to Zeus, "Father, look at how my wife treats me. I am crippled, so she sleeps with Ares because of his handsome looks. Right now, they are in my bed, locked together in the act of lovemaking by chains that only I can loosen. Come, look and laugh at the lovers. I will keep them bound until I receive my bride-gifts back. The goddess I married is a bitch."

The gods entered Hephaestus' bedroom and looked at the unhappy and embarrassed Ares and Aphrodite, naked and stuck together. The goddesses, however, were embarrassed and stayed away.

The gods laughed, and one god said to another, "Hephaestus one, adulterers zero. The blacksmith god conquers both the god of war and the goddess of sexual passion."

Apollo asked Hermes, "Would bedding Aphrodite be worth the embarrassment of being caught by Hephaestus?"

Hermes replied, "Of course! Look how beautiful she is!"

Only Poseidon did not laugh; he was a friend to Ares. He begged Hephaestus to release the lovers, saying, "Ares will pay you whatever you ask for sleeping with your wife."

Hephaestus replied, "Ares is a worthless god, and a promise from a worthless god is a worthless promise, so don't ask me to release him from my chains."

But Poseidon said, "If he won't pay the fine, I will. My word is good."

"So it is," Hephaestus said. He released the two lovers, who ran away in opposite directions to friends who would not laugh at them.

Odysseus listened to the comic song, and he was reminded of Paris and Helen, whose adulterous love affair had caused the Trojan War. He did not want to think about what could possibly be happening on Ithaca.

Now King Antinous asked two Phaeacians, his sons Laodamas and Halius, to dance, as they were the best of the Phaeacians at dancing while tossing a blue ball as the other men pounded out a beat with their feet.

Well entertained, Odysseus praised the dancers: "King Alcinous, I am amazed. Your Phaeacian dancers certainly live up to their reputations."

Pleased, King Alcinous said, "Phaeacians, let us give our guest the gifts that such a man deserves. Our land has twelve lords. Let each lord, including myself, give our guest a cloak and a shirt and a bar of gold. Bring the gifts to the palace tonight so that our guest may see the gifts and rejoice. And

Broadsea must apologize to our guest as well as give gifts. Earlier, he insulted our guest."

Each noble sent away for the gifts, and Broadway apologized to Odysseus, "King Alcinous, of course I will apologize to our guest. And I will give our guest this sword. I am sure that he will value it. Guest, sir, please accept my apology for what I said earlier. I wish you a swift and safe journey home to your loved ones."

Odysseus replied, "I accept your apology. May you enjoy good fortune throughout your life."

I can see why this society works so well, Odysseus thought. *Look at the king. He is like a good father to these young men. When they do something wrong, he lets them know it and he lets them know how to make up for the wrong they have done.*

The sun set, and all of Odysseus' gifts from the lords were carried into the palace. King Alcinous then spoke to his queen and requested of her, "Please, queen, give our guest a cloak and a shirt, and I will give him a golden cup so that he will remember us."

The serving-women prepared a hot bath for Odysseus, and all of Odysseus' gifts were put in a chest, ready for him to carry away. The queen invited Odysseus, "Tie the lid of the chest with a strong knot. You don't want to be robbed during your journey home."

That's good advice, Odysseus thought. *Even with a good king and queen, the common people can go astray. It's best to keep them away from temptation, to make it difficult for them to rob me.*

He tied the chest with a good strong knot. Circe had taught it to him; it was difficult to untie unless you knew how.

Odysseus bathed and dressed, and then he met Nausicaa as he walked to the dining hall to join the Phaeacian nobles. Nausicaa said to him, "Farewell, friend. I know that you are leaving to go to your home soon. Remember me when you are at home. I helped you when you needed help."

"Yes, Nausicaa," Odysseus replied. "I will always remember you, and I will pray to you as if you were a goddess. You saved my life."

He entered the dining hall, and he sat by King Alcinous. The meat was brought to the table, and Odysseus cut a savory portion from the roast boar, tender and tasty, and he sent it to Demodocus, the blind bard, saying,

"Herald, take this to Demodocus, and ask him to eat. The gods love a bard — the Muse herself gives bards their gift."

The bard rejoiced at the honor shown him, and all ate their fill. Odysseus then said to Demodocus, "I respect you and all bards. You have been given a great gift. You have sung of the Greeks' war against the Trojans. Now sing of the wooden horse filled with warriors — the trap that Odysseus thought up and that Epeus built. Sing that for us, and I will speak to men of your genius for epic song."

The bard knew the song. He sang of the Greeks' pretending to return to their homes, leaving behind a wooden horse that was pregnant with warriors. The Trojans debated what to do with — or to — the horse, but their city was fated to fall, and they brought it inside Troy. That night, the Greeks crept out of the wooden horse, opened the gates of the city to let in Agamemnon and the rest of the Greek army, and conquered the city. Odysseus and Menelaus fought side by side, going together to the house of Deiphobus, Helen's newest Trojan husband.

So the bard sang, and Odysseus wept just like a woman weeps whose husband has died in battle as his city is conquered. She clings to his corpse, but the enemy soldiers force her to leave the body and become a slave.

So Odysseus wept, perhaps out of recognition that the Trojan War had brought grief both to the victors and to the vanquished. Odysseus may also have wept because of the atrocities that the Greeks had committed during the fall of Troy. Little Ajax raped the virgin Cassandra in Athena's own temple — a place where the virgin should have been respected. The Greeks killed Hector's son by throwing him from the high walls of Troy. The Greeks sacrificed Polyxena, a daughter of King Priam, following the fall of Troy. Such atrocities should not be committed — even against an enemy.

Only King Alcinous noticed Odysseus crying, and he said, "Let Demodocus stop singing now. His song is not pleasing to all here. Our guest has been crying throughout the song. We must treat a guest the way that we would treat a brother — that is the civilized way. But now, guest, tell us who you are. Who are your parents? From which land are you? We will sail you home. No land bordering the sea is too far for our ships to reach. We return all wanderers to their homes.

"Such has been the case so far, but my father once told me a prophecy. Poseidon is angry at us. He is the god of the sea, and he thinks that we are disrespecting him by returning travelers to their homes in our ships that can cross the sea and never sink. According to the prophecy, someday Poseidon will crush one of our ships as it returns home and he will put a mountain in our harbor to keep us from using the port to send travelers home.

"But guest, friend, tell us your story. Where have you traveled? What have you seen? Why do you cry when you hear a song about Troy? Did a relative of yours die at Troy? Or a friend?"

Chapter 9: Odysseus and the Cyclops

Odysseus said, "King Alcinous, it's a wonderful thing to listen to a bard, to hear his stories and songs. Nothing is better than to listen and to feast and to drink in times of peace. But since you want to hear the tale of my hardships, so be it. I have suffered so much. But first let me tell you my name. Some day to come, perhaps you will visit me and be my guest.

"My name is Odysseus, and as the songs of the bard have shown, my fame has reached the skies."

King Alcinous and the Phaeacians marveled. Here before them was *the* Odysseus, a hero of the Trojan War, a hero who had vanished and no one knew whether he was alive or dead. They had known that their guest must be a man of some importance in his own land, but they had not expected *this*.

"My father is Laertes, and my home is Ithaca," Odysseus continued. "I am the man of twists and turns, and I long to see my home. For years, I lived with the goddesses Calypso and Circe, but even then I longed for home. Nothing is better than one's own home — not even foreign luxury. Let me tell you my story, everything that happened after the Fall of Troy."

Tell a good story now, Odysseus thought. *Tomorrow you will return home. You are generously laden with gifts, but if you can impress the Phaeacians with your story, they may give you more gifts. You have lost everything you gained from the Trojan War, and this is a chance to make up for what you have lost.*

"We sailed first to Ismarus, the city of the Cicones. We attacked and conquered the city, gaining more booty that we hoped to take home with us. We killed all of the men, and then we divided the Cicones' wives and booty equally — no one went without a fair share. I urged my men to sail away quickly, but they did not listen to me. No. They were more interested in drinking the wine of the Cicones and feasting on their cattle. Meanwhile, the refugees from the city sought relatives and friends, armed themselves, and attacked at dawn. We fought all day, but in the end the Cicones defeated us, killing six men from each of my twelve ships.

"We fled in our ships, mourning the men we had lost, and Zeus sent a storm against us, blowing us way off course for nine days. Finally, we reached the land of the Lotus-eaters. We landed, we ate, and I sent out three men to scout the territory to see who, if anyone, lived there. They ran across the Lotus-eaters, a gentle people who would never attack anyone, but who were addicted to the Lotus, a plant that contains a drug that takes away all ambition. Anyone who eats the Lotus forgets about goals and forgets about trying to achieve something important with their lives. All they want to do is to eat the Lotus. That is no life for a human being. The scouting party ate the Lotus, and they forgot about seeing home again, but I forced them to return to the ships and continue our journey.

"Then we reached the land of the Cyclopes, a one-eyed race of giants who do not farm. They herd animals and gather wild plants. They make wine from wild grapes. They have no laws, no courts, no councils. They have no ships. They live wild and uncivilized. Each Cyclops rules his own wife and children, if any, and they do not care for neighbors or for strangers.

"We landed on an island by the home of the Cyclopes. We slept and ate there for a day, and then I became curious. I did not know then that the Cyclopes lived just across the water, but I could see the smoke from their fires, and I could hear the sounds made by their animals. I could even hear the voices of the Cyclopes.

"The next morning, I issued orders: 'Most of you will stay here on this island. I will sail in my ship across the water and investigate what is on the land over there. Who lives there? Are they wild and do not follow the rules of *xenia*? Are they civilized and follow the rules of *xenia*?'

"We crossed the water and landed. Most of my men stayed behind with the ship, but twelve warriors and I set off to investigate a cave that was home to one of the beings that lived here. I took along fine wine as a gift to my host. The wine was a gift from Maron, a man whom we had rescued — him and his family. Even when mixed with water, the wine was strong and delicious.

"We went to the cave, but no one was at home. We looked around. We saw the cheeses. We saw the young animals: lambs and kids. We saw the buckets the owner used for milking.

"My crewmembers urged me to be a pirate — to steal the cheeses first and then to come back and steal the lambs and kids. But I was curious and would not be a pirate, although it would have better for my men and me if I had been a pirate rather than a curious but bad guest.

"We made ourselves at home. We built a fire. We ate most of the cheeses. We also sacrificed some of the cheeses to the gods. We were bad guests. Then the Cyclops returned home, carrying logs with which to build a fire. We saw him — one-eyed, immense — and out of fear, we hid ourselves in the shadows in the rear of the cave.

"The Cyclops blocked the opening to his cave with a boulder that was impossible for us — even with our strength combined — to move. We were trapped in the cave of the Cyclops. He milked his animals, and then started a fire — and saw us.

"He cried out, 'Strangers, who are you? Where' you come from? Are you merchants sailing the seas? Or are you pirates, robbing everybo'y you can?'

"I replied, 'We are men from Troy, trying to sail home but driven far off course. We fought for Agamemnon, but now we are your guests. We hope that you will welcome us, even give us a guest-gift. That is what the gods would want you to do — especially Zeus, the god of *xenia*.'

"The Cyclops replied, 'Stranger, we Cyclopes 'o not fear Zeus or any other go'. We 'o what we want, and we have no 'uties except to 'o what benefits us. But tell me, where is your ship?'

"I was suspicious. I did not want to tell him where our ship was, so I lied: 'We are shipwrecked. Our ship has been broken by Poseidon, god of the sea.'

"Hearing that, the Cyclops grabbed two of my men, knocked their heads against the rocky floor of his cave, dashing out their brains, and then ate them raw. We were horrified. We prayed to Zeus, god of *xenia*, but we heard no reply. Having filled his belly, the Cyclops slept.

"My first thought was to kill the Cyclops as he slept, but I could not. We were trapped inside the cavern, and all of us together could not move the boulder that blocked the opening of the cave. If I had drawn my sword and killed the Cyclops, we would have been trapped in the cave with his decomposing corpse. And once we had eaten all the cheeses and all the animals inside the cave, we would have starved to death.

"The next morning, the Cyclops awoke and milked his ewes, and then he killed and ate two more of my men. He drove the mature animals out of the cave so they could go to pasture, but he made sure to block the opening of the cave with the boulder so that we could not escape.

"We needed a plan. We could not do nothing and allow the Cyclops to devour us. I gave orders. We found a club that the Cyclops had in the cave — it was big enough to be the mast of a ship with twenty oars. We cut off six feet of the club, and we planed it to make it smooth. I myself sharpened one end of the club to a sharp point. We hardened the point in a fire, and then we hid our new weapon well. By lot we chose four good men to help me that night as the Cyclops slept.

"That evening the Cyclops returned to the cave. He drove all of his animals into the cave, blocked the opening with the boulder, performed his chores, and then ate two more of my men. I poured some of my wine — my gift to my host — into a mixing-bowl and offered it to the Cyclops, saying, 'Drink this fine wine. I brought it as a gift. I had hoped to meet a friendly host, but you have been the opposite of friendly. Instead of making your guests a meal, you have made your guests your meal!'

"The Cyclops took the wine and drank, and then praised the wine, 'This is ambrosia, the 'rink of the go's. More! Give me another bowlful! And tell me your name — I will give a guest-gift to you.'

"I gave the Cyclops another bowlful of wine. He drank three bowlfuls — enough to cloud his brain and make him drunk and sleepy. I said to him, 'You want to know my name, Cyclops? I will tell you, but give me a guest-gift. My name is Nomad, wanderer of the sea.'

"'Your name is Noma'?' the Cyclops replied. "I will give a guest-gift to Noma'. I will eat your men first. I will eat you last of all. That is the guest-gift I will give to you.'

"Having said that, the Cyclops fell down drunk and vomited up chunks of human flesh mixed with wine. Then he slept.

"My men and I got out the sharpened log hardened in fire, and we put it in fire again — to make it red-hot. Then I told my men, 'Be brave. We can't afford to be cowards now.' We then drove the red-hot stake into the sleeping Cyclops' eye — I myself directed the point into his eye and used all my strength to drive the stake deep. The eye sizzled and blood ran from the socket. The Cyclops awoke, roaring with pain, and he grabbed the stake and pulled it from his eye.

"The neighboring Cyclopes arrived to see if he needed help, but I was too clever for them. I had foreseen what would happen and had planned a trick. The Cyclopes shouted, 'Polyphemus, what man now is hurting you?'

"As I had foreseen, Polyphemus, the one-eyed Cyclops who had been keeping us captive, replied, 'Noma' now is hurting me.' The other Cyclopes replied, 'If no man now is hurting you, then the go's must be angry at you and are sending you an illness. Pray to your father, Posei'on, for help.' Then they left.

"Polyphemus wanted revenge. When it was time to take his animals to pasture, he moved the boulder from the opening of the cave and he squatted in the opening and used his hands to feel whatever left his cave. He hoped to catch my men and me and kill us, but I was too smart for him. I tied rams together — three rams were enough to camouflage one of my men so that they could escape the hands of the Cyclops and escape from the cave. I myself hid under the oldest and the biggest of the rams, leaving the cave last of all.

"Polyphemus felt the back of the old ram, and with newfound sympathy learned from suffering said, 'Ol' ram, why are you the last of the flock to leave the cave? When you were younger, you were the first of the flock to reach the pasture and feast on grass. When you were younger, you were the first of the flock to hea' for home in the evening. Now you are last of all. Why? 'o you mourn for your master, whose eye has been put out by Noma', the cowar' who got me 'runk and attacked me while I was asleep? I will have my revenge against him. He will not escape retribution. How I want to kill him!'

"Polyphemus let the ram — and me — go. When I was out of the cave, I left the ram and gathered my men together and we drove Polyphemus' flocks to my ship — the Cyclops was floundering, unused to being blind. The crewmembers we had left behind with the ship mourned the men who had died, but quickly loaded the animals on board our ship. We set sail.

"But I spoke when I should have remained silent. I yelled to Polyphemus, 'You devoured the men of a captain who is no coward! You ate your guests, and now you have been paid back!'

"Furious, Polyphemus grabbed a boulder and hurled it in the direction of my voice. It fell past my ship, and the wave it made drove us toward Polyphemus. My men rowed frantically to save their lives.

"Again, I taunted the Cyclops, although my men urged me not to, saying, 'We almost died. Why risk death a second time? If he had heard us when we were close to shore, he would have killed us all!'

"But I insisted on taking the credit for my exploit. I yelled to the Cyclops, 'Do you want to know who blinded you? It was I, Odysseus, son of Laertes. My home is Ithaca.'

"The Cyclops moaned, 'Once I heard a prophecy that O'ysseus would blind me. I have always looked for him, but I expected him to be a giant, a magnificent warrior, not a puny human. If you return, O'ysseus, I will give you a guest-gift. My father, Posei'on, will heal my eye if he wants to.'

"I was not about to return to the Cyclops' shore. I shouted at him, 'I wish that you were dead! I hope that your eye is never healed!'

"Polyphemus, angry, prayed to Poseidon, 'Father, curse O'ysseus, son of Laertes. O'ysseus' home is Ithaca. May he never return home. Or if he 'oes return home, let it be only after years of wandering, and let him find 'anger and trouble at home.'"

As soon as I heard the Cyclops' prayer, I knew that I had made a mistake, thought Odysseus. *If I had not told the Cyclops my identity, he would not have been able to pray to Poseidon and curse me. Poseidon may never have found out that it was me who blinded his son, and he would not have known to hate me.*

"Poseidon heard the Cyclops' prayer. Gods can do that. Polyphemus lifted and hurled another boulder. It fell short of my ship, and the wave it made pushed us across the water to our other ships. We landed, and we divided the Cyclops' animals equally, so that all had a share. My crew voted to award me the big, old ram, which I sacrificed to Zeus, god of *xenia*, but the sacrifice did not move Zeus. He still plotted to destroy my ships and my men.

"We feasted, and then we slept. In the morning, we rowed away to new lands, mourning still for the men who had died."

Chapter 10: Odysseus and Circe

"Next we reached the island over which lorded Aeolus, god of the winds, who welcomed us. Aeolus and his wife and his six daughters and six sons live happily in his palace, feasting continually. Aeolus asked me for news of Troy as he hosted us for one whole month, and when we left he gave me the best possible guest-gift: a sack in which all the contrary winds were tied up. The only wind left out of the sack was the one that would blow my ship straight to home — my men and I would see Ithaca once more!

"For nine days and nights we sailed, with me as pilot — I would not trust that job to anyone but myself. I even saw the smoke rising from the fires burning on Ithaca, and then I was so weary that I fell into a deep sleep. My crewmembers — greedy as they were — began to complain among themselves: 'Odysseus gets heaps of treasure from Troy, and he gets a guest-gift from Aeolus. We get nothing.' Another of my crew suggested, 'Let's open the sack that Aeolus gave Odysseus and see what's inside.' Bad luck — they opened the sack and the contrary winds stormed out and blew us away from Ithaca and back to the island of Aeolus. He was not pleased to see me, saying, 'Why are you here, Odysseus? How could anything keep you from reaching Ithaca? Do the gods hate you?' I replied, 'It was my crewmembers — they untied the sack.' Aeolus told me, 'Get away from here, and don't expect any more help from me. If the gods hate you that much, it would be a crime for me to help you.'

"I pleaded, but Aeolus would not be moved. We had to leave without the guest-gift that I wanted so much. We traveled for six days and nights, rowing all the way, until we reached the land of the Laestrygonians. They had a fine harbor, and all of the other ships pulled in close to shore. I alone ordered my ship to remain outside the harbor. I have learned to be cautious in this world.

"I sent three men to scout the land. They met the daughter of Antiphates, King of the Laestrygonians, a huge girl, much larger than our girls. She took them to the palace and summoned her father, who grabbed one of the men and tore him to pieces so he could eat him.

"The other two men ran for their lives, but the king summoned his Laestrygonians, who gave chase. The Laestrygonians hurled boulders from the cliffs, breaking the ships. Other Laestrygonians waded in the water, spearing men as if they were fish, to take them home and eat them.

"I fled to safety, cutting the ropes that moored us and yelling at my men, 'Row quickly now — or die!' We made it to safety; all of the other ships and men were lost. We mourned the loss of our companions, but we were glad that we had escaped.

"Next we reached Aeaea, the island of the goddess Circe. We sailed into a harbor and stayed for two days and nights, mourning for our lost companions. Then I went exploring. I climbed to a lookout point and surveyed the land. In the distance, I saw smoke rising from a palace. I didn't want to go to the palace until my men were fed, so I returned to my ship. On the way, I killed a stag, meat enough for all of my men and me.

"I carried the meat to my men, and then I said to them, 'Be brave. We aren't dead yet. Let's eat and drink.' We cooked the meat, feasted and drank wine, and slept. The next morning I told my crewmembers about the smoke I had seen. Thinking of the Laestrygonians, they regarded the smoke as a bad sign — a sign of another race of cannibals who wished to feast on our bodies.

"But I divided everyone into two groups. I was the leader of one group, and Eurylochus was the leader of the other group. We shook lots, and it fell to Eurylochus and his men to investigate the house of the rising smoke. I stayed by my one remaining ship with the other group of men.

"Eurylochus and his men found Circe's palace. Mountain lions and wolves — beasts that she had bewitched — guarded it. The mountain lions and wolves did not attack, but they watched Eurylochus and his men. Circe was inside, singing as she worked at her loom. Eurylochus was hanging back, suspicious, so Polites took command and called to Circe, who invited all of them inside.

"Eurylochus alone stayed outside of her palace. Inside, Circe fed the men a potion, and then she waved a wand and transformed them into pigs, which she drove into a pigsty. Only the minds of the men remained human.

"Eurylochus ran back to me and my ship and told me what he had witnessed: 'I saw the men go into the palace with the singing female — whether she was immortal goddess or mortal woman, I do not know. The men never came out of the palace again, although I waited outside a very long time.'

"I armed myself with sword and bow and arrows and prepared to go in search of my men, but Eurylochus begged me to set sail and leave the men behind. I refused. He begged me not to make him return to the palace, so I ordered him to stay behind at the ship. I set off, alone. I was not going to leave the island without my men.

"As I drew near the palace, Hermes, the messenger of the gods, appeared and gave me advice: 'So, friend, you go in search of your men. They are with Circe, turned by her into swine. Without my help, you also would fall under her enchantments. I will help you. Here is an herb called moly that will keep you safe from Circe's enchantments. Take it with you into her palace. She will give you a potion, and then she will draw her wand to enchant you. When she does that, draw your sword and rush at her. She will invite you to go to bed with her. If you want her to release your men from her enchantment, take her to bed. But first make her swear that she will do nothing to hurt you.'

"Hermes left, and I went to Circe's palace. I called to her, and she invited me inside. She mixed a potion for me to drink, but the herb that Hermes had given me protected me. She then waved her wand, saying, 'Now, pig, go into the sty with the other pigs.' I drew my sword and rushed at her. Goddesses are immortal and cannot die, but they do feel pain.

"Circe avoided the blade of my sword and fell at my feet, begging me not to stab her. She said, 'Why didn't my potion and wand have any effect on you? You must be Odysseus. Hermes told me that you would arrive one day. Put away your sword, and let's go to bed.'

"I remembered what Hermes had told me. 'Go to bed with you?' I said. 'Why? So you can get me naked and vulnerable? You turned my men into swine, and you tried to do the same thing with me. I won't go to bed with you unless you swear an oath that you will not hurt me.'

"Circe swore the oath, and I took her to bed. Her handmaids prepared a meal, and after Circe and I had finished making love, Circe gave me a bath and then invited me to eat. But I, thinking of my men, could not eat. I said to her, 'How could any man eat, knowing that his men are still in the shape of swine? If you want me to eat and drink, give them back their human shapes.'

"Circe went to her pigsty, rubbed an ointment on each pig, and my men returned to their human shapes. Each man was thankful to me for not abandoning them on the island. Circe herself invited me to get my other men and bring them to her palace.

"I did as she asked. I returned to the ship and found my men worried — but glad that I was alive and glad at the good news that I brought them. I told him, 'Let us go to the palace of Circe and enjoy her hospitality.' But Eurylochus was overly cautious; he was still worried about Circe and her tricks. He did not want to be turned into a pig.

"I wanted to kill Eurylochus right by the ship — a crewmember should obey his captain. But my men persuaded me not to, advising instead that I leave him by the ship if he did not want to go to Circe's palace and feast. We left for Circe's palace — and Eurylochus followed, reluctantly.

"Circe had bathed the men left behind in her palace, and now they were feasting. We all rejoiced to be together again, safe. Circe said to me, 'Eat and drink now. All of you have had a long, hard journey. Now it is time to relax.'

"We stayed at Circe's palace — for an entire year. It was my companions who grew homesick and urged me to set sail again — it was time to look for our homecoming. I had delayed too long. I knew that my men were right.

"That night I entreated Circe to let us go. I did not want to make her angry, so I made it clear that my men were the ones who were restless and wanted to leave, but I also said that I too longed for my homecoming.

"She told me, 'Leave if you wish — I won't hold you here against your will. But before you return home, you must make another journey. You must visit Persephone's land — the Land of the Dead. There you must see Tiresias, the blind Theban prophet who can tell you what lies ahead for you. Although he is dead, his spirit has retained its wits. The other ghosts of the dead have lost their wisdom.'

"This was not a journey I wished to make. I asked her, 'Circe, what living man has ever reached the Land of the Dead in a ship?'

"Circe gave me directions and advice. She said, 'To reach the Land of the Dead is easy. Simply spread your sail and let the North wind blow you out into the Ocean and to Persephone's land. Beach your ship and find the rivers that flow into a flood of grief — a River of Fire and a River of Tears flow into Acheron, the Flood of Grief. That is where you need to be. When you arrive there, dig a trench, and all around it pour milk and honey and wine and then pour barley — these are the offerings to the dead. Vow that once you are home on Ithaca you will slaughter a heifer and offer treasures to the dead. In addition, vow to sacrifice a black ram for Tiresias alone. Then slaughter a ram and a black ewe, but as you do so look toward the ocean. Let their blood flow into the pit. The ghosts of the dead will smell the blood and come out of the pit of the Underworld. Order your men to skin the carcasses of the sheep you have slaughtered and to say prayers to Persephone and her husband: Hades, God of the Underworld. You, Odysseus, draw your sword and keep the ghosts of the dead away from the blood until you have talked to Tiresias and heard his prophecy. He will tell you what you need to know, what you need to do, and what you need to avoid doing. He will tell you how you may reach home.'

"Dawn came, I dressed, and I spoke to my men: 'Today we leave. Let us set sail.' But one man did not sail with us. Elpenor had drunk too much. To find a cool place to sleep in the hot night, he had climbed up to Circe's roof, but at dawn, still drunk, he got up and fell off the roof. He broke his neck and died. His soul reached the Land of the Dead before we did.

"As we were walking to the ship, I gave my men the news: 'We are not sailing for home. Circe has set for us a different destination. We must visit Persephone's land: the Land of the Dead. We go there to consult Tiresias, the blind Theban prophet.'

"My men groaned, but it did them no good. Moaning and groaning never does. When we arrived at the ship, we saw that Circe had prepared everything for our voyage, including giving us a ram and a black ewe to sacrifice. The gods and goddesses can move quickly and silently."

Chapter 11: Odysseus in the Land of the Dead

"We launched the ship, and filled with grief, embarked on our journey to the Land of the Dead. Circe sent us a favorable wind, and we sailed quickly past the inhabited lands and into the Ocean. When we reached Persephone's land, we disembarked and found the rivers that flow into a flood of grief. There I dug a trench and after I had made all the vows that Circe had advised me to make, I sacrificed the ram and the black ewe, spilling their blood into the trench. The ghosts of the dead smelled blood and came out of the Land of the Dead, but I drew my sword and would not let them drink blood — I first wanted to speak to Tiresias.

"But first I saw my crewmember, the newly dead Elpenor, whose corpse we had not yet buried because we wanted to undertake this important journey. I called to him, 'Elpenor, how did your ghost arrive here so much faster than our ship?'

"'I died too soon,' the ghost of Elpenor replied. 'I slept on the roof of Circe's palace but fell from her roof and broke my neck. Then my ghost traveled here. But when you leave Persephone's land, I beg you to return to Circe's island and hold a funeral for me. Until you give me a decent funeral, I cannot enter the Land of the Dead but must remain just beyond its boundary.'

"I promised him, 'I will do that for you.'

"Then I saw the ghost of my mother, Anticleia. Until this moment, I had not known that she was dead. I grieved, but even so I would not let her drink blood — not until I had questioned Tiresias.

"Tiresias arrived, and he immediately recognized me, saying, 'Odysseus, why are you here? Seeking prophecy and knowledge of the future? I have my wits in the afterlife, but I need to drink blood in order to regain the gift of prophecy.'

"I allowed him to drink blood, and then he began to prophesy: 'You hope for an easy journey home, but you have made Poseidon angry at you. You blinded the one-eyed Cyclops Polyphemus, his son. Poseidon will make your journey home difficult. Still, you may make it home quickly, despite difficulties, if you can control yourself and your crewmembers. You will reach Thrinacia, the island of the Sun-god, where you will find his immortal cattle and sheep. Leave the immortal animals alone. If you do, you and your men will reach home. But if you harm the animals in any way, your ship will be destroyed and your men will die. You will return home to Ithaca, but not quickly, and you will be alone and you will find a world of trouble waiting for you. You will find young men courting your wife, trying to marry her although you are still alive. No doubt you are intelligent and brave enough to kill all of the suitors — either by trickery or in open battle. After you have killed the suitors, you must undertake a journey. You must travel inland while carrying an oar. When you meet a people who have no knowledge of the sea and who call the oar a winnowing fan, plant the oar in the ground and sacrifice to Poseidon. By carrying knowledge of Poseidon to a people who know nothing of him, you will make peace with Poseidon and the god will no longer be your enemy. At that time, you may return home to Ithaca. You will meet your death there — it will be an easy death. When you die, you will die of old age, surrounded by family and friends. I have told you the truth.'

"I replied, 'Tiresias, all that you have said is fated to occur, but I have one question for you. I see the ghost of my mother before me, but she does not recognize me or speak to me. What can I do to have a conversation with her?'

"Tiresias replied, 'It's very simple. Any ghosts you allow to drink blood will recover their wits for a short time — long enough for you to speak with them. If you do not allow a ghost to drink blood, that ghost will return to the Land of the Dead.'

"Tiresias left me then and returned to the Land of the Dead, and I allowed the ghost of my mother to drink blood. She recognized me and cried, saying, 'Why are you here — you are still alive! Have you just left Troy? Have you been home to Ithaca yet to see your wife?'

"I replied, 'Mother, I have not yet been home. First I had to visit the Land of the Dead to see Tiresias and to hear him prophesy. But tell me how you died. Did you die a slow death of illness? Or did the goddess Artemis bring a quick death to you? Tell me about my father and my son. Is someone else King of Ithaca now because people do not think I will ever return home? Tell me about my wife. Has she married someone else by now?'

"My mother told me, 'I am sure that Penelope has not remarried. No one else is King of Ithaca. Telemachus is the head of your house. As for your father, he stays on a farm, working hard in his old age, wearing rags, and grieving for you. As for me, I died out of grief for you. I so longed for your return, with you gone so long, that I died.'

"I wanted to embrace my mother. Three times I tried to hug her in my arms, but she was insubstantial. Three times my arms closed on nothing. She was a ghost. I said to her, 'Mother, I long to hug you. Are you a wraith that Persephone has sent to torment me?'

"My mother replied, 'No, I am not a wraith sent to torment you. This insubstantial form is simply what ghosts are like in the Land of the Dead. This is what death is. The body is gone, and all that remains is a ghost. But you must want to return soon to the Land of the Living. Go soon, and remember all that you have learned so that you can tell Penelope.'

"Then many famous women of the past came to me. I wanted to speak to them, so I allowed only one at a time to drink blood. I saw and spoke to many famous women. I saw and spoke to Alcmena, the mother of Heracles and wife to Amphitryon. Zeus wanted to sleep with her, so he disguised himself as her husband. Looking exactly like Amphitryon, Zeus slept with her and she gave birth to Heracles, the greatest hero Greece has ever produced, at the same time she gave birth to Iphicles, the son of Amphitryon.

"I saw and spoke to Megara, the wife of Heracles. I also saw and spoke to Epicaste, the mother of Oedipus. Horror — she married her son, Oedipus, who had killed his father, her husband. I also saw and spoke to Leda, the mother of the twins Castor and Polydeuces, who after their deaths, take turns being alive. When one is alive for a day, the other is dead.

"So many famous women I saw in the Land of the Dead, I cannot name them all. But it is late now; it is time for sleep. I could even sleep on a ship as it carries me home."

Odysseus thought, *This is a perfect time to stop telling my story. Queen Arete has much influence among the Phaeacians, and I have been careful to speak about the women she is most interested to hear about. I have also been careful to tell an interesting story to the Phaeacians. In addition, I have been careful not to tell everything. For example, I have not spoken about seeing any of the dead heroes of the Trojan War. If I have told my story well enough, King*

Alcinous and the other nobles will want me to continue telling my story. They won't want me to go to sleep now and leave for home in the morning. If that were to happen, they would never hear the rest of my story. Instead, they will encourage me — with more gifts — to stay awake all night and tell them what else I saw in the Land of the Dead — and what happened afterward. I will be able to return to Ithaca with more possessions. My twenty years away from Ithaca will not have been spent without gaining material wealth.

"Queen Arete, who had enjoyed hearing about the famous women in the Land of the Dead, spoke first: 'Phaeacians, isn't our guest an impressive storyteller and an impressive man? Let's not be quick to send him on his way, and let's be generous in giving him gifts. We are a wealthy people, and he washed up on our shore with nothing.'

"Echeneus, advisor to the king, said, 'Our queen speaks wisely. We should do as our queen says, if the king agrees.'

"King Alcinous said, 'Yes, by all means, let us give gifts to our guest, who must stay here until we can gather all of his gifts.'

"I replied, 'King Alcinous, now, if you should wish me to stay here for an entire year and then send me home with many gifts, I would be willing. If I return to Ithaca laden with many gifts, I will be much more respected than I would if I should return home with empty hands.'

"King Alcinous told me, 'Odysseus, you are an honest man. Frauds rove the world, but you are not one of them. You tell your story like a bard! Please tell me, when you were in the Land of the Dead, did you see any of your fallen comrades from the Trojan War? Please keep telling us your story — I want to hear it all.'

"'King Alcinous,' I replied, 'there is a time for sleep and a time for storytelling. Since you want to hear my story, I will continue. I will tell not only my own story, but the story of a leader who escaped death during the war, only to be killed at home.'

"After the ghosts of the famous women had left, I saw Agamemnon, leader of the Greeks during the Trojan War. I had not known that he was dead. He drank blood, and he recognized me. He wanted to embrace me, but he was a ghost so he could not. I wept. I said to him, 'Famous Agamemnon, why are you in the Land of the Dead? Did you drown during your voyage home? Were you killed as you tried to sack another city?'

"He replied, 'Odysseus, I did not drown during my voyage home. I made it safely home, but I was not safe at home. My wife, Clytemnestra, had taken a lover named Aegisthus while I was at Troy. Together, they killed me. Aegisthus invited me to his palace for a feast. As I was eating, he slaughtered me. All of my comrades also died in his palace. He showed no mercy. You, Odysseus, have seen hundreds of men killed in battle, but this slaughter would have made you feel pity. As I lay dying, Clytemnestra killed Cassandra, the woman I was awarded after the fall of Troy. As I lay pierced by the sword of Aegisthus, Clytemnestra turned away from me. When I was dead, she did not close my mouth or my eyelids.'

"Agamemnon continued, 'Such is the way of vengeful women. They have no pity on those they slaughter! Clytemnestra also ruined her own reputation throughout the ages, and she makes it much harder to believe that any woman can be honest, faithful, and true.'

"I said to Agamemnon, 'Your family has suffered much at the hands of the gods. So many of us died to get Helen for Menelaus, your brother. While we were dying, Clytemnestra was plotting how to murder you.'

"'That's true,' Agamemnon said. 'So learn from my death. Don't trust a woman, even if you are married to her. Never tell her everything. Still, Odysseus, your wife is unlikely to murder you. Penelope is wise. When we left to go to Troy, Penelope was very young. She was nursing her newborn son. That boy is becoming a young man. How fortunate he is — he will see his father returning home. I myself never saw my son. Clytemnestra killed me before I could see him. Remember what happened to me. Be cautious — don't trust a woman! But have you heard anything of my son?'

"I replied, 'I have heard nothing. I have run across no news of him during my travels.'"

Odysseus thought, *At the time I visited the Land of the Dead, Agamemnon's son, Orestes, had not killed Aegisthus yet. Orestes' fame had not yet spread throughout the world. Of course, if he had killed Aegisthus, Aegisthus' ghost would have told Agamemnon how he had died.*

"We grieved together, and then Achilles, the greatest warrior of the Trojan War, strode up to me. He was pleased to see me and said, 'What are you planning for your next exploit? Can you ever top visiting the Land of the Dead while you are still alive? Why are you here?'

"I replied, 'Achilles, I needed to consult the ghost of Tiresias, the Theban prophet, to get advice on how to reach home. I have not been home since I left to fight at Troy. I have had many troubles. But Achilles, you have been blest! While you were alive, we honored you. And now that you are dead, you are honored in the Land of the Dead. You should not grieve at being dead, Achilles.'

"Achilles replied, 'Don't praise death to *me*. I have experienced both life and death. I know this to be true: Being the slave of an impoverished farmer in the Land of the Living is vastly preferable to having the very highest status in the Land of the Dead. Being dead sucks. But can you tell me about my son? Did he ever fight at Troy? Did he become a hero? Can you tell me about my old father, Peleus? Is he still respected at home, or do people take advantage of him because he has grown old? I wish I were alive again, even for a day, so I could see my father and teach his tormentors not to victimize an old king.'

"I replied, 'Achilles, I can't tell you anything about your father, but I do know the story of your son, Neoptolemus. I myself brought him to Troy to fight. He understood the strategy of war — only old wise Nestor and I were better than he at devising plans. As a fighter, he was always in the front ranks. He killed and killed again. He even killed the magnificent hero Eurypylus, the leader of the Ceteans. When we entered the Trojan Horse, many warriors were afraid — what if the trick did not work? Your son was not afraid — he was eager to sack Troy. Even after fighting so hard before and during the sack of Troy, his body remained without scars — he was such a skillful warrior that he could fight yet avoid wounds that scar.'

"Achilles was proud of his son. He strode off, thinking of his son and glorying. Now all of the other dead came crowding around the blood — with one exception. The ghost of Great Ajax kept his distance. Great Ajax was still angry at me. After Achilles died, his mother, the goddess Thetis, wished to give his armor that was made by the god Hephaestus to one of the Greek warriors. They voted. I came in first; Great Ajax came in second. Great Ajax was so angry that he lost his sanity. He tortured and killed sheep, thinking that they were Agamemnon and I. When he returned to his senses and realized what he had done, he was so ashamed and felt so dishonored that he committed suicide. I wish that I had not won the armor. It would be better by far for Great Ajax to live.

"I called to Great Ajax, 'Please stop being angry at me. The gods tormented the Greeks by setting up the contest for the arms of Achilles. We lost a mighty warrior when you died. We grieved, and we gave you a funeral as magnificent as the funeral we gave Achilles. Please talk to me, Great Ajax.'

"Still angry at me, he did not answer, but walked away.

"I saw still more illustrious dead. I saw Minos, the King of Crete who was renowned for his justice. I saw the hunter Orion.

"I also saw famous sinners. Tityus had once kidnapped and tried to rape Leto, the consort of Zeus and mother of Apollo and Artemis. For this infamous deed, he had been sentenced to lie chained on the ground as two vultures eternally dug into his body and ate his liver.

"And I saw Tantalus, so proud that he tried to fool the gods. He killed and cooked his own son, Pelops, and he put the meat into a stew that he served the gods. The gods knew the trick, however, so they did not eat the stew — with the exception of the goddess Demeter, who ate part of Pelops' shoulder. Outraged, the gods brought Pelops to life again and gave him a shoulder made out of marble, and they sentenced Tantalus to eternal torment in the Land of the Dead. He stands in a stream of water, and branches heavily laden with ripe fruit are overhead, yet Tantalus is eternally thirsty and hungry. Whenever Tantalus bends over to drink from the stream, the water dries up. Whenever Tantalus reaches overhead to seize a piece of fruit, a breeze blows the fruit just out of his reach.

"And I saw Sisyphus, a trickster who even tricked the God of Death. When Sisyphus was on his deathbed, he ordered his wife not to give his corpse a funeral. After his death, his spirit went to the Land of the Dead and complained to Hades, King of the Dead, that he had not yet had a funeral. Hades allowed him to return to the Land of the Living so that he could tell his wife to give him a funeral, but once he was back in the Land of the Living, he refused to return to the Land of the Dead. He lived to an advanced old age and then died again. Now he is punished to forever roll a boulder up a hill. Just as he reaches the top of the hill, he loses control of the boulder and it rolls back to the bottom of the hill again. Sisyphus can never accomplish his goal.

"And I saw Heracles — his mortal part, of course, since his immortal part is among the gods on Olympus. Such accomplishments that man is known for! He immediately recognized me, and he hailed me, 'Odysseus! You're unlucky like me. Like me, you had to go to the Land of the Dead while you were still alive.'"

King Alcinous and the other Phaeacians thought, *Heracles himself recognized Odysseus! The greatest hero ever of the Greeks treated Odysseus like an equal! Wow!*

"Heracles continued, 'Like you, I was luckless while I was alive. I had to slave for a man who was not my equal. I had to visit the Land of the Dead so that I could take Cerberus, the three-headed dog of Hell, to the Land of the Living.'

"Heracles then left and returned to his home among the dead. I hoped to see more heroes, but so many dead crowded around the blood that I was overcome with dread and horror. I was afraid that Persephone, the Queen of the Dead, might send some monster to keep me there and not allow me to return to the Land of the Living. I returned to my ship, and we set sail."

Chapter 12: Odysseus and the Cattle of the Sun-god

"We returned to Circe's island, and there we buried Elpenor. We burned his body, and we heaped earth over his bones to create a burial-mound.

"Circe welcomed us back to her island: 'Twice-dying men, come and eat and drink. But tomorrow, you must undertake your journey home. I will advise you where to sail.'

"After we had feasted, Circe drew me aside and gave me advice. No easy journey would we have, but instead we would face many dangers.

"Circe told me, 'First you will come to the island of the Sirens, who enchant men with their lovely song. Sailors who hear their song crash their ships on the Sirens' island, whose shores are strewn with the bones of men. Sail quickly past the Sirens! Your men must not hear their song. Soften beeswax and plug their ears with it. But if you must hear their song, have your men tie you to the mast so that you don't jump overboard and swim to their island and die. Tell your men that when you order them to untie you, they must tie you tighter.'

"Circe continued, 'Next you have a choice of routes to take. On one side are the Crashing Rocks. If you try to go between them, they will crash together and destroy you, your men, and your ship. No ship has ever gone between them and survived, except for the *Argo*, which was piloted by Jason. The only way the *Argo* and the Argonauts made it between the Crashing Rocks was through the divine aid of Hera, wife of Zeus. She sped the *Argo* between the Crashing Rocks.

"'Your other route is between Scylla and Charybdis. Scylla is a man-eating monster with twelve legs and six necks. If you sail too close to Scylla, she will shoot her six long necks out of the cavern she lives in, and each of her mouths will seize a man to devour. Charybdis is a whirlpool. If you sail too close to Charybdis, it will suck your ship down into the ocean and destroy it. It is better to sail close to Scylla. You will lose six men, but you will not lose your entire ship and all the men on board.'

"'But, Circe,' I asked, 'isn't there some way to fight Scylla so that I don't lose any men?'

"

"'Odysseus,' Circe replied, 'sometimes you try to do more than mortal men can do. Scylla is not mortal; she is an immortal monster. You cannot stop her from devouring six of your men if you sail by the cliff where she lives. No. Simply row as fast as you can, so you don't lose more than six men.

"'Next you will reach the island of Thrinacia, where the cattle and sheep of the Sun-god graze. Do not harm his cattle and sheep. They never breed, and they never die. If you do not harm his cattle and sheep, you will still face hardships, but you and your men will reach Ithaca. However, if you or your men harm the cattle and sheep of the Sun-god, your ship will be lost and your men will die. And if you survive, you will return to Ithaca alone and in danger.'

"When Circe finished speaking to me, dawn arrived, and I went directly to my ship and we set sail. Circe sent us a favorable wind to help us on our way. I told my crewmembers, 'I will tell you everything — everything that Circe told me. Dangers await us. We will come to the island of the Sirens. Circe said that only I would hear their song. You must tie me to the mast so that I cannot jump overboard, swim to their island, and die.' I did not tell them everything, as I had promised. I did not tell them about Scylla — I feared a mutiny.

"As we approached the island of the Sirens, I melted beeswax and stopped the ears of the crewmembers with it so that they could not hear the song of the Sirens. They tied me tightly to the mast. I heard the song of the Sirens: 'Come to us, Odysseus. Your fame has reached the sky. Hear our song and become wise. We know what happened at Troy, and we know what will happen on the Earth.'

"I wanted my crewmembers to untie me. They tied me tighter to the mast. They rowed quickly to escape from danger. Once we were past the island of the Sirens, they removed the beeswax from their ears and untied me.

"We avoided the Crashing Rocks — we went the other route, the one that lay between Scylla and Charybdis. I told my men, 'We will get through this alive. You see the whirlpool. Stay clear of it. Sail close to this cliff, away from the whirlpool.' I did not mention Scylla. I remembered that Circe had told me that it was useless to try to stop Scylla from devouring six of my men, but I put on my armor, got my spears, and watched and waited. We saw Charybdis suck water down, down, down, and then vomit it up again. While we were watching Charybdis, Scylla struck. Each of her six long necks snaked down from her lair and grabbed one of my men. They shrieked my name, they screamed for help, but I could do nothing. She ate them raw. I have seen much evil in my life, but this made me feel the worst.

"Next we reached the island of the Sun-god. I could hear the lowing of the cattle and the bleats of the sheep. I remembered the warnings that I had heard, both from Tiresias and from Circe. I did not want to land on the island. I told my crewmembers, 'Race past this island! Danger lies here! So Tiresias and Circe have told me!'

"Eurylochus opposed me, saying, 'Odysseus, you are hardy, but your men are exhausted and they need rest and a hot meal. We need time on land so that we can cook and sleep without having to worry about the ship. Let us land on the island for just one night. In the morning, we will set sail and leave.'

"My crewmembers cheered Eurylochus. I feared trouble. I said, 'Eurylochus, you and the men wish to land here against my orders. I am outnumbered. Promise me something. Cattle and sheep are on the island. Promise me not to harm them. We have food on board ship — the food that Circe gave us.'

"They promised, and we landed. The men ate and slept, but during the night the winds changed, and we could not set sail in the morning. Again, I warned my crewmembers not to harm the cattle and the sheep of the Sun-god. For an entire month we stayed on the island as the winds blew in the wrong direction for us to set sail. We ran out of food. We tried to hunt and to fish, but we had no luck. I went inland to be alone to pray to the gods for help. I prayed, and then I slept.

"While I was gone, Eurylochus misled the men, telling them, 'No death is a pleasant death, but to die of hunger is the worst way to go. Here we see cattle and sheep. Let us sacrifice them to the gods and eat. When — if — we make it home to Ithaca, we will build a magnificent temple to the Sun-god. But if the Sun-god wants revenge and sinks our ship so that we all drown, I prefer to die that way than to die of hunger.'

"Immediately, they began to sacrifice the cattle and the sheep of the Sun-god. They roasted the meat. I awoke, I smelled the meat, and I knew what they had done. They had acted like bad guests. I groaned, but I could do nothing. The cattle and the sheep were immortal. Their skins lay on the ground, but they moved, creeping around. Their meat roasted on spits, but the meat lowed and bleated. I complained to Zeus about the actions of my men and the disaster that I knew would occur. The Sun-god quickly found out about the sacrifice of his herds and flocks. He complained, 'Father Zeus, look at this outrage! The crew of Odysseus has sacrificed my cattle and my sheep. I want revenge! Unless I get satisfaction, I will no longer shine my light on the Earth. Instead, I will go down to the Land of the Dead and shine my light there.'

"Zeus quickly promised, 'This sacrifice of what is yours shall be avenged. Keep shining your light on the Earth. I will destroy these impious men's ship with a thunderbolt.'

"So Calypso told me when I was on her island.

"I upbraided my men, but I could not undo the damage that they had done. For six days, they feasted on the meat of the cattle and sheep of the Sun-god. I did not eat. Then the winds changed, and we set sail.

"As he had promised, Zeus sent a storm against us and hit my ship with a thunderbolt. The mast fell and crushed the skull of my helmsman. My men fell into the sea, I with them. I made a raft from some of the wreckage. Another wind drove me to Charybdis. As Charybdis sucked my raft underwater, I grabbed a branch growing from the side of a cliff. I hung on until Charybdis vomited my raft to the surface of the water again. In the evening, a judge goes home after a day of dispensing justice, and in the evening, Charybdis vomited my raft. Zeus' work as judge was done: My ship was destroyed and my men were dead. I climbed aboard the floating timbers. Scylla did not see me — thanks to Zeus, the father of gods and men. For nine days and nights, I drifted. On the tenth day, I reached the island of Calypso. I have already told you about Calypso. There is no need to repeat the story that I have already told so clearly.

"And so I end the tale of my Great Wanderings."

Chapter 13: Odysseus Arrives on Ithaca

The Phaeacians had been listening intently to Odysseus' story, and now King Alcinous said, "Odysseus, we will make sure that you will arrive home safely. What's more, we will give you even more guest-gifts. Lords of Ithaca, let each of us give Odysseus a tripod and a cauldron. We will be able to recoup the cost of the guest-gifts by taxing the common people of our land."

The Phaeacian lords applauded the king and then went home to sleep. The next day, they arrived at the palace bearing tripods and cauldrons. The sailors stowed the guest-gifts on board ship.

King Alcinous gave a feast for everyone, and Demodocus sang, but Odysseus was eager to set sail for home. A farmer hard at work is eager for the day to end so that, weary, he can go home and eat. Odysseus was also eager to return home. When the sun set, he pleaded, "King Alcinous, please send me on my way. Make your offerings to the gods, and let your sailors and me set sail. May I be happy with what I find when I return home: a loyal wife and all of my loved ones safe. And may all Phaeacians find good fortune throughout their lives!"

King Alcinous ordered his herald, "Bring wine so that we can drink and then pray to Zeus, king of gods and men. Then Odysseus will go to his home."

The herald poured the wine, and Odysseus toasted the queen: "May good health attend you all your days until death, which comes to all mortals, arrives. I go home now, and I wish you good fortune and good family relationships all your life."

Odysseus walked to the ship with the herald as an escort, and Queen Arete sent along a sea-cloak, a shirt, the chest stuffed with guest-gifts, and food and wine. Everything was stowed on board the ship, and Odysseus climbed on board, lay down, and slept.

The sailors rowed quickly and reached Ithaca when the morning star rose. They entered a harbor where an olive tree grew by a cave. Two ways go into the cave: Mortals use one way, while nymphs use the other way. The way of mortals and the way of immortals are different.

The Phaeacian sailors lifted Odysseus, who was still asleep, out of their ship. They also lifted out all of his guest-gifts and placed them on shore by the olive tree. Then they set sail again and headed for their home.

Poseidon, still angry at Odysseus, witnessed all. He complained to Zeus, "Mortal men do not respect me. Look at the Phaeacians. I made it difficult for Odysseus to return home. I did not block his passage home forever — I would not go against fate and your orders. But look at what the Phaeacians do and have done! They have helped Odysseus return home safely with many valuable guest-gifts, and the Phaeacians do the same thing for other travelers. They are renowned for their hospitality, and they sail any traveler who arrives on their island to his home, using *my* sea."

Zeus replied, "The gods still respect you, Poseidon. You are among the oldest and the most powerful gods. Mortals count for little. Do to them whatever you would like to do."

"I want revenge immediately," Poseidon said. "I have held my anger back out of respect for you, the god of *xenia*. But now I will blast the Phaeacian ship to pieces, and then I will put a mountain in the harbor of the Phaeacians' island so that they can't sail travelers home anymore."

Zeus advised, "Why not wait until the Phaeacian ship reaches its harbor and then turn it to stone as the people on the shore watch? Then you can put a mountain in the harbor of the Phaeacians' island."

Poseidon flew to the island of the Phaeacians. As the Phaeacian ship came into the harbor, Poseidon turned it to stone.

The Phaeacians on shore saw this and gasped, and King Alcinous stood up and addressed his people, "I remember a prophecy that my father made years ago. My father told me that Poseidon hated us because we used his sea to safely sail travelers to their homes. Poseidon felt that it should be up to him — not to mortals — whether someone sailed home safely. My father said that one day Poseidon would turn one of our ships into stone as it entered our port, and then Poseidon would put a mountain in our harbor, thus keeping us from safely returning travelers to their homes. Part of the prophecy has come true! Let us immediately sacrifice twelve bulls to Poseidon and pray to him not to put a mountain in our harbor. We will promise Poseidon that we will no longer safely return travelers to their homes using his sea. In the future, we will leave it to Poseidon whether or not travelers return home safely."

Odysseus had no knowledge of this; he still slept soundly on Ithaca. He had wished only good, not evil, on the Phaeacians, yet his visit to their island had completely changed their way of living. No longer would they be renowned for their fast ships and for *xenia*. Perhaps Odysseus would not have been surprised that Zeus, the god of *xenia*, had allowed Poseidon, his brother, to do this. The gods have a touchy sense of pride and often care little about mortals.

On Ithaca, Odysseus suddenly woke up. He looked around, but he did not know where he was. The land he had been away from for twenty years was covered with fog. The fog was the work of Athena, who worried that Odysseus might wake up, run to his palace, and put himself in danger — but Odysseus was too intelligent to do that. Athena also wanted to meet Odysseus and plot strategy with him before he went to his palace.

Odysseus looked around and said, "Man of misery and son of pain. Where are you? Who lives here? Are they wild and do not follow the rules of *xenia*? Are they civilized and follow the rules of *xenia*?"

He noticed the guest-gifts piled by the olive tree and said, "The Phaeacians are partly honest, anyway. They did not steal my guest-gifts. But they did drop me off somewhere, I don't know where. I hope that Zeus, the god of *xenia*, pays them back!"

He counted the guest-gifts — nothing was missing. But Odysseus still longed for his homecoming, not realizing that he was home — he was on Ithaca, at least, but more time would pass before he could be reunited with his family.

Athena, disguised as a shepherd boy holding a spear, appeared before Odysseus. He was happy to see someone, and he said to her, "Hello, you are the first person whom I have seen on this land. Help me to put these treasures — tripods, cauldrons, and chest — somewhere safe. Help me, also. Please tell me where I am. Am I on an island or the mainland?"

Athena replied, "This land is well known. It is rugged — good for goats, not for horses. Grain grows well here, and grapes and other food. This is Ithaca, and its name has traveled as far as Troy, which is very far from here."

I am home on Ithaca, Odysseus thought, and he was happy. And yet a sense of sadness quickly followed. *I have wanted to see my day of homecoming, and yet I did not see my homecoming. I wanted to see the smoke rising from the fires on Ithaca. I wanted to see the island rising in the distance. I wanted to recognize the landmarks of Ithaca. I wanted to see the harbor. And I wanted to step off the ship onto the solid ground of Ithaca. I did not see my day of homecoming, but at last I am home.*

Odysseus said to the shepherd boy in front of him, "I think that I have heard of Ithaca. I come from Crete, and I am a fugitive. I killed a man there, and when you kill a man, that man's relatives will try to kill you. I did kill him for a good reason. He tried to steal all the treasure that I had won fighting at Troy, where I declined to fight at the command of his father. Instead, I was the leader of my own men. I lay in wait for him with a friend, and I killed him with one thrust of my spear. I then begged a Phoenician crew to take my treasure and me away from Crete. I wanted to go to Pylos or to Elis. A wind blew them off course, and they dropped my treasure and me off here and then they returned to their home."

Athena was amused by his lies. She touched his arm, and she transformed herself from shepherd boy to goddess. "You are a talented liar," she said. "Not even here at your own home will you stop lying — you are the man of twists and turns. I also am known for my cunning: You were unable to recognize me in disguise. I have been watching out for you. When you were among the Phaeacians, I made sure that you were treated well. Now I am here to make sure that you stay alive. I will tell you the trials that you will face — even in your own palace. You must endure hateful insults — you have no choice. And you must tell no one who you are — Odysseus, the great wanderer come home at last."

"Goddess Athena," Odysseus said, "a mortal cannot recognize you when you are in disguise. You are a shape-shifter extraordinaire! You used to look out for me. While I was a soldier at Troy, you were there to make sure that I survived the war. But after we conquered Troy, I have not seen you. You could have helped me."

Odysseus thought, *If you had warned me, I would not have visited the land of the Cyclopes, and I would not have blinded Polyphemus, the son of Poseidon. Poseidon would not be angry at me. And when we were on the island where the*

Sun-god kept his cattle and sheep, you could have sent a favorable wind to us. I could have arrived home years earlier. I could have returned home with my ships and crewmembers. I could have arrived home before the suitors took over my palace and tried to take over my wife. I could have watched my son grow up.

"I do like you, Odysseus," Athena said. "You are intelligent. Anyone else who just returned home after twenty years would have run off to his palace to see his wife and son. But not you. You are cautious. First you gather information to determine the best course of action. You will even test your wife to see if she has been loyal to you, loyal woman that she is."

Yes, I like you, Athena thought, *but I remember the atrocities that the Greeks committed when they conquered Troy. I remember that Little Ajax raped the virgin Cassandra in my own temple, a place where she — and I — should have been respected. I remember that the Greeks killed Hector's son by throwing him from the high walls of Troy. I remember that the Greeks sacrificed Polyxena, a daughter of King Priam, following the fall of Troy. I remember all of these atrocities committed by the Greeks. It took me a long time to get over my anger at all of the Greeks, including you.*

Athena continued, "I always knew that you would return home. I did not want to fight Poseidon, my father's brother, to get you home quicker."

The way of mortals and the way of immortals are different, Odysseus thought. *Gods and goddesses look at time differently from the way mortals look at time. Time is not important to immortals — they have the time of eternity. For mortals, time is valuable. If I had come home sooner, I would not have to worry about being killed by the suitors. If I had come home sooner, Penelope and I could have had more children. If I had come home sooner, I could have raised my son, Telemachus. But I must not criticize Athena more than I have already. The gods and goddesses make powerful enemies for mortals.*

"You are home now," Athena said. She dissipated the fog, and Odysseus recognized landmarks and knew for certain that he was home. He felt joy, and he prayed to the nymphs who lived in this part of Ithaca: "I never thought that I would see you again, but soon things will be normal again and I will give you gifts. I pray that Athena will help me to fight well and will encourage my son to become a man."

"Let us put away your treasures in this cave," Athena said. "Then we will make plans for you to regain your position on Ithaca."

After the treasure was hidden away, Athena and Odysseus sat by the olive tree, sacred to Athena, and thought. Athena said, "Plan how you will be able to recover your palace from the suitors who have been partying there for years while courting your wife, who remains faithful to you. She has been leading them on, making them think that soon she will choose a husband, but in her heart knowing that she is already married to a good man who is much better than any of the suitors besieging her."

"I have avoided the fate of Agamemnon — killed by enemies when he returned home," Odysseus said, "but please help me now. With you by my side as you were at Troy, I would dare to fight 300 men."

"I will stand beside you," Athena promised. "Soon enough at least some of the suitors will splatter your floor with their blood and brains. But for now let me transform you. I will make you old. I will wrinkle your skin, make you bald, dress you in rags, and blear your eyes. Even your wife and son will think that you are an old beggar. But go first to the swineherd, who is loyal to you and your family. Talk to him and gather information. I myself will go to Lacedaemon, see your son, and tell him to return home. Telemachus traveled to Lacedaemon to ask Menelaus for news of you."

"Why didn't you tell him that I was alive?" Odysseus asked. "Is my son going to have a life like mine? Will he travel and suffer hardships while strangers devour our household here?"

"I myself encouraged him to make the journey," Athena replied. "He needs to grow up, and I wanted him to undertake the journey to make a reputation for himself. He is safe — Menelaus is an excellent host. True, some suitors have set an ambush to kill Telemachus when he returns home. Will the suitors' ambush succeed? I doubt it. Before that should happen, the suitors will be dead."

Athena transformed Odysseus with a stroke of her wand. He aged. She gave him the clothing of a beggar, and his disguise was complete.

This disguise will work well, Odysseus thought. *The world is filled with beggars, and no one will pay much attention to one more beggar. The suitors think that I am dead, and they think that if I have survived I will return home with men and ships. They won't be expecting their king to look like an old beggar.*

Odysseus walked off to find the swineherd, while Athena flew to Lacedaemon to see Telemachus.

Chapter 14: Odysseus and the Loyal Swineherd

Odysseus climbed up a rugged path to find the swineherd — Athena had shown him which path to take. The swineherd was loyal to Odysseus. He worked hard to keep Odysseus' pigs safe from wild animals. He had built walls to enclose the pigs, and he had built sties for them. He also had four dogs to protect the pigs, and now he was making a pair of sandals — he had worn out his old sandals in service to his master. Men worked under him. Three men were attending to the pigs; a fourth was driving a hog to the palace for the suitors to slaughter.

The four dogs saw Odysseus and ran snarling toward him. The swineherd came quickly, calling off the dogs, and then saying to Odysseus, "You're lucky to be alive. The dogs are not friendly to strangers. Your death would have been a disgrace to me — I observe *xenia* although my life is hard. Not only has my own life been hard, but also my master is gone. Suitors eat up his wealth in his palace, while he — if he is still alive — wanders the earth homeless, hungry, and without friends, begging for enough food to keep him alive. Come into my hut, eat and drink, and then you can tell me your story."

The swineherd led Odysseus into his hut and gave him a place to sit. Odysseus was happy to receive such good hospitality, and he said a prayer out loud for the swineherd: "May Zeus and the other gods reward you for the hospitality you have given me."

The swineherd — whose name was Eumaeus — replied, "*Xenia* is a duty given to us by the gods. All strangers and beggars come from Zeus, and sometimes the gods disguise themselves as strangers and beggars to test us. We servants can at least give a stranger some food. I wish my old master were home. He would have treated me well. He would have given me a house, some land to farm, and a wife. When a slave such as myself works hard for a master, the master will reward the slave. But my old master is dead now. It would be better by far if Helen of Troy were the one who is dead! She got so many men killed at Troy! My master was one of the men fighting in the Trojan War to return Helen to Menelaus and to save the honor of Menelaus and Agamemnon."

Eumaeus went to a pigsty, picked out two pigs, slaughtered and cooked them, and set them down on a table for Odysseus and him to eat. Eumaeus said, "Eat, friend, although it is a poor meal. The suitors eat fat hogs, while we must be satisfied with scrawny pork. The suitors care nothing for the gods, but the gods take notice of who is good and who is evil. Most criminals know that — even pirates with much stolen treasure know that Zeus is aware of what they are doing and will someday take vengeance against them. But the suitors don't care about the gods, and since they are sure that Odysseus is dead, they besiege his palace and eat his sheep, pigs, cows, and goats and drink his wine. For them, it's a party every night. My master was a wealthy man, but now his wealth goes to feed the suitors. I guard these pigs, but everyday I have to send one of the best to the palace for the suitors to slaughter!"

Odysseus, of course, was disguised as an old beggar. He was hungry, so acting like a hungry beggar was easy. He ate the pork and drank the wine, all the while listening to Eumaeus and thinking about how to kill the suitors. When he had satisfied his hunger, he asked Eumaeus, "What is the name of your master, the one who died because of the Trojan War? Perhaps I have seen your master. Perhaps I have news of him."

"Many men have claimed to have had news of him," Eumaeus replied, "but they lied. Tramps wash up on Ithaca, and when they claim to have news of my master, Penelope sends for them and questions them. They give her good news, lying that he will return soon, and she rewards them with a shirt and a cloak, crying all the while because of hearing the good news that her husband is still alive. Maybe you too would lie in order to receive clothing. What has really happened to my master? No flesh is on his bones — the dogs and the birds have eaten his flesh. Or perhaps he drowned at sea, and the fish ate his flesh, and now his bones are buried deep in sand on a distant shore. Those he left behind are broken-hearted — especially me! He was a kind master, and I will never again have a master as kind as he was. Even if I could return to the home where my parents raised me, I would not find anyone as kind as he was. I grieve for my parents, but I grieve most of all for my lost master — Odysseus, who is dead."

Odysseus, still in disguise as an old beggar, told the swineherd, "I swear that Odysseus is on his way home. I take a sacred oath that this is true. Am

I looking for a reward for bearing this good news? Give me my reward when Odysseus sets foot as master in his palace. Give me handsome clothing — a shirt and a cloak — at that time, not before. I know that people will lie when it is to their advantage, but to lie to a woman about a long-gone husband is despicable. I swear by Zeus that Odysseus will return to his palace this month. He will return to his palace, and he will get vengeance against anyone who has disrespected his wife and his son."

Odysseus thought, *I need to convince this slave and anyone else who is loyal to me that Odysseus is — that is, I am — returning soon. That way, when I reveal myself to them, they will believe that I am Odysseus. I do not want anyone who is loyal to me to think that Odysseus is never going to return to Ithaca. If they believe that, they will not be willing to fight for me.*

"That is good news," Eumaeus said, "but it is not true news. My master is dead, and he will never return. But drink your wine and we will talk of other things. I wish that Odysseus would return — and so does Penelope, and Telemachus, and old Laertes, Odysseus' father. I have high hopes for Telemachus. He has grown up, and he is like his father, but I wonder at what he has done — is it a wise thing to do? He left to visit the mainland to seek news of his father. He left the suitors behind to plot their treachery. Who knows what will happen? Will Telemachus be safe, or will the suitors beat him down?

"But, friend, what is your story? How did you come to Ithaca? You did not walk here."

"I will tell you the whole truth," Odysseus lied. "I have suffered many hardships. I was born the son of a rich man on Crete. His other sons were legitimate — not I. My mother was one of his slaves. But my father — a good man — died, and his legitimate sons inherited his wealth. I got very little, but I did get a poor house. By myself, I got a wife. I have had talents, and I could fight back then. But now, I am old. Look at me now, and you cannot imagine the man I used to be. At one time, I could lead troops in battle or plot an ambush. I was in the first line in battle.

"I did not care for farming. Instead, I was a wanderer. Ships and battles delighted me. Even before the Trojan War, I wandered the sea, fought, and got rich through raids. The Cretans honored — and feared — me.

"When Helen and Paris fled to Troy, I went with the Greek army that pursued them. We fought at Troy for nine whole years, and in the tenth year we conquered the city. I went home, but not for long. I was home only a month with my wife and children and treasure, but then my wanderlust led me to go to Egypt. Nine ships I had. For six days my crewmembers and I feasted and sacrificed to the gods, and on the seventh day we set sail.

"We reached the mouth of the Nile River, and I sent scouts ahead. They disobeyed orders and began raiding immediately. They became greedy when they saw the rich Egyptian farms and the Egyptian wives. They killed men, and they captured women and children to make slaves. The Egyptians armed and attacked. They killed the raiding party and attacked the ships. Anyone they did not kill became a slave. I took off my armor and cast aside my weapons. I went to the Egyptian king and supplicated him, begging for my life. He respected Zeus and did not let his men kill me. He also let me keep my freedom. I stayed in Egypt for seven years and became wealthy — the Egyptians treated me well. In the eighth year, a Phoenician — an evil man — talked me into setting sail with him with all my wealth. I stayed with him a year, and then we sailed to Libya. I was supposed to help him with his cargo, but the Phoenician regarded *me* as cargo — he intended to sell me as a slave. I became suspicious, but I could not leave the ship. Zeus sent a storm against the Phoenician's ship. A thunderbolt hit it, it sank, and all drowned — except me. I grabbed the mast and floated for nine days. On the tenth day I reached Thesprotia. The king's son rescued me, and the king took care of me. That is where I heard about Odysseus. The King of Thesprotia told me that he had hosted Odysseus, who had left his wealth with the king to protect it. Odysseus had left to go to Dodona to consult an oracle of Zeus and receive advice. Should he return to Ithaca openly? Should he return to Ithaca secretly? The King of Thesprotia had a ship ready to take Odysseus home to Ithaca.

"The king sent me to visit Dulichion, but the Thesprotian sailors who were supposed to take me there were treacherous. They stripped my good clothing from me and gave me rags to wear. When they reached Ithaca, they tied me up while they went ashore. I got free of the ropes and swam to shore. When the sailors missed me, they searched for me, but I hid. They gave up searching for me and sailed away. The gods then led me here to you."

I hope that my story has been effective, Odysseus thought. *I need to convince the swineherd first to pity me and to give me* xenia. *But I also need to convince the swineherd that Odysseus will return to Ithaca soon and that Odysseus may return to Ithaca in secret — disguised. That way, the swineherd will believe me when I reveal my identity later.*

"You have suffered much hardship. That is clear," Eumaeus said, "but I will not believe one part of your story. Odysseus will never return to Ithaca. It would have been better if Odysseus had died at Troy. Then we could have held a funeral for him and mourned his death. Instead, we have strangers coming to Ithaca and telling lies about Odysseus to Penelope, who rewards them with clothing. I fell for the lies of an Aetolian once. He had killed a man, and to escape being killed by the man's relatives, he had run away and traveled the earth. He told me that he had seen Odysseus in Crete with the king and that Odysseus would soon be home with his ships, his men, and his treasure. All lies. I won't believe any more lies about Odysseus and his non-existent homecoming. But still, I will treat you well and give you *xenia*. I respect Zeus, the god of *xenia*, and I pity you and your hardships."

"You are suspicious despite the oath I made," Odysseus said to the swineherd, "so let's make a pact. If Odysseus returns, I will receive clothing and passage to Dulichion. If Odysseus does not return this very month, then you and your friends will fling me off a cliff and kill me."

"I would never kill you," the swineherd said. "I am not the man to violate *xenia* so horribly. But it is almost time to eat. The herdsmen should be home soon and we can prepare a meal."

Odysseus and Eumaeus continued talking, and soon the herdsmen arrived and put the pigs in the sty for the night. Eumaeus really did like Odysseus, so he ordered the herdsmen, "Bring me your fattest hog. We will slaughter it and eat it ourselves. All too long the suitors have had the fattest hogs. This one we will have for ourselves and for the guest." Eumaeus plucked a few hairs from the hog and threw them in the fire, praying to the gods, "Please allow Odysseus to come home soon."

Odysseus, in disguise as an old beggar, thought, *Perhaps my story has had an effect. Despite what he said earlier, Eumaeus seems more open to the possibility that Odysseus is alive and will return to Ithaca.*

Eumaeus and the herdsmen slaughtered the hog and cooked it, giving portions to the gods. Eumaeus honored his guest by giving the old beggar the choice portion of the hog — the cut of honor.

Odysseus thanked Eumaeus: "You honor me. I hope that Zeus will reward you."

Eumaeus replied, "Eat, guest. As for Zeus, he will give whatever he will give."

Mesaulius served everyone bread. He was a slave whom Eumaeus had bought for himself — he was the slave of a slave. After everyone had finished eating, Mesaulius cleared the table, and it was time for bed.

The night was cold, and Odysseus needed a cloak to keep him warm throughout the night. He said to the loyal swineherd, "Let me tell you a story about your master. Odysseus and I fought together at Troy. Once we were together in a raid. Odysseus was in command, and I was third in command. We were near Troy and camped out there that night. It was freezing cold, and I had forgotten to bring my cloak. The other men had shirts and cloaks and were warm — not me! I said quietly to Odysseus, 'The night is cold, and I will freeze and die.' Odysseus immediately came up with a plan. He called to his fellow fighters, 'A god has sent me a dream — a warning. We are camped too close to Troy. Someone go to Agamemnon and ask him to send us reinforcements.' Thoas jumped up, dropped his cloak to the ground, and went to the ships to find Agamemnon. I wrapped myself in the cloak and slept. I wish I were young and strong again, and I also wish I had something to keep me warm."

"You tell a good story," Eumaeus said, "and your story has a point. Here is my winter cloak, but it is just a loan for tonight. We slaves don't have much clothing ourselves."

Odysseus, now warm, slept inside the hut, and so did the herdsmen. But Eumaeus went outside to sleep so he could guard the pigs of his master.

Chapter 15: Telemachus Returns to Ithaca

Athena went to Lacedaemon to find Telemachus and tell him to return to Ithaca. She appeared to him as he lay in bed, unable to sleep. Athena, her eyes blazing in the night, told him, "It is wrong for you to stay here, Telemachus. It is time for you to return home. The suitors are in your palace, devouring your wealth. You need to go back to your home. Tell Menelaus that you need to leave. Your mother, Penelope, is being begged, even by her parents, to marry Eurymachus. If she does, she may carry away your wealth for her new husband. Don't allow her to do that! Sail home — quickly! Keep your wealth for yourself — and for the wife you will have one day.

"Listen carefully. The suitors have set an ambush for you — but I will not allow it to succeed. They wait for you in between Ithaca and the island Same. Avoid that part of the sea when you return home. Land on Ithaca, and then visit the swineherd. He is loyal to you. Stay there that night, and send the swineherd to the palace to tell your mother that you have returned safely."

Athena thought, *This will allow Odysseus and Telemachus to meet.*

Athena flew to Olympus, and Telemachus awoke Pisistratus and said to him, "It's time to head for home — right now."

"No," Pisistratus objected. "It's still night. Morning will come soon enough, and then we can see to drive the chariot. Let's wait awhile. Let's collect the guest-gifts that Menelaus has promised to give to us. We will remember him and his gifts to us as long as we live."

At dawn, Menelaus woke up and went to see his guests. Telemachus said to him, "Menelaus, it is time for me to return to my home."

Menelaus replied, "If you want to return home, so be it. I am not the man to keep a guest here longer than the guest wishes. A host must find a balance — not be too stingy or too generous with his hospitality. Allow me to put my guest-gifts to you in your chariot, and let me feed you before you leave for home. But if you would like to tour all of Greece, I will be your guide. Each person we visit will give us a gift: a tripod, a cauldron, a pair of mules, or a cup made of gold."

Telemachus replied, "I must go home. No one is guarding my possessions. I must not lose anything valuable — my life or my possessions — while I search for news of my father."

Hearing this, Menelaus ordered that a meal be prepared. He and Helen went to their storeroom, and Menelaus chose a two-handled cup and a silver mixing-bowl with a lip of gold to give to their guests. Helen went to the chests and lifted out a robe that she had made.

They went to Telemachus and presented the gifts to them. Menelaus said, "Please take this silver mixing bowl with a lip of gold — Hephaestus himself made it." He also placed the two-handled cup in Telemachus' hands. And Helen added, "Here is another gift for you. It's a robe that your future bride can wear on her wedding day. Let your mother keep it until that day."

Pisistratus put the gifts in the chariot. Everyone ate, and then Telemachus and Pisistratus prepared to set off on their journey. Menelaus prayed to the gods for the boys' safety and said to them, "Farewell. Give my regards to Nestor, who was always as kind to me as a father at Troy."

As Menelaus spoke, an eagle flew past on his right side — the lucky side. The eagle had killed a goose and was carrying it off. Pisistratus said, "It's a lucky omen, but who is it for? Is it a lucky omen for us, or for you?" Menelaus thought a moment, wondering how best to interpret the omen, but Helen said, "I will be a prophet and interpret the omen. The gods have told me what the omen means. The fierce eagle killed the defenseless goose. Just so, Odysseus — fierce in his anger — will return home and kill the suitors, who are as defenseless as geese against him, although they do not know it. It's even possible that Odysseus has already set foot on Ithaca and is awaiting the right time to strike."

Telemachus said to Helen, "May Zeus bring all to pass that you have stated. If he does, I will pray to you as if you were a goddess."

Telemachus and Pisistratus set off, traveling all day. They received *xenia* at the house of Ortilochus, a good man, where they slept, and at dawn they journeyed again.

As they approached close to Nestor's palace, Telemachus said to Pisistratus, "I need to return home now. I don't want to go to your father's palace. He loves to be hospitable, but I am eager to leave. I don't want to be a guest any longer. Please drop me off at my ship!"

Pisistratus did as Telemachus asked. He dropped Telemachus and his guest-gifts off at the ship, and then urged him, "Leave quickly. Set sail at once. I know my father. He will come after you and urge you to stay at his palace. It is hard to tell him no."

Telemachus sacrificed to Athena first, and before he set sail, a stranger arrived. The man was a prophet who had killed a man and then had fled his country to keep from being killed by the man's relatives. This prophet, whose name was Theoclymenus, asked Telemachus, "Who are you? What is your story? Who are your parents?"

Telemachus replied, "My country is Ithaca, and Odysseus is said to be my father. I am Telemachus. I left my home to seek news of my father."

"Like you, I have left my home behind," Theoclymenus said. "In my case, I killed a man and now I am trying to escape his many relatives — they want me dead. I am a fugitive, and I beg you as a fugitive — take me to Ithaca with you! Don't let the dead man's relatives find me and kill me!"

"Poor man," Telemachus replied. "Yours is a desperate situation. Of course, I will take you to Ithaca. That is what Zeus, the god of *xenia*, would want me to do." He took Theoclymenus' spear on board and told Theoclymenus to sit behind him. They set sail, and Athena sent them a good wind. Telemachus steered, keeping in mind Athena's warning about the suitors waiting to ambush him. He wondered, *Will I live or will I die?*

That night, Odysseus, the herdsmen, and the swineherd finished their evening meal, and Odysseus tested Eumaeus, wondering whether the loyal swineherd would extend further hospitality to him or send him out to beg somewhere else: "Eumaeus, in the morning I plan to go and beg in town. I don't want to be any further burden on you. But help me — give me a guide to show me the way to town. From there I will be on my own. I would like to visit the palace of King Odysseus and talk to his wife, Penelope, so that I can give her news of her husband. Perhaps the suitors will give me food — they certainly have enough that they can spare some for me! I could do chores and run errands for them: I can build a fire, I can split kindling, I can carve meat, and I can pour wine. In short, I can be a good servant."

"Don't do something rash," Eumaeus said. "Why do you want to go to the palace and see the suitors? They already have servants — finely dressed men who look nothing at all like you. Stay here. You are not a burden. Stay here until Telemachus comes back. He will give you clothing and passage to wherever you want to go."

"You are good to me, Eumaeus," Odysseus said, "and I wish that Zeus were as good to you. You have fed me and given me a place to sleep. You have stopped for a while my wandering across the world without a friend. I must do that in order to find food to fill my belly. But since you want me to wait until Telemachus comes back, please tell me about his grandmother and his grandfather. Are they still alive?"

"Friend," Eumaeus replied, "old Laertes is still alive, but he prays for death to relieve his misery. He mourns for his son and for his wife. He is older than he should be by the count of his years. His wife died of mourning for her son, absent for so long. No parent should die that way. She was always good to me — she raised me after I came here. I was a friend with her daughter until she married and moved away. Telemachus' grandmother gave me a shirt and a cloak and a pair of sandals and sent me here to work. She was good to me, and I always have enough to eat and drink. Penelope is different. She is so burdened by the suitors that she ignores me. I miss seeing her."

"You must have been very young when you came to Ithaca," Odysseus said. "How did you become a slave? Was your city conquered? Were you kidnapped by pirates?"

I already know your story, Odysseus thought. *After all, I am your king, although you do not now know it, but I would like to hear you tell it. It is a way to pass the time and a way for us to bond. Later, I may need your help when I kill the suitors. My bonding with you now may help me convince you to fight for me later.*

"This is my story," Eumaeus replied. "The nights are long now, and we have lots of time for telling stories. Sleep is a blessing, but the nights are so long now that we can get too much sleep. You and I will stay awake and remember our sorrows.

"I was born on the island Syrie, a good place for raising crops and herds, but not many people live there. Two cities are there, and my father ruled both. I am the son of a king. One day, some good-for-nothing Phoenicians landed there. One of my father's household servants was a Phoenician woman. When she was alone washing clothes, with no man from the palace guarding her, one of the Phoenician sailors seduced her — even the best women alive like being seduced — and then he asked who she was and where she was from. She replied that she worked as a slave in my father's palace, but she added, 'Originally, I came from Sidon, and my father was a wealthy man, but Taphian pirates kidnapped me and sold me as a slave.'

"The Phoenician sailor then said, 'Why not escape with us? When we leave, come with us. I have heard about your family — I have heard that they are rich!'

"Cautious, the woman said, 'I am tempted to run away with you, but first swear to me an oath that you will take me home and not hurt me in any way.'

"The Phoenicians swore the oath she required, and the woman said, 'It's a deal! No one speak to me in the palace. I don't want anyone to suspect what I am going to do. But when the cargo is packed in your ship and you are ready to set sail, let me know and I will come running with as much gold as I can steal — and with something else that will pay for my passage home. I take care of my master's son — a toddler. I will bring him with me, and you can sell him. He'll bring you a lot of money!'

"The Phoenician scoundrels stayed with us for a year, and then, with their cargo stowed away in the ship, the Phoenician who had seduced my nurse came to the house. He displayed beautiful jewelry — and nodded to my nurse. She went through the house, grabbing golden goblets, and she grabbed me and took me to the Phoenician ship. I was innocent. I willingly went with her. The Phoenician took us on board and set sail. For six days and nights we sailed, and then my nurse died. The Phoenicians treated her body with contempt. They heaved the corpse overboard — no fitting funeral rites for her! I was left alone. When we reached Ithaca, Laertes saw me and bought me."

"You have suffered much hardship," Odysseus said, "but good is mixed with the bad. You may be a slave, but you have enough to eat and drink — not like me! I wander the earth without enough food to eat, without enough wine to drink, and alone."

As they continued to talk, Odysseus thought, *Anyone passing by would see an old beggar and a slave, but actually we are a king and the son of a king. Take note of Eumaeus' life. He was the son of a king, but now he is a slave. Odysseus, what will happen to you? Unless you can find a way to kill the suitors and reestablish yourself as King of Ithaca, you will be condemned to spend the rest of your life as a beggar. Such changes of fortune can be permanent!*

They talked, and then they slept.

Meanwhile, Telemachus and his crew reached Ithaca — safely. They landed, and they prepared a meal and ate. Then Telemachus ordered, "Take the ship off to the town. I am going to visit some of my herdsmen. Later, I will go to the town, and I will repay you for all you have done for me — I will give you a feast and wine."

Theoclymenus quickly asked, "Where should I go? Where can I stay? Will one of the lords of Ithaca be my host? Or should I stay at your palace?"

Telemachus bitterly replied, "I would and should invite you to my palace, but I am not master there. I will be away from the palace for a while, and I am afraid that the suitors will not show you respect. My mother stays away from the suitors as much as she can, so she will not be able to protect you. You might stay with Eurymachus. He is regarded as a fine, upstanding young man, although he is one of the leaders of the suitors and wants to marry my mother and seize my property. Zeus knows whether or not that will ever happen."

As Telemachus spoke, a hawk flew by on his right side — the lucky side. The hawk had killed a dove and was carrying it away.

The prophet Theoclymenus immediately knew what the bird-sign meant: "This is good news for you, Telemachus. Your line will remain intact. No one will wrest the kingship of Ithaca from you or your family."

"I hope that what you say is true," Telemachus replied. "You would soon know my gratitude and my hospitality."

Telemachus then turned to his friend Piraeus and said, "You have always been good to me. Please do me a favor. Let Theoclymenus be your guest for a while until I can be his host and make sure that the suitors do not harm him."

"Of course, Telemachus," Piraeus replied. "I will be the man's host. Attend to your business as long as it takes. He will have a place to sleep and food to eat."

Piraeus, Theoclymenus, and the other men boarded the ship and headed for town.

Telemachus headed for the hut of the swineherd, just as Athena had ordered, where, unknown to him, his father was waiting.

Chapter 16: Odysseus and Telemachus

As Telemachus neared the swineherd's hut, the dogs caught his scent. The dogs did not growl, so Odysseus knew that one of Eumaeus' friends must be arriving. Telemachus stood in the doorway of the hut, and Eumaeus went to him and kissed his face and his eyes, crying with happiness that he had come safely home again. Eumaeus greeted Telemachus the way that a father who has been absent from home for ten years would greet a son whom he had not seen for those ten years.

Eumaeus said, "You're home, Telemachus. I worried about you when you were gone, and I thought that I might never see you again. I am so happy to see you. You have stayed away from the farm for so long."

Hearing this, Odysseus thought, *This is Telemachus, my son. I would love to greet him the way that Eumaeus is greeting him, but I cannot. I must remember that I am disguised as an old beggar. I must stay in character.*

Telemachus said to Eumaeus, "I have come to you, who have been like a father to me all these years, to find out news about my mother and the palace. Does she still resist the suitors? Or has she married again?"

"I am sure that she still resists the suitors," Eumaeus replied. "Her life is so hard. She cries both day and night."

Eumaeus took Telemachus' spear, and Telemachus walked into the hut. Odysseus stood up and wondered, *How will my son act? Does my son observe xenia? Has he been raised properly? Does he know how to treat strangers? What kind of young man is he?*

Telemachus told the old beggar, his father, "Go ahead and sit down. Eumaeus can get me another chair."

Good, Odysseus thought. *He knows how to properly treat a stranger.*

Eumaeus brought a chair for Telemachus, and then he brought food for all. As was proper, Telemachus did not ask about the old beggar, whom he did not know was his father, until all had eaten. Then Telemachus asked Eumaeus, "Old friend, who has acted like a father to me for so many years, who is this stranger and what is his story? How did he get here? I don't think he walked."

"He comes from Crete and claims to have traveled much," Eumaeus replied. "He just escaped from a Thesprotian ship and came here. Now he is your guest. You may treat him as you think proper. He needs both food and shelter."

"It is difficult for me to offer shelter to a stranger," Telemachus said. "I am young, and I have troubles. I don't know what my mother will do. Will she marry again? Will she continue to resist a second marriage? But I will give him clothing — a shirt, a cloak, and sandals. I will also give him a sword and passage to wherever he wishes to travel next. Or he can stay here, if you like, and I will send food and clothing here. But the suitors in the palace are dangerous. It is not wise for him to go among them. They are abusive, and I cannot restrain them — I cannot make them observe *xenia*. They are a mob, and they are much stronger than I."

This is disappointing, Odysseus thought. *My son is not the master of his own home. He allows himself to be bullied by the suitors. He has not yet become a man.*

Odysseus said to Telemachus, "Friend, may I speak? I am saddened to hear about the suitors besieging your palace. Tell me about them and yourself. Do you allow yourself to be bullied? Do the people of Ithaca, at the prompting of a god, despise you? Don't you have any brothers to help you? If I were young again, or if I were the son of Odysseus, or if I were Odysseus himself returned to Ithaca, I would fight the suitors. I would kill them all or die trying. And what if the suitors should overcome me and kill me? It is better to fight the suitors and die than to be bullied in my house and watch them mistreat strangers and serving-women and also watch them waste my wealth partying all the time."

"The suitors run wild," Telemachus said to the old beggar, his father. "The people of Ithaca are not my enemies. My brothers are not at fault because I have no brothers. I am an only son, as was my father and his father and grandfather before him. The suitors moved in when I was young, when I was too young to resist them. Now I don't know what to do. Is my mother planning on marrying one of them? Is she planning on continuing to resist them? She never has decided what she wants to do. Someday, the suitors may kill me. But everything depends on the will of the gods.

"Eumaeus, go to Penelope and tell her that I have safely returned home. Tell only her, and then return. Don't tell the suitors that I am back."

"Of course," Eumaeus said. "Do you also want me to tell Laertes, your grandfather, that you are back? Since you went away, he has grieved. He has not eaten, and he has not worked on his farm."

"Don't tell Laertes," Telemachus replied. "Come back here after your errand is done. But tell Penelope to send a housekeeper — in secret — to tell Laertes that I have safely returned."

Eumaeus put on his sandals and left. Ever-watchful Athena appeared in the doorway of the swineherd's hut and motioned to Odysseus to come outside. Odysseus could see her, but Telemachus could not. The gods appear only to those whom they wish to appear. The dogs saw her — they did not bark, but only whimpered.

Outside the hut, Athena told Odysseus, "Now is the time for you to reveal yourself to your son. The two of you must work together to kill the suitors. I also will help — I want the suitors dead."

Athena waved her wand and made the old beggar into Odysseus again. His skin was unwrinkled, his eyes were clear, and his head had curly hair. He stood tall and strong and handsome.

Odysseus returned to the swineherd's hut, and afraid, Telemachus stared at him. Telemachus exclaimed, "You have been transformed! You are no longer an old beggar! You must be a god! Mortals don't transform themselves! Please don't hurt me!"

"I am not a god," Odysseus replied. "I am a mortal. I am your father, Odysseus. I have returned to you after twenty years."

Odysseus kissed Telemachus, and Odysseus cried, but Telemachus did not believe him: "No! You can't be my father! You can't be Odysseus! This must be a trick! No mortal can do what you have just done! Unless you had help from a god!"

"Telemachus," Odysseus said, "don't be disbelieving. I am the only Odysseus who will ever come to you. I am the man who fathered you and has been away from you for twenty years. How did I transform? That is the work of Athena. She can make me appear as an old beggar or as myself. The gods have that power."

Telemachus believed Odysseus, his father. They wept together, just as eagles will mourn when farmers steal the eagles' nestlings. Telemachus and Odysseus wept for the lost years.

I have missed so much time with my son, Odysseus thought. *I never saw Telemachus as a toddler, as a youngster, as a young teenager, or as an older teenager. When I left Ithaca, Telemachus was an infant. Now I have finally returned to Ithaca, and he is a young man, on the verge of maturity. I never saw my son grow up.*

Telemachus thought, *This is the father I don't remember and have never known.*

After they had wept, Telemachus asked his father for his story: "How did you get here, father? What ship brought you?"

"The Phaeacians carried me in their ship to Ithaca," Odysseus said. "They brought treasure, too, which I have stored in a cave. Athena helped me return to Ithaca so that together — you and I — we can plan how to kill the suitors. Tell me how many of them there are. Then I will decide if you and I can defeat them, or if I should seek allies before confronting them."

"There are over a hundred suitors," Telemachus replied. "I know that you are a warrior, but the thought that you and I can defeat over one hundred suitors is staggering. I don't see how we can fight them and win. Can you think of an ally who can help us?"

"Of course I can," Odysseus replied. "You and I, fighting together, with Athena and Zeus as our allies, can defeat over one hundred suitors. Do you think that we need better allies than these two champions?"

My father thinks that he and I — fighting together — can kill over one hundred suitors, Telemachus thought. *I have always heard great things about my father, but wow!*

"I trust you," Telemachus said. "If you say that we can do it, then we can do it."

Yes, we can do it, Odysseus thought, *but I need you to completely grow up. I am your father, I am here now, and I can help you to grow up and become a man. Right now is a good time to start. I will give you some responsibilities to take care of.*

"The time that we fight the suitors is not long off," Odysseus said. "You need to return to the palace quickly. I will arrive soon. The swineherd will lead me there. Once again, I will look like an old beggar. Listen carefully. When I am in the palace, if the suitors abuse me, you must endure it. They may beat me or throw me out of the palace or throw things at me, but you must endure it. You can't treat me with any special consideration; if you do, you will draw the attention of the suitors to me. The suitors are evil, and they will treat me evilly. They cannot change, not at this late date.

"When I am in the palace, Athena will let me know when it is the right time to give you a signal. When I signal you, take all of the weapons hanging on the walls of the Great Hall and stow them away in the storeroom. If anyone asks you what you are doing, say that you are putting the weapons in the storeroom away from the smoke that is damaging them. Say that the weapons are in much poorer shape than they were when Odysseus left Ithaca. But leave two swords, two spears, and two shields. They will be for us to seize and use. The rest of the weapons and armor will be in the storeroom out of the reach of the suitors. When we fight, we will be armed — the suitors will not. Athena and Zeus will do their parts — they will panic the suitors so that they cannot think well.

"Here is one more responsibility for you. Don't tell anyone that I have returned to Ithaca. Don't tell Laertes. Don't tell Eumaeus. Don't tell Penelope. You and I will test the servants. Some of them may be willing to help us, but many of them are probably on the side of the suitors."

"I will do as you say," Telemachus replied, "but I don't think it is a good idea to go from farm to farm investigating the men, unless Zeus has advised you to do that. It will take much time, and throughout that time the suitors will be running wild in the palace. We can test the women in the palace, though. Some of them may be willing to help us."

As Odysseus and Telemachus plotted against the suitors, the ship that had brought Telemachus home pulled into port. The crewmembers sent a herald to tell Penelope that Telemachus was home, and the herald met Eumaeus and together they entered the palace. Both had the same task to perform, but they performed it differently. Eumaeus told Penelope quietly, so that no one could hear, that Telemachus had returned home and that she should send the news to Laertes, and then Eumaeus left the palace. The herald, however, loudly announced, "Your son, Queen Penelope, has returned to Ithaca."

The suitors heard the news, and they were shocked — Telemachus was still alive! Eurymachus said, "Telemachus is asserting himself and becoming dangerous to us. We thought that he would be dead by now. Send a ship to go to Antinous and the other men waiting to ambush Telemachus. They have been outwitted."

But Amphinomus said, "No need to send the message. Look in the harbor. Our friends have returned in their ship. Perhaps a god told them the news, or perhaps they saw Telemachus' ship but were outrowed."

The suitors met together. Antinous was angry: "Telemachus escaped the ambush although we kept watch for his ship. We failed to kill him during his journey home, so we will have to kill him here on Ithaca. Now that he has begun to assert himself, he is too dangerous for us to allow him to live. He made a speech against us, and the people of Ithaca heard him and are on his side. Then he went to the mainland to spread news of our outrages. What if a king pities him and sends an army to help him? We had better kill him quickly and take all he owns, splitting it among ourselves. But whoever marries Penelope will keep the palace. Either we murder Telemachus, or we give up our life of partying here."

Amphinomus, one of the less evil suitors, said, "I don't want to murder Telemachus — that is an evil deed. Let us find out what the gods think of this plan. If the gods are in favor of killing Telemachus, then I myself will kill him. But if the gods don't want us to kill Telemachus, then we must restrain ourselves."

Amphinomus' plan was agreeable to the suitors, and for now they did not plot to kill Telemachus.

Now Penelope appeared before the suitors. The herald Medon was loyal to her, although the suitors forced him to serve them. Medon told Penelope all that the suitors had been plotting — she knew that they had wanted to ambush and kill her son. Penelope said, "Antinous, people of Ithaca say that you are among the finest young men here. They are wrong. You are violent! You are vicious! You want to commit murder! Why do you want to murder Telemachus? You need to remember how your father came to Ithaca. He had been a pirate, and mobs were after him. He fled to Ithaca to save his life. Odysseus protected him, kept the mob from tearing him to pieces. Knowing this, you should treat Odysseus' wealth, Odysseus' wife, and Odysseus' son with respect. Stop your outrages, and stop the outrages of the other suitors, too!"

Eurymachus tried to calm her down: "Penelope, don't worry. No one will ever harm Telemachus while I am near him to protect him. If anyone tries to kill Telemachus, that man will feel my spear — deep in his belly! I am old enough to remember Odysseus. When I was a young boy, he held me in his lap and fed me bits of roasted meat and gave me sips of wine. I love your son, and I will protect him. As long as I am around, the suitors will not harm him. But what the gods send him is something that I can't control."

So Eurymachus spoke, but he lied. Telemachus' death would please him, even if he had to make that death occur faster than the gods wanted.

Penelope returned to her quarters and wept.

Eumaeus returned to his hut, where Telemachus and the old beggar — transformed again by Athena — were cooking supper.

Telemachus greeted Eumaeus, "Welcome back, friend. How are the suitors? Have they recalled the ambush they set against me?"

"I did not stay to ask," Eumaeus said. "I was eager to return here. But as I was heading home, I saw a ship filled with armed men pulling into the harbor. Perhaps they are the men who plotted to ambush you, but I am not sure."

Telemachus was sure that they were the men. He smiled, and he glanced at his father. All ate, and then they slept.

Chapter 17: Odysseus Enters His Palace

The next morning, Telemachus put on his sandals and said, "I'm off to my palace to see my mother. I know that she will not stop crying until she sees for herself that I am safely back on Ithaca. Take this stranger to town so that he can beg for his food. I have troubles of my own to take care of, so I can't take care of every stranger who comes around begging. I am blunt because I have to be."

"Friend, that suits me," Odysseus said. "Beggars do better in town than on a farm. Someone will feed me. I am too old to work on a farm. Your servant will take me to town later. It is too early for me to go now. I am wearing rags, and I would freeze. Soon enough, the sun will warm the air."

Telemachus walked home. When he entered the palace, his old servant Eurycleia saw him and rejoiced. She hugged and kissed him.

Penelope came down to see her son and said, "Telemachus, you're home! I was afraid I would never see you again. Did you get any information about your father — or even see him yourself?"

Telemachus replied, "Mother, don't bother me about that now. I have narrowly escaped death. Take a bath and get dressed, and then stay in your quarters with your serving-women. Offer a sacrifice to Zeus. I am off again to welcome a guest, a man I met while I was roving. Piraeus has been taking care of him, but now I am ready to host him."

Penelope did as her son ordered her. She wanted Telemachus to grow up, and in ancient Greece, women obeyed men.

Telemachus walked out of the palace and went to the meeting-ground with two dogs at his heels. He looked like a god. The suitors saw him and welcomed him with warm words on their lips and black murder in their hearts. Telemachus avoided the suitors and sat with loyal friends and advisors: Mentor, Antiphus, and Halitherses. Soon Piraeus arrived with Theoclymenus. Piraeus requested Telemachus, "Now please send men to pick up the gifts that Menelaus gave you on your travels."

"Not yet, Piraeus," Telemachus replied. "I don't know what the future holds. Perhaps the suitors will murder me. If that happens, they will get everything in my palace. In that case, I prefer that you get the gifts. But if, however, I can rid my palace of the suitors, then I will send for the gifts."

Telemachus led Theoclymenus home to his palace. Women bathed both of them and massaged them with oil, and then Telemachus and Theoclymenus enjoyed a meal with Penelope while the suitors were still at the meeting-ground.

Penelope said, "Telemachus, I am going to return to my quarters, but before I do, please tell me, while the insolent suitors are still away, whether you have heard any news about your father."

"Yes, mother," Telemachus replied, "I will tell you everything. We visited King Nestor in Pylos, and he treated me like a father, away from home for many years, would arrive home and treat his son. Unfortunately, Nestor had no news of Odysseus, so he sent me to visit King Menelaus of Lacedaemon. I saw Helen, the cause of the ten years of war between the Trojans and the Greeks, the cause of so much death and suffering.

"Menelaus asked me why I had come. I told him the purpose of my journey, and he said, 'The suitors don't know what they are doing. They want to crawl into Odysseus' bed, but they don't realize what kind of man he was. Should he return home, he will slaughter them all.'

"Menelaus told me that he had received news of Odysseus. He had spoken to the Old Man of the Sea and learned that the god had seen Odysseus on an island, longing for his homecoming, held back from returning by the goddess Calypso, who kept him on her island by force. Around three years ago, Odysseus was still alive.

"Having learned all that I could, I returned to Ithaca. The gods sent me a good wind."

Penelope was reassured by the news, and Theoclymenus reassured her further: "Queen Penelope, Menelaus could give you no more recent news, but I am a prophet who is skilled in the interpretation of bird-signs. I can tell you — and I swear by Zeus that I am saying the truth — that Odysseus is on Ithaca right now! He is either ready to attack or he is gathering information, but either way, he will wreak havoc on the suitors. I saw a bird-sign that told me these true things."

"I hope that you are right," Penelope said. "If you are, you will be rewarded with many gifts. All will call you fortunate."

The three talked together, while the suitors stayed outside, amusing themselves by throwing the discus and spears. In addition to partying, they sometimes played sports. Always, they amused themselves. They did no work. Evening came, and Medon the herald announced that it was time for them to go to the palace and prepare their feast.

The suitors went to the palace and butchered sheep and goats and pigs and a cow — no stinting on the feast when it was someone else's meat they were eating.

Meanwhile, Eumaeus and Odysseus, still in disguise as an old beggar, left the hut and headed to town. Eumaeus said to Odysseus, "I know that you want to go to the palace, but if it were up to me, you would stay here — it's safer. No swaggering suitors will hurt you here. But I am a slave, and I must follow Telemachus' orders. I will take you to town and the palace."

"I believe you when you say that it is safer here," Odysseus replied, "but let's set off. Please give me a walking stick — you say that the road to town is rough and rocky, and it's easy to fall while walking on it."

Odysseus slung his beggar's sack — tattered like his clothing — over his shoulder, and the two set off. The dogs and the herdsmen guarded the pigs. When they reached the fountain where the people in town got their water, they met Melanthius, the goatherd, who was the son of Dolius. He sneered at them and said, "Two pieces of dirt walking along together! A pig-boy and his pig! Pig-boy, where did you find this beggar? He is worthless. What can he do? Just scratch his back and eat. Give him to me, and I will teach him to work. He can clear the shit out of the goat-stalls. But, no. He wouldn't do that! It's much easier to beg for a living — much easier than doing actual work! If he goes into King Odysseus' palace, he had better watch out! The suitors will fling stools at him and knock him silly!"

Melanthius did more than insult Odysseus with words. He kicked him in the ribs. Zeus, and everybody, knows that this is no way to treat a king — or an old beggar!

What should I do? Odysseus thought. *Should I kill this treacherous goatherd right here, right now? Should I merely beat him up? What is the best thing to do? It is best for me to stay in character — to remember that I am disguised as an old beggar. It is best to do nothing now and avenge the insult later.*

Eumaeus, shocked at this treatment of a stranger, prayed, "Nymphs of the fountain, Odysseus has made many sacrifices to you. Help him to come back to his home."

Eumaeus then said to Melanthius, "If Odysseus does come back to Ithaca, you will not go unpunished. You spend all of your time in town instead of taking care of Odysseus' goats."

"What do *you* care?" Melanthius replied. "*You* can do nothing about what I do. Someday I will tie you up and give you to some sailors who will sell you far from Ithaca. I will do that just as soon as the suitors kill Telemachus, and I am just as sure that that will happen as I am sure that Odysseus will never return to Ithaca."

Melanthius left them behind and went to the palace, where he sat with the suitors, facing Eurymachus, who liked him. As they did with the suitors, the servants brought him meat and bread to eat.

Eumaeus and Odysseus drew near the palace. They could hear the lyre of Phemius the bard. Odysseus said to Eumaeus, "This must be Odysseus' palace. The wall around it is strongly built — it can hold off attackers. I can smell the feast inside, and I can hear the suitors as they party. I can also hear the music of the bard."

"You are intelligent," Eumaeus said, "but it is easy to guess that this is Odysseus' palace. What should we do now? Is it better for you to go into the palace first, or should I? We should not linger here. Someone may see you, think that you're an intruder, and order you to leave. The suitors are not friendly to strangers."

"I have endured many hardships," Odysseus said. "You go in first — they know you. I am prepared for whatever happens. Another hardship matters little. Bring it on. My belly is empty, and I will endure much to be able to fill it."

As they talked just outside the palace, an old dog lying on a dung heap heard them. The old dog lay on the dung heap because it was warm there, but the dung should have been carted off long ago to fertilize the fields — no dung heap should be near a palace!

The old dog recognized Odysseus. The old dog was named Argos. When Argos was a puppy, he and Odysseus had hunted together before Odysseus left Ithaca to fight at Troy. Now Argos was old, abandoned, and covered with ticks. The ticks were sucking away Argos' blood just like the suitors were wasting away Odysseus' possessions. But with the little strength left to him, Argos wagged his tail weakly. He had no strength left to crawl to his master.

Odysseus saw Argos, but he could not show that he recognized the old dog — Eumaeus was still present. Odysseus said to Eumaeus, "How strange, Eumaeus, the way that this old dog is neglected. You can see that it used to be a handsome dog. But I don't know if it was a good hunter."

"Yes, this dog was once a good hunter," Eumaeus replied. "He and Odysseus used to hunt together. This old dog was strong and swift. He was a champion tracker. But now his master is gone, and the serving-women neglect him. Many slaves slack off when their master is not around. When a person becomes a slave, that person usually becomes lazy."

Eumaeus entered the palace, and Odysseus followed him. At exactly that moment, Argos died.

This death is significant, Odysseus thought. *The old way of doing things is dying now, and a new order of things is starting. Now I will set my palace to rights. Soon the suitors will be dead, and order will reign again in Ithaca. I will see to it. The king has returned.*

Telemachus saw Eumaeus and waved him in. Eumaeus took a stool and moved it across from Telemachus, and then a servant served them. Odysseus stood in the doorway, waiting to be noticed. Telemachus saw him. Telemachus gave Eumaeus a loaf of bread and as much meat as he could hold in his hands and ordered him, "Take the food to the stranger and tell him to eat and then beg from each of the suitors. A beggar cannot be shy."

Telemachus thought, *This will give my father a chance to see the suitors and learn what kind of men they are.*

Eumaeus did as Telemachus ordered and gave the old beggar the food and the message. "Stranger," he told Odysseus, "Telemachus wants you to eat and then beg food from the suitors. He says that a beggar cannot be shy."

Smart boy, Odysseus thought. *This will give me a chance to see the suitors and learn what kind of men they are.*

"Your master is intelligent," Odysseus told Eumaeus. "May the gods bless him."

Odysseus ate the food first, and as all ate, the bard sang. After eating, the suitors continued to drink. Athena appeared before Odysseus — no one else could see her — and she advised him, "Go to each of the suitors. See what kind of men they are. Are any of the suitors better men than the others?"

But Athena knew that all of the suitors were guilty of outrage against Odysseus, his family, and his possessions. They had been evil for so long that they were no longer capable of change even if they had wanted to become good men. People who do not use their free will to be good soon become incapable of being good. They are incapable of making the effort of the will that is needed to change. They are slaves to their evil desires.

Many of the suitors gave the old beggar food. They pitied him — he looked wretched. They wondered who he was. Melanthius the treacherous goatherd loudly told what he knew about the stranger, "The swineherd led the stranger here — I saw them earlier. But I don't know who the stranger is or what is his story."

Antinous sneered at Eumaeus and said, "Swineherd, why bring a beggar here? Don't we see enough disgusting beggars as it is? Why bring yet another beggar to lick other people's plates? Aren't we eating enough of your master's animals without help from beggars?"

Eumaeus replied, "Antinous, you are a noble, but you lack intelligence. No one would invite a stranger in to eat away one's possessions unless he had skills such as prophesying, healing, working in wood, or singing. You are the hardest on the servants, but I endure it all as long as Penelope and Telemachus are still alive."

"Stop, Eumaeus," Telemachus said. "Don't argue with Antinous. He simply likes to cause trouble."

Telemachus then said to Antinous, "What kind of a man are you? You want me to order this stranger away from the palace. You want me to disrespect the laws of Zeus. Not I! Give food — *my* food — to the beggar. You have much more than enough to stuff your face and your belly. Why not give to the hungry?"

"You need to shut up, Telemachus," Antinous said. "I would like to give the stranger a gift, indeed. The gift I would give him would keep the palace free of beggars for months!" He lifted a stool and pretended to throw it at the old beggar.

All of the other suitors gave Odysseus food, but he wanted to see Antinous close-up, so he stood in front of Antinous and said, "Give me some food, friend. You look like a king. Please act like one and be generous. If you do, I will pray for you. I once led a far different life. I had a fine house, and I often gave to strangers. I was rich. But all went wrong. I sailed to Egypt with some other pirates. I sent out scouts to gather information, but they went wild. They robbed the farms and carried off the women and children. Armed men gathered and hunted us down. My men were killed or made slaves. I went to Cyprus and then to Ithaca, worn down by hardship."

"Stay away from me, you loser," Antinous replied. "I can bring much more hardship into your life! I can't believe that the other suitors are giving you food, but then again, it is not their food that they are giving you. They are being generous with food that does not belong to them."

"Why shouldn't you be generous, too?" Odysseus asked as he walked away. "Look around. There is more than enough food here. You wouldn't even feed your own servant — not if you won't give me some food from the feast of someone else's food that is spread before you."

"Now you've done it," Antinous said. "I can't ignore an insult such as that."

He grabbed a stool and threw it at Odysseus, hitting him under the right shoulder. Odysseus bore the blow, but he wanted to kill Antinous. He went to the doorway, set down his beggar's sack, and then said to all the suitors, "Taking a blow as one fights to save one's possessions is honorable, but Antinous hit me because I was begging — something that I have to do to fill my belly. If beggars have gods to look after them, I pray that Antinous will die before he marries!"

"Shut up, stranger," Antinous shouted. "Sit and eat, or leave! If you keep on talking that way, we will beat you so badly that you will regret ever talking."

Even the suitors were outraged at how Antinous had treated the beggar:

"By hitting the stranger, you violated the laws of Zeus, the god of *xenia*!"

"What if the stranger is a god is disguise? Then you're dead!"

"The gods know everything that we do — good or bad!"

Antinous did not care about what the other suitors — or the gods — thought of him.

Telemachus obeyed the orders that his father had given him earlier. He sat still and did not defend the beggar. But he thought about the best way for Antinous to die and how to make that happen.

Soon the news reached Penelope of how Antinous had thrown a stool at the old beggar, violating the laws of Zeus in Odysseus' palace. She prayed, "May Apollo, whose arrows cause death, hit Antinous as hard as Antinous hit the old beggar."

A loyal housekeeper, Eurynome, added, "If the gods would answer our prayers, none of the suitors would be alive tomorrow morning!"

"Antinous is the worst of the suitors," Penelope said. "The other suitors gave food to the old beggar, but Antinous threw a footstool at him. That is no way to treat a hungry guest."

Penelope gave instructions for Eumaeus to come to her. She then gave him orders: "Tell the old beggar to come to me so that I can talk to him. I want to find out if he has any news of my husband."

"Queen," Eumaeus replied, "you will be impressed with the old beggar. He spent three days and nights with me, and we talked — I was the first person he saw on Ithaca. Even after three days of talking, he could not finish his tale of troubles. A bard is marvelous to listen to, and the old beggar talks like a bard. The old beggar says that he knew Odysseus' father. The old beggar comes from Crete, and he has heard news of Odysseus. The old beggar swears by the gods that Odysseus is in Thesprotia and will return to Ithaca soon!"

"Go to the old beggar," Penelope said, "and tell him to come to me. I want to hear what he has to say. The suitors will party, as they always do. They are wasting Odysseus' possessions, not their own. They squander everything. If only Odysseus were to return to Ithaca, he and Telemachus would take care of the suitors — easily."

As Penelope said these words, Telemachus sneezed — a lucky sign. Penelope was happy to hear the sneeze, and said to Eumaeus, "Go and quickly bring the old beggar to me. The omens are all in our favor. Soon the suitors will be dead, and I will be happy again. If I believe that the old beggar is telling the truth, I will give him a shirt and a cloak."

Eumaeus went to the old beggar and said, "Penelope wants to talk to you and ask you questions. If she believes all that you say in answer, she will give you a shirt and a cloak. Those are things you need — it's easier to beg and get food than to get a shirt and a cloak."

"Of course, I will talk to the queen," Odysseus said, "but now is not a wise time to talk to her. Look at the suitors — they drink and they party! I am afraid to turn my back on them. Antinous just threw a footstool at me and hit me. Who would protect me from violence? Telemachus will not — he said nothing to Antinous. No one would protect me. Please tell Penelope that I will see her after the sun has gone down and the suitors have left. She can ask me anything, but let her give me a seat close to the fire — my clothing is rags and will not keep me warm."

Now is not a good time to talk to Penelope, Odysseus thought. *There is lots of light, and she may recognize me. She will have serving-women with her to act as chaperones. Penelope would never meet a man alone whom she is not related to — and she does not know that I am her husband. And I know that some servants are not loyal to me, to Telemachus, or to Penelope. If Penelope were to recognize me and call out my name, a disloyal servant would run to the suitors and say, "Odysseus has returned — come quickly and kill him!"*

Eumaeus returned to Penelope, who was surprised that the old beggar was not with him. "Where is the old beggar?" she asked. "Why didn't he come with you? Is he afraid or embarrassed?"

"The old beggar is a smart man," Eumaeus replied. "He wants to avoid trouble with the suitors. He requests that you wait to ask him questions until after the sun has gone down and the suitors have left the palace."

"He is right," Penelope said. "It is a good idea to avoid angering the suitors. I will wait and talk to him later."

This is interesting, Penelope thought. *When a queen asks an old beggar to come to her, the old beggar will come — quickly. Is this old beggar different from other old beggars, or is he simply afraid of the suitors?*

Eumaeus returned to the Great Hall, where he said quietly to Telemachus, "I need to return to the pigs to watch after them. You must, of course, remain here to look after things — including your own hide. The suitors are dangerous, and I pray that Zeus kills them before they kill you."

"You are right," Telemachus said. "Eat some more, and then leave. But bring some boars to the palace in the morning so that we can slaughter them. I will watch after things here."

The swineherd ate, and then he left to watch after the pigs. The suitors partied, as they always did.

Chapter 18: Odysseus in His Palace

A tramp arrived at the palace. His name was Arnaeus, but his nickname was Irus because he ran errands and carried messages for the suitors just like the rainbow goddess Iris carried messages for the gods. He was big, with an enormous belly but no muscle. He was also unfriendly to rivals for the suitors' scraps.

Seeing Odysseus, still disguised as an old beggar, Irus told him, "Get lost, tramp! The suitors don't want you here, and I don't want you here! Either leave, or take a beating!"

"I have at least as much right as you to be here," Odysseus replied. "There's plenty of food to feed both of us. You have no right to try to make me leave the palace. Don't try to fight me, or you're the one who will take a beating!"

Irus loudly made his threats so that the suitors could hear, "This beggar talks big, but I am handy with my fists. One uppercut from me, and he'll be lying and bleeding in the dust — among his teeth! Beggar, if you want to try to fight me, I'm ready. You're old; I'm not. How can you hope to beat me?"

Antinous, a man who enjoyed entertainment that involved the pain of other people, told the suitors, "Listen to the beggars threaten each other! Let's have them fight!"

All the suitors crowded in a ring around the two beggars, and Antinous named a prize for the winner of the fight: "We are cooking goat sausages — filled with tasty fat and blood — for supper tonight. The winner of the fight will step up and take his pick of the sausages. In addition, he will be the only beggar who eats here. All other beggars we will drive away from the feasts!"

This will work out well, Antinous thought. *Not only will we have the entertainment of the fight, but also we will be down to only one beggar here — and we will have a reason to drive away any other beggars who show up at the palace. No beggars need come here looking for* xenia*!*

Odysseus, cautious as ever, wanted to be sure that it would be a fair fight: "Friends, I am old. He is young. Swear to me that you will not interfere in the fight. Swear that you will not hit me or trip me to give my opponent even more of an edge."

The suitors swore the oath that Odysseus requested, and Telemachus vowed, "Stranger, have no fear of an unfair fight. Anyone who hits you or trips you will have to answer to me — and to Antinous and Eurymachus, the leaders of the suitors."

That was clever of Telemachus, Odysseus thought. *He mentioned the names of Antinous and Eurymachus as referees of the fight. They are two people whom the suitors will respect, even if they don't respect Telemachus.*

Odysseus prepared for the fight, pulling up his rags and tying them around his waist so that he would not trip on them. As he did so, he revealed massive muscles — Athena had made him stronger.

The suitors were amazed by Odysseus' muscles, which had been hidden by his rags:

"Irus hasn't got a chance!"

"Whoever would have thought that an old beggar could look like that!"

Irus heard, and he was afraid, but he could not back out of the fight now — the suitors wanted their entertainment. Antinous sneered at Irus and said to him, "Don't be afraid of this broken-down beggar. I want a good fight. If the stranger wins, I will send you to King Echetus on the mainland. He is renowned for cruelty and will cut off your nose and ears and private parts — his dogs will eat them raw!"

Irus was shaking with fear, but he put up his fists.

Odysseus thought, *What is the best thing for me to do? Should I go for a knockout punch that might kill him? Would that draw too much attention to me? Or would it better for me simply to hit him hard enough to knock him down? Yes, that way seems best.*

Irus threw a punch, but Odysseus threw a much harder punch. Odysseus' fist caught Irus in the neck, and Irus' bones cracked, and he sprawled on the floor with blood coming from his mouth. He was not unconscious, but lay kicking the ground and howling with pain.

The suitors laughed. Irus' pain made them happy.

Odysseus grabbed Irus' leg and pulled him to the outer gate in the courtyard, and then he gave him his walking stick and said, "Don't bother strangers any more. If you try to be the king of the beggars, something worse will happen to you — I guarantee it."

Odysseus returned to the Great Hall of the palace, and the suitors congratulated him:

"Fill up your begging sack with food!"

"All that you want!"

"We're glad that you got rid of Irus — the tramp!"

As promised, Antinous gave a goat sausage to the winner of the fight. Amphinomus added two loaves of bread and said to him, "Well done, old man. I wish you good luck."

Odysseus knew that the suitor's name was Amphinomus and he knew whose son he was because he had heard other suitors call him by name and mention his father's name. Odysseus believed that Amphinomus was less evil than the other suitors, so he said, "Amphinomus, you are intelligent. You have sense, just like your father."

Whoa, Odysseus thought. *Be careful. How would I, who am supposed to be an old beggar from Crete, know Amphinomus' father? I would like to warn Amphinomus subtly and have him leave the palace — if he leaves the palace, I will have one fewer suitor to kill. Still, I don't want to reveal my identity and get killed because I am trying to warn this man.*

"At least I have heard that your father is a man of sense," Odysseus said. "Listen to me. The life of a man is filled with hardship. When a man is young, life is good, and the young man thinks that it will continue to be good. But hard times come to all men, and old age comes to all men, unless the man dies young. Once I was a young man, and I thought that my happy days would continue, but they did not. I engaged in violence, and my fortune changed.

"I look around and I see the suitors also engaged in violence, eating the animals of another man and wanting to marry that man's wife. But that man will return. I say that he is near — nearer than you think! Why not go home now? If that man returns, much blood will flow in this hall."

Amphinomus listened to the old beggar, and the old beggar's words made him uneasy, but he stayed in the Great Hall with the other suitors. He had partied at another man's house for so long that he was unable to make the effort of will needed for him to change. Athena saw this, and she knew that Amphinomus would die — stabbed by the spear of Telemachus. The gods and goddesses know how men are fated to die.

Athena also knew that it was time for Odysseus to see his wife, Penelope, for the first time in twenty years. Athena inspired Penelope to appear in front of the suitors — and to trick them.

Penelope said to her faithful servant Eurynome, "I want to appear before the suitors and talk to them. I also want to talk to Telemachus and warn him that he is spending too much time with the suitors."

Eurynome replied, "As you wish, but first take a bath. Don't appear before the suitors with tears streaming from your eyes. You have grieved too much. You have something to be happy about — your son has grown up, as you can tell from his beard."

Yes, Telemachus does have a beard now, Penelope thought. *That gives me an idea.*

"Eurynome," Penelope said, "I have grown old in grief. I have cared nothing for how I look since Odysseus sailed away. Please call my servants Autonoë and Hippodameia to me. I would never appear before the suitors without chaperones."

Eurynome obeyed Penelope's orders. After Eurynome left, Athena caused Penelope to go to sleep, and then Athena beautified her. Athena washed away the stains of tears from her face, made her taller, and gave her curves. Eurynome and the other servants arrived and Penelope woke up from her nap, feeling much refreshed.

Penelope went into the Great Hall, attended by two women. The suitors saw her and wanted to take her to bed. First, Penelope said to her son, "Telemachus, you had more sense when you were a boy. Now that you are a young man, you have forgotten how to treat strangers. Just now, in the Great Hall, our guest the old beggar was mistreated and had to fight. That is no way to treat a stranger — strangers are protected by Zeus."

"You are right, mother," Telemachus said. "I have grown up, but I am outnumbered by the suitors. No one is on my side. Fortunately, the fight between the stranger and Irus did not end the way the suitors desired — the stranger clobbered Irus! I wish the suitors would suffer the same fate as Irus — flattened, punch-drunk, unable to stand or walk."

Eurymachus thought, *Now is a good time to change the subject of conversation.*

He said, "Penelope, you are beautiful. If more young men could see you, you would have even more suitors."

"No, Eurymachus," Penelope replied. "I was beautiful when Odysseus was home on Ithaca, but not now. I lost my beauty when Odysseus sailed away. I remember what he told me when he left, 'Not every Greek will return home again. The Trojans are good fighters. I do not know if I will ever see Ithaca again. You must watch over things here and take care of my mother and father. Wait for me until Telemachus grows a beard, and then if I have not returned home, find a husband and leave the palace behind for Telemachus.' The time has come. I must get married, although I would rather not. But I am bothered by your behavior — you don't court me the way you should. When a man courts a woman, the man sacrifices his own animals and provides the feast, and the man brings gifts for the woman. The man does not devour the food of the woman and give nothing in return."

Good going, Odysseus thought. *This is a trick, I know. I have heard from Athena that you are faithful to me. This is a way for you to recover some of the wealth that the suitors have wasted through the years. You are beautiful, Penelope. You are as beautiful as the day I married you, but I married you for more than your beauty. You are as sly as the day I married you — as sly as I am.*

"Gifts?" Antinous said. "We will be happy to give you gifts. Please accept them — we won't leave until you choose a man to marry."

Each of the suitors sent a servant to get a gift and bring it to the palace. Antinous gave Penelope an elegant robe. Eurymachus gave her a necklace of amber. Eurydamas gave her earrings. Pisander gave her a choker. Suitor after suitor gave Penelope a gift; all of the gifts were valuable. Penelope's servants carried away her gifts to her chamber.

The suitors now began to party and to dance. The serving-women of the place kept the fires and the torches lit, but Odysseus, disguised as an old beggar, told them, "Servants of Odysseus, please attend to your queen. I can attend to things here. I will tend the fires and keep the torches lit."

The women laughed at him, and Melantho, the daughter of Dolius and the sister of Melanthius, mocked him. Penelope had always treated Melantho well, but Melantho was not loyal to Penelope. Melantho was loyal to Eurymachus, whom she slept with.

"Are you proud, old beggar?" Melantho mocked. "Has defeating that braggart Irus made you proud? Why are you still here? Shouldn't you seek shelter with the other tramps? You may have beaten Irus, but soon someone else will beat you."

"Bitch," Odysseus said, "I'll tell Telemachus what you said and how you treat a guest. He'll take care of you! If he wants to, he'll kill you — you're his slave!"

Melantho and the other female slaves ran then. Yes, masters can kill their property, their slaves.

Odysseus attended to the fires and to the torches, and he thought about what he must do and how to do it.

Athena watched. She knew that the suitors would engage in outrage — would make Odysseus even more eager to kill them. Change is impossible for those who do not wish to change and who have lost their free will and become slaves to evil.

Eurymachus mocked the old beggar first: "It's fortunate that we have the old beggar to tend to the fires and to the torches. His bald head is as good as a torch — it shines!

"I could give you a job, old beggar. You could build a stone wall or plant trees. Or could you? No, you're too lazy to do real work. It's much easier to beg for a living."

"Eurymachus," Odysseus replied, "I can work. If you and I should compete in plowing or reaping, you would be impressed by my work. Or if Zeus ever made it necessary for us to fight in a battle, you would see that I would fight in the front ranks. But you, you're too proud! You are one of the leaders of the suitors — a weak band! Let Odysseus come home, and you would run as quickly as possible and wish that you could be quicker!"

"Are you drunk, old beggar?" Eurymachus asked. "I will make you pay for your insults."

He grabbed a stool and threw it, but it missed Odysseus — he ducked — and hit the wine steward in the right hand. He dropped his cup, and he dropped to the floor in pain.

The suitors were outraged:

"This old beggar causes trouble! I wish that he had never shown up here!"

"Why should we be concerned about an old beggar? We should be enjoying the party!"

Telemachus ordered, "Enough! You have partied enough for one day. You are drunk. Go home and sleep it off. Leave if you're ready, for I don't want to throw a guest out of my house."

Amphinomus said, "Telemachus is right. We are fighting too much. Let us have one more drink and then leave. We shall leave the old beggar here. He came to Telemachus' palace, so he is Telemachus' problem."

The suitors drank, and then they went home.

Chapter 19: Odysseus and Penelope

Odysseus and Telemachus were the only mortals left in the Great Hall, but Athena was present, too.

Odysseus said to Telemachus, "Now we have the opportunity to take the weapons from the walls and put them in the storeroom, out of the suitors' reach when the fighting starts. When the suitors ask you where the weapons are, say that you put them in the storeroom away from the smoke that is damaging them. Say that the weapons are in much poorer shape than they were when Odysseus left Ithaca. Also say that when you, the suitors, are drinking and a quarrel breaks out, you suitors might grab the weapons and someone could get hurt, so it is better for the weapons to be out of your reach."

Telemachus obeyed his father. He ordered Eurycleia, "Shut the serving-women in their quarters. I am going to take my father's weapons to the storeroom, away from the smoke in the Great Hall. The weapons are in much poorer shape than they were when Odysseus left Ithaca. I have grown up, and I realize now that I must protect them from the smoke."

"Good idea," Eurycleia said. "Who will carry the torch?"

"This old beggar will," Telemachus said. "If he is going to eat my food, then he needs to do work for me."

Odysseus and Telemachus both carried weapons and armor — it was Athena who lit the way for them, although Telemachus could not see her.

"Look, father," Telemachus said. "A god must be present. Our way is brightly lit, but I see no person or torch."

"Don't talk so loudly, Telemachus," Odysseus said. "Yes, a god is present. This is the way of the gods. Now that we have the weapons and armor stowed away, go to bed. I will see your mother now. She will ask questions of the old beggar."

Odysseus returned to the Great Hall, and Penelope came down from her quarters. As always, she was not alone. Serving-women attended her. One of them was Melantho, who saw the old beggar and spat, "What are you doing here, old beggar? Are you leering at the women now? Be glad for the food you have gotten and get lost! Or we will throw you out!"

Odysseus replied, "Why are you so angry at me? Is it because I'm old? Because I'm poor? Because I have to beg for a living? Once I was well off. I had a home. I gave to beggars. I had many servants, and people called me rich. But the will of the gods was to make me poor. Be careful! One day you may lose all you have. Perhaps your mistress will punish you. Perhaps Odysseus will return one day and punish you. Or perhaps Telemachus, who is finally growing up, will punish you."

Penelope overheard their conversation and warned Melantho, "You bitch, I see what you are doing and I am aware of what you have done. You don't obey orders. You know that I intend to ask this old beggar questions, and yet you want to drive him away! I want to see if this old beggar knows anything about my husband."

Penelope then turned to Eurycleia and asked her to bring a chair for the old beggar so he could sit while she asked him questions.

Be careful, Odysseus thought. *Penelope and I are not alone. I cannot reveal myself to her. Melantho is present, and if Melantho finds out that I have returned to Ithaca, she will run to the suitors and tell them to kill me. I cannot speak openly.*

When Odysseus was seated, Penelope asked him, "Stranger, what is your story? Who are you? Where are you from?"

Odysseus replied, "You are a queen, and you are known for your virtue. Please, ask me anything, but don't ask me that."

Ask me anything but that, Odysseus thought. *I can't reveal who I am to you yet, so I will have to lie, and Penelope, I don't want to lie to you.*

Penelope looked at the old beggar, and she thought, *Is this old beggar my husband? Odysseus might look like this if he is still alive. Let me tell this old beggar my situation just in case this old beggar is Odysseus. I must be careful. If this old beggar is Odysseus and Melantho were to find out, she would run to the suitors and tell them to kill him. I cannot speak openly.*

"My life is horrible," Penelope said to the old beggar. "The palace is filled with suitors who court me against my will. They also waste my husband's and my son's property. They party all the time and do no work. They kill our animals and feast on them. They take and they take, and they give nothing in return. I want my husband back.

"I thought of a trick to keep the suitors at bay. I told them that Laertes, Odysseus' father, was growing old and would need a funeral shroud. I told them that I would weave the shroud, and I would marry one of the suitors when the shroud was finished. For three years I wove by day and unwove by night. But my disloyal servants told the suitors about the trick. They caught me unweaving the shroud. I had to finish the shroud — they forced me.

"Now I don't know what to do. The suitors are pressing me to marry one of them now that the shroud is finished. My parents want me to get married again. My son has grown up and is angry at the suitors for wasting his possessions. If I were to marry again, the suitors would not have an excuse to be in the palace partying all the time. I don't know what to do. I don't know whether I am a wife or a widow.

"But now tell me: What is your story?"

Does Penelope recognize me? Odysseus thought. *A queen just poured her heart out to an old beggar. Is she giving me information, letting me know how desperate her situation is? Or is she pouring her heart out simply to make herself feel better? But now, I must answer her question. I must lie to her. I have no choice.*

"I come from Crete," Odysseus said. "My father is Deucalion, and my brother is Idomeneus. My name is Aethon, the fiery one. We saw Odysseus on Crete when he was going to Troy. He became my friend. He was looking for Idomeneus, but Idomeneus had already sailed. I took him to my home and hosted him for twelve days. Then he went to Troy."

Penelope replied, "I will test you. You say that you hosted Odysseus. What kind of clothing was he wearing?"

Odysseus answered, "Twenty years have passed since I saw him, but I remember that he was wearing a purple cape made of wool with a gold brooch that was a work of art that depicted a hound with a fawn in its mouth. He also wore a tunic that was yellow like the sun. I gave him guest-guests — a sword and a cloak. One more thing: Odysseus was accompanied by a friend named Eurybates."

Penelope cried briefly, and then she said, "You have described Odysseus' clothing well. I myself gave him those clothes. When he left to go to Troy, I fastened the gold brooch you mentioned. But Odysseus will never return home."

Does Penelope recognize me? Odysseus thought. *I gave her a strong hint of who I am by describing the clothing of a man whom I am supposed to have last seen twenty years ago. Penelope is intelligent. If she recognizes me, she deliberately said that 'Odysseus will never return home' to keep Melantho from knowing who I am. If Penelope recognizes me, perhaps I can give her a message.*

"I can't blame you for crying over your husband," Odysseus said. "Any wife would cry if she thought that her husband would never return home. But I have more recent news about Odysseus. He is near. He is in Thresprotia, but he is alone. He has lost his ships and his men, but he does have treasure. His men sacrificed and ate the cattle of the Sun-god, and because of that his men were destroyed. But Odysseus remained alive, clinging to the floating wreckage of his ship that Zeus destroyed. He made his way to the land of the Phaeacians, who would have sailed him to Ithaca. But Odysseus wanted to gather treasure before returning home, and so he has been wandering through the world and picking up wealth. But now he is ready to return to Ithaca — so the King of Thesprotia said. I saw Odysseus' enormous treasure. But Odysseus went to Dodona to consult an oracle and hear the will of Zeus — should he return to Ithaca openly, or in secret? So, queen, Odysseus is alive and he is near. Soon he will return to Ithaca."

Is this old beggar my husband? Penelope thought. *Is he giving me a message? Is he telling me that he lost his men but will nevertheless try to reestablish himself on Ithaca?*

"I hope that what you say is true," Penelope said. "I would give you many gifts. But now, stranger, let one of the serving-women wash your feet and make up a soft bed for you. Tomorrow you can eat breakfast with Telemachus. We will show you good hospitality. We will take care of you. It is the right thing to do."

"Wait," Odysseus replied. "A soft bed? That's too fancy for a man like me. All I need is a blanket. I have led a rugged life. I also don't want anyone to wash my feet unless it should be an old woman who has known troubles like I have."

"I do have an aged servant who has known troubles," Penelope said. "She can wash your feet. Eurycleia, please do this. You took care of Odysseus from the day he was born. Now wash your master's ... equal in hardship. Odysseus has suffered so much hardship that he must have aged like this old beggar by now."

Eurycleia loved her master. She cried at the mention of his name, and she said to the old beggar, "My master must have suffered hardship like you. He was denied his homecoming, and he had to seek hospitality at many houses. At some of those houses serving-women must have treated him the way that you have been treated here. The young serving-women mock you, so you will allow only an old woman to wash your feet. You even look like my master. Many people have visited here, and of them all you most resemble my master."

"Yes, I have heard that before," Odysseus said. "Other people have noticed a resemblance."

Eurycleia poured water into a basin, and suddenly Odysseus remembered his scar — if Eurycleia saw the distinctive scar on his knee, she would know that he was Odysseus.

Long ago, Odysseus had visited Parnassus to see his mother's father, Autolycus, who had visited Ithaca when Odysseus was born and who had named Odysseus. Eurycleia had put the baby in the man's lap and had said, "Autolycus, you must name your grandson."

Autolycus had replied, "I have the perfect name for him. Call him Odysseus, the son of pain. In his life, he will both give and receive pain. When he becomes a young man, send him to visit me so that I can give him gifts."

When Odysseus came of age, he visited his grandfather at Parnassus. He was welcomed with hugs and kisses, and with a feast and a hunt. The hunt was for a wild boar. Odysseus was in the lead, ahead of Autolycus' sons, when the boar rushed from a thicket and gouged Odysseus' knee as Odysseus drove his spear deep into the boar, and so Odysseus both gave and received pain. The gouge left a distinctive scar on Odysseus' knee — a scar that he was afraid that Anticleia would recognize now.

Anticleia bathed Odysseus' feet — and she saw the scar. She dropped the basin, which clanged on the floor, and turned to get Penelope's attention, but Odysseus grabbed her by the throat and whispered fiercely to her, "Don't get me killed! Yes, I am Odysseus, and I have returned home after twenty years.

But be quiet about it! Don't tell anyone. Or if I succeed in killing the suitors, I will kill you, too."

"I will keep quiet," Eurycleia replied, "and if you succeed in killing the suitors, I will tell you which serving-women are loyal and which are disloyal."

Does Penelope recognize me? Odysseus thought. *The basin clanged on the floor, but Penelope seems not to have noticed. Maybe she did not want to draw the attention of disloyal Melantho to me.*

Penelope then said to the old beggar, "Friend, I have a question to ask you. I keep wondering what I ought to do. Ought I to stay here in the palace and wait for Odysseus to return? Or ought I to get married again and move out of the palace so that Telemachus can have it? But my question is about a dream I have had. Can you interpret it for me, please? In my dream, an eagle killed all of my geese. But then the eagle spoke to me with a human voice, saying, 'This is not a dream. It is the truth. The geese represent your suitors. I was an eagle, but now I am Odysseus. I have returned to Ithaca, and I am going to kill all of the suitors.' Please interpret this dream for me."

Does Penelope recognize me? Odysseus thought. *This dream does not need to be interpreted. It already has its own interpretation. Perhaps Penelope is asking me what I plan to do. Do I plan to try to kill all of the suitors? Or have I given up and decided that I will leave Ithaca to save myself from a bloody death at the hands of the suitors?*

"Queen," Odysseus said, "interpreting your dream is easy. Odysseus shall return, and he shall kill all of the suitors. None of them will escape death."

Is this old beggar my husband? Penelope thought. *Is he telling me what he plans to do? If so, is there anything that I can do to help him?*

Penelope then said, "Tomorrow I will hold a contest in the Great Hall. Whoever wins the contest will make me his bride. Twelve axes will be lined up in a row. Each ax will have a hole at the end of its handle. Whoever shoots an arrow through all the holes of all twelve axes will have me for his bride."

Does Penelope recognize me? Odysseus thought. *Is she helping me to get a weapon in my hands? Is she telling me that she will get my old bow in the Great Hall and then it will be up to me to get the bow into my hands? A bow and arrows would be an excellent weapon to use when I am outnumbered — with a bow and arrows I can kill at a distance. Or is Penelope simply finding a way to humiliate the suitors? No ordinary man can string my bow, much less shoot it. Penelope knows that. She may know that the suitors are weak from their partying and unable to even string my bow. This may be a way for her to insult the suitors, to tell them that none of them is the man I was.*

"Queen," Odysseus said, "that is an excellent idea. Hold the contest tomorrow. Before any of the suitors can even string the bow, Odysseus will be here with you."

"Stranger," Penelope said, "it is time for sleep. You can sleep on the floor with a blanket, if you wish. Or the serving-women can make up a soft bed for you."

Penelope went to her quarters, but she did not immediately sleep. Instead, she cried because of Odysseus.

Chapter 20: Deadly Omens for the Suitors

Odysseus put his blanket on the floor of the entrance-hall, but he found it difficult to sleep. He thought, *Tomorrow is the day that I kill the suitors, or they kill me. Tomorrow is the day that Penelope brings my bow into the Great Hall. I need to get my hands on it and then kill and kill again.*

He heard the disloyal serving-women of his palace leave to meet their lovers. He thought, *These are the female slaves who would like me to be dead. If they knew that I — the old beggar — am Odysseus, they would run to their lovers and tell them to kill me. Once I am dead, the suitors would kill Telemachus.*

Odysseus was angry. He was tempted to kill the disloyal female slaves immediately, but he knew that it was too early for him to do that. He thought, *Odysseus, you have been in tough spots before. Remember when you and your men were trapped in the cave of the Cyclops, who used a boulder to close off the exit from the cave? You got out of the cave alive although most men would have given up. Now you are in a tough situation again. You will have to use your cunning, but you will succeed.*

He kept thinking about ways to kill the suitors, and he thought about other problems. Athena appeared before him and asked, "Why are you still awake? You are at home now. You are with your wife and your son."

"Goddess," Odysseus replied, "you are right, but I am thinking about tomorrow. First, I need to find a way to kill all of the suitors. Second, what happens if I kill all of the suitors? They have families who will want revenge against me. Many men will come after me to kill me. What can I do then? If I succeed in killing the suitors, well and good. But I don't want to die at the hands of their avengers."

"Odysseus," Athena said, "think of who your ally is. I am a goddess. I will protect you. Even if fifty bands of avengers would come against you, still you would live. So go to sleep. Don't stay up all night worrying."

Odysseus slept then, but his wife, Penelope, awoke. She thought of the upcoming archery contest, wept, and then prayed, "Artemis, you are the goddess who shoots arrows at women and kills them. Kill me now! Kill me the way that Pandareus' daughters were killed. First the gods killed their parents. Then Aphrodite and other goddesses raised the daughters until they were young women ready to marry. But storm spirits snatched the daughters before they were married and gave them to the Furies, goddesses of vengeance. Just so, kill me! I married Odysseus and was happy, but then he left and the suitors came. Even my dreams torment me! I dreamed that Odysseus was here, lying beside me, but then I awoke and discovered that it was a dream!"

Goddesses know much. Artemis had seen Odysseus and Athena together. Artemis also heard Penelope's prayer. Artemis thought, *Yes, mortals have changes in fortune, from bad to good to bad. Odysseus' palace is overrun with suitors. Bad. Odysseus returns and kills the suitors. Good. The suitors' families possibly kill Odysseus. Bad.*

The gods kill the parents of Pandareus' daughters. Bad. Aphrodite and other goddesses adopt the daughters and raises them until they are young women ready to be married. Good. Storm spirits snatch the daughters before they are married and give them to the Furies. Bad.

The suitors try to marry Penelope against her will. Bad. Penelope dreams that Odysseus is lying in bed with her. Good. She awakes, discovers that it is only a dream, and wishes to die. Bad.

So it goes with human beings and the wheel of fortune. Still, Odysseus and Penelope have a mighty ally in Athena. Good.

Penelope cried out in grief, and her cry awoke Odysseus. It was dawn. Odysseus thought about Penelope, and he daydreamed that they were together again. He prayed, "Zeus, you have brought me home to Ithaca. Now please let me have a good omen — an omen that good things are fated for me this day!"

Zeus heard the prayer and answered it. The sky was clear, but thunder rumbled — a lucky sign! Another lucky sign followed — lucky words! One of the twelve serving-women who were already up so they could grind grain for the suitors' supper heard the thunder and said, "Zeus, the sky is clear, but I heard thunder — a lucky sign! No doubt you have said 'yes' to somebody's prayer. Please hear my prayer now. Let this be the last day of life for the suitors. Let all of them die, choking on their own blood."

The lucky signs pleased Odysseus. He was confident that this day he would kill all of the suitors.

Telemachus arose and asked Eurycleia, "Where did the stranger sleep? Did he get a soft bed? Did my mother neglect him?"

"Your mother is blameless," Eurycleia replied. "She offered him a soft bed, but he declined. He slept in the entrance-hall with a blanket, which is all he wanted."

Telemachus went to the meeting-ground to see other lords of Ithaca, while Eurycleia gave orders to the serving-women to clean the palace. Today was the feast day of Apollo, and all had to be clean for the god. As always, the suitors would eat at the palace that day.

The swineherd Eumaeus arrived at the courtyard with three fat pigs to be slaughtered. He asked the old beggar, "How are you doing at the palace? Are the suitors treating you well or badly?"

"Eumaeus," Odysseus replied, "they treat me badly. They are wild and reckless. I wish that Zeus would punish them."

The goatherd Melanthius arrived with goats to be slaughtered. Seeing the old beggar, he said to him, "Get lost! Why are you still here? Are you looking for a fight?"

Odysseus ignored him.

The cowherd Philoetius arrived with more animals to be slaughtered. He noticed the old beggar and asked Eumaeus, "Who is this stranger? Who are his relatives? He is dressed as an old beggar, but he looks like a king! The gods send troubles to all men, rich and poor."

Philoetius shook hands with Odysseus and said, "Welcome, friend. You have seen troubles. Zeus sends troubles to all men. But when I saw you, I noticed your resemblance to Odysseus right off. My old master, if he is alive, must be wearing rags like the rags that you are wearing. He put me in charge of his cows, and his herds have grown! But they would have grown much greater if it were not for the suitors. They eat and eat, and they disrespect Telemachus. I have thought about running away and going elsewhere, but I don't want to leave Telemachus and I pray that Odysseus will return."

"Cowherd," Odysseus replied, "you're a good man. You are neither a coward nor a fool. I swear to you by Zeus that Odysseus will return — and soon! You yourself will see all of the suitors lying dead in their own blood."

"Stranger," Philoetius said, "I hope that what you say is true. I would fight for Odysseus against the suitors."

Eumaeus also joined in the wish that Odysseus would return to Ithaca.

At the same time, the suitors were talking together — they were planning how to kill Telemachus. Suddenly, a bird-sign appeared: An eagle holding a dove in its claws flew past on the left — the unlucky side!

Amphinomus saw the bird-sign and told the other suitors, "This is an unlucky omen. Our plot will not be successful — not at this time. Let's stop talking and start getting ready to feast."

The suitors went to the palace and started butchering animals. They butchered, they cooked, and they ate and drank.

Telemachus situated his father in the doorway just inside the Great Hall, next to the courtyard. He gave him food and said to him, "I'll make sure that you are left alone." He then said loudly, "Suitors, control yourselves! Don't insult the guest, and don't fight — or you'll have to answer to me! Odysseus built this palace, and now it is mine."

Antinous was angered by Telemachus' words: "Suitors, Telemachus is becoming high and mighty, but let's obey him — for now. He should be dead now, a casualty of our spears, but some god has saved him."

Telemachus ignored him.

People all over the island celebrated the feast of Apollo, god of archery. All ate.

Inside the palace, the feast continued. Athena was present, although no one saw her. She wanted Odysseus to see just how depraved the suitors had become. At this point, no one could save them. They were so far gone in debauchery that the only thing that could be done was to kill them. They had used their free will to do evil for so long that they were no longer capable of doing good.

Ctesippus was wild, reckless, out of control, evil. He told his fellow suitors, "The old beggar has eaten well. He has been treated as a guest. Guests get guest-gifts, and so I have a guest-gift for him."

He picked up an ox-hoof from a basket — a remnant of the recent slaughter — and he threw it at the old beggar. Odysseus ducked, and the ox-hoof missed him.

Telemachus shouted at Ctesippus, "You should thank Zeus that you missed the old beggar with that throw! Otherwise, you would be dead — with my spear stuck in your belly! Suitors, enough! I have seen enough outrages in my palace! No more! Otherwise, it would be better for you to kill me. Death is preferable to watching you feast in the palace day after day, taking and taking and never giving anything in return. Death is preferable to watching you abuse my guests and mistreat my serving-women."

The suitors were silent for a moment, and then Agelaus said, "Telemachus has spoken well. Why should we fight or start a fight? Suitors, leave Telemachus' guests and servants alone!

"But, Telemachus, listen to me. You and your mother keep hoping that Odysseus will return. But clearly, he will never see his day of homecoming. So, Telemachus, talk to your mother. Convince her to marry one of us. When that happens, you will be the master of your palace and your mother will live in the home of her new husband."

"Agelaus," Telemachus replied, "I don't hold my mother back. I want her to marry the man she chooses. But I am not going to force my mother to marry again. I am not going to force her out of the palace."

The suitors laughed at Telemachus. It was not normal laughter. It was the laughter of mad men. Athena made the meat they were eating bleed. And she did more.

Theoclymenus, the seer and prophet, saw and heard all. He cried out, "Suitors, what is happening to you? I look at you, and I see ghosts! I hear cries of mourning! I see tears of grief! The sun is dark! All is night! This is a sign! Death is coming, and you don't know it!"

The words of the prophet made the suitors laugh even more. Eurymachus brayed like a donkey and said, "This guest of Telemachus says that everything is dark here. Let's send him into the courtyard where he can see the sun."

"I don't need your help to leave the Great Hall," Theoclymenus said. "This is not a place where I want to be. I can see what will happen here soon. Death. Blood. Destruction. None of you suitors will escape."

Theoclymenus left the Great Hall and walked to the house of Piraeus to seek hospitality. It was safe there, with no ghosts and with no premonitions of the slaughter of humans in the Great Hall. Being a prophet has its advantages.

The suitors continued their outrages:

"Telemachus has the worst guests!"

"First he has a dirty old beggar who is too lazy to work!"

"Then he has a guest who claims to be a prophet and to see ghosts!"

"Telemachus, let me give you some advice. Tie up your guests, put them on board a ship, and then sell them as slaves!"

"You'll make a lot of money if you sell them on Sicily!"

Penelope was nearby, outside the Great Hall, but close enough to hear the suitors' drunken conversation. She was waiting for the right moment to hold the archery contest.

Soon, the suitors began to butcher more animals for another feast that day. They were unaware of the feast that Odysseus, Telemachus, and Athena were planning for them — a feast of blood.

Chapter 21: Odysseus and the Archery Contest

Penelope realized that the time for the archery contest had come. She went to the storeroom and found Odysseus' bow. The bow was a guest-gift that Odysseus had received while on a mission to recover sheep stolen from Ithaca. He had met Iphitus, who was also trying to recover stolen animals. Iphitus died, a victim of bad *xenia*, killed by Heracles while he was Heracles' guest because Heracles wanted Iphitus' horses. Iphitus gave Odysseus the bow, originally a gift by Apollo to Iphitus' father. Odysseus gave Iphitus a sword and a spear. They were friends, and they understood the way that *xenia* is supposed to work.

That bow, a guest-gift, was the bow that Penelope found in the storeroom. She wept briefly, and then she carried the bow and quiver of arrows to the Great Hall, where she told the suitors, "Listen to me. You have been partying here every day for over three years, claiming that you are courting me. Today is the day that one of you can win me as your bride! This is the bow of Odysseus. Today we will hold an archery contest, and the winner will take me as his bride. Twelve axes will be lined up in a row. Each ax will have a hole at the end of its handle. Whoever shoots an arrow through the holes in all twelve axes will have me for his bride."

Penelope ordered Eumaeus the swineherd to carry the axes to the Great Hall and to put them before the suitors. Both Eumaeus and Philoetius the loyal cowherd grieved when they saw Odysseus' bow, remembering their master, but Antinous told them, "Fools, stop grieving. Sit down and eat and drink. Leave Odysseus' bow and the axes in the Great Hall. I remember Odysseus from when I was young. Stringing his bow will not be easy."

Although Antinous knew that stringing the bow would not be easy, he hoped to be the suitor who would win the archery contest and take Penelope as his wife. He did not know that he was fated to be the first suitor killed — struck down to the Land of the Dead by an arrow shot by Odysseus.

Telemachus was giddy with excitement and nervousness — he knew that today he would fight the suitors, but he did not know whether he would be alive at the end of the battle. He laughed and told the suitors, "Take a good look at Penelope. She is the bride whom you will win if you are victorious in the archery contest. I myself will also try to string my father's bow and shoot an arrow through the twelve axes — to see how I match up to my father."

Telemachus then dug a trench, lined up the axes, and planted them. The axes were all in a row, and the suitors marveled at his competence in lining up the axes although he had never seen them lined up before.

He then attempted to string the bow. Twice he came close but did not succeed. On his third attempt, Telemachus would have strung the bow, but he saw his father shake his head not to. Odysseus did not want the suitors to waste the arrows shooting in the archery contest — Odysseus had a much better use in mind for the arrows.

"I must be a weakling," Telemachus told the suitors. "I must still be a boy because I am unable to string my father's bow. Suitors, see if you are able to string the bow."

No, you are not a weakling, Odysseus thought. *You could have strung the bow, but you chose not to, at my command. By not stringing my bow, you have ensured that we will have more arrows to use to kill the suitors. Good work, Telemachus.*

Antinous then invited the suitors to try to string the bow in order, going from left to right. The first suitor to try to string the bow was Leodes, but he gave up almost immediately. His palms were soft — they had no calluses. He said, "Suitors, I can't even bend the bow, much less string it. All of you, try to string the bow. This is a bow that can take the life out of us, but that might be preferable to always staying in the palace and never being able to marry Penelope. Try the bow, but I don't think that you will succeed in stringing it. Soon you will try to marry a different woman, wooing her with gifts. I don't think that any suitor will win the archery contest. Whoever wins Penelope will have to woo her with gifts."

Antinous did not care for anything that Leodes, who was reputed to be a seer, had said, "Are you trying to prophesy when you say, 'This is a bow that can take the life out of us'? That is a bad omen. You shouldn't talk like that just because you can't string the bow. We may very well be capable of it."

Antinous then ordered Melanthius the disloyal goatherd, "Build up the fire in the fireplace bigger, and bring us some lard. We will warm the bow in the fire and rub it with lard. Doing that will make the bow easier to bend and to string."

The suitors conditioned the bow — the bow that Odysseus would use to kill many of them. On this day, Apollo's feast day, Odysseus would use to kill the suitors a bow that had been owned by Apollo. They warmed it and they rubbed it with lard, and then they tried to bend it. They failed. Two suitors did not try to bend the bow: Antinous and Eurymachus. They were hoping that the attempts by the other suitors to bend the bow would make it easier for them to string it, and they were afraid of failing in front of the other suitors — and Telemachus and Penelope.

Eumaeus the loyal swineherd and Philoetius the loyal cowherd were tired of watching the suitors. They went into the courtyard, and Odysseus followed them. No one else was there. Odysseus asked them, "What if Odysseus were to suddenly appear? Would you fight for him, or would you fight on the side of the suitors?"

"I wish to Zeus that Odysseus would return home," Philoetius said. "I would fight for him. I want all of the suitors to die."

Eumaeus said the same.

Odysseus then said, "Odysseus has returned to Ithaca. I am he. Here's how you can know that I am who I say I am. You remember the scar on my knee that I received while hunting on Mount Parnassus. Look — here is the scar."

Odysseus lifted his rags, and his loyal servants knew that he was telling the truth. They rejoiced, and Odysseus told them, "Fight for me, and after we kill the suitors, this is what I will give you: I will give you your freedom — you will no longer be slaves. I will find you wives. I will give you land and a house. You will be able to work for yourself and earn a living. You will be friends to my family and me. All of this I will give you after we kill the suitors."

All knew that killing the suitors would not be easy, and the rewards for making the attempt needed to be great. Even with two loyal servants on their side, Odysseus and Telemachus would find it difficult to kill over one hundred suitors. It was much more likely that the suitors would kill them and the two loyal servants.

Odysseus then told the loyal servants, "Let's go back in the Great Hall one at a time. Let's not draw attention to ourselves. Eumaeus, when I ask you to, carry the bow to me. The suitors will yell at you and threaten you, but bring the bow to me. I need it to kill the suitors. Then you must tell the serving-women to stay in their quarters. I don't want the loyal serving-women to get hurt, and I don't want the disloyal serving-women to help the suitors. Tell the serving-women that no matter what they may hear they must stay in their own quarters.

"And Philoetius, you must lock the outer gate of the courtyard. I don't want passersby to hear the noise of battle and be able to come running to help the suitors."

Odysseus entered the Great Hall first and then the two loyal servants entered the Great Hall, one at a time.

Eurymachus was trying to string Odysseus' bow, but he failed. He complained, "This is galling to me. Not only have I failed to string Odysseus' bow and win Penelope as my wife, but I — we — have failed in public. People will hear about this, and they will know that we have failed."

"Eurymachus," Antinous said, "don't worry about that. We don't need to worry about the contest today. Today is the feast day of Apollo, so let us feast. Tomorrow we will feast again, and then we will resume the archery contest. We can leave the axes as they are. Right now, let us drink."

Odysseus let them drink for a while, good strategy on his part: *That's right*, he thought. *Drink your fill. Befuddle your wits with wine. Then I will take action.*

Once the suitors had drunk and drunk again, Odysseus said, "Let me try to string the bow. I am old and gnarled now, but I used to have some strength. Let me see if any of my strength remains. You may find my attempts to string the bow amusing."

"Old beggar," Antinous shouted, "don't even attempt to touch the bow! You must be drunk! Remember what happened to the Centaur Eurytion when he got drunk at a wedding while visiting the Lapiths. He tried to rape the bride — the worst violation of *xenia* possible — and the Lapiths cut off his nose and ears."

Antinous thought, *The old beggar just might string the bow — he displayed some impressive muscles when he fought Irus. How will that make us suitors look? We could not string the bow — a bow that an old beggar was able to string.*

Odysseus thought, *Yes, I know that story about the Centaur and the Lapiths. But who is drunk here? Not I. You, the suitors, are the ones who have been drinking. And who is trying to rape a bride? You suitors want to marry Penelope, but she does not want to marry any of you. I know what the Lapiths did to the Centaur, but I am going to do worse to you.*

Penelope spoke up, "Antinous, the old beggar is a guest in the palace — a guest whom Telemachus has welcomed. We should let the old beggar try to string the bow. After all, even if he strings the bow, do you think that he will take me away and make me his wife? That will never happen."

True, Odysseus thought. *I will not take Penelope away from here and make her my wife. We are already home, and she is already my wife.*

Eurymachus said to Penelope, "Yes, we know that the old beggar will not take you away and marry you. But we don't want to be shown up by an old beggar. If he strings the bow, men will talk about us. They will say that the suitors were too weak to string the bow — a bow that an old beggar was able to string. Years from now, people will still be talking about the failure of the suitors to string the bow. We will be shamed."

"Aren't you already shamed?" Penelope replied. "Look at how you and the other suitors have been acting for the past three years. Can anything shame you more than that? Give the bow to the old beggar and let him attempt to string it."

"Mother," Telemachus said, "let me attend to this. I am the man of the palace, and men are concerned with weapons. Go to your quarters and stay there."

Telemachus thought, *Please, go quickly. A battle is going to be fought in a few minutes, and I don't want you to get hurt or killed. My father and I are going to try to kill over one hundred suitors, and the odds are very much against us. We will probably die, and I don't want you to see us die.*

Odysseus thought, *This is a sign of maturity. My son is protecting his mother.*

Penelope left the Great Hall and went to her quarters. She wept briefly, and then Athena blessed her with sleep.

After Penelope left the Great Hall, Eumaeus, the loyal swineherd, picked up the bow and started carrying it to Odysseus, who was at one end of the hall with Telemachus and Philoetius, away from the suitors.

The suitors yelled at Eumaeus:

"Slave, put that bow down!"

"Where do you think that you are going with that bow?"

"We'll kill you unless you put that bow down!"

Eumaeus, a slave who was accustomed to obey, stopped.

Telemachus shouted out orders of his own: "Carry that bow to the old beggar, or you'll suffer at my hands! I am younger and stronger than you!"

Eumaeus obeyed and carried the bow to Odysseus, and then he went to Eurycleia and told her, "Telemachus orders you to keep the serving-women locked up in their quarters. Don't let any of them out, no matter what sounds you hear coming from the Great Hall — even if you hear the sounds of dying men."

Eurycleia obeyed quickly — she knew that the old beggar was Odysseus.

Philoetius slipped outside and locked the outer yard of the courtyard.

Odysseus stood by Telemachus with the bow in his hands. He and Telemachus were blocking the gateway to the courtyard and the door leading to the rest of the palace. The suitors were trapped inside the Great Hall, although they did not know that yet.

Odysseus looked his bow over, turning it back and forth. The bow was faultless — it had not decayed or been damaged during his twenty years away from Ithaca.

The suitors laughed at him:

"The old beggar appears to be a connoisseur when it comes to bows!"

"Perhaps he has a huge collection of bows in his palace!"

"Look at the way he twists and turns the bow!"

"Good luck to the old beggar — exactly as much luck as he will have when he attempts to string the bow!"

Quickly and easily Odysseus bent the bow and fastened the top of the string to the top of the bow. Now the bow was ready for shooting arrows. But first Odysseus plucked the string — and its sound carried throughout the Great Hall the way the sound of a lyre string carries throughout a great hall when a bard plucks it. The suitors listened, and Zeus threw a lightning bolt from Mount Olympus that thundered to the ground. The suitors felt fear.

Odysseus grabbed an arrow, fitted it to the string, and then shot an arrow that went through the holes in the handles of all twelve axes. He then said to his son, "Telemachus, your guest is not a disappointment to you. I strung the bow and I shot an arrow through all twelve axes. But we have work to do. The suitors have mocked us both. Now it is time for us to pay them back."

Telemachus strapped a sword around his waist and grabbed a spear — one of the two spears left in the Great Hall. Then he stood beside his father — the bronze point of his spear glittered like fire.

Chapter 22: The Battle in the Great Hall

Odysseus poured the arrows from the quiver. There they lay in front of him, within easy reach, so that he could kill and kill again. He yelled to the suitors, "The contest is over — I won. But I see another target in the Great Hall — let me see if I can hit it."

Odysseus then shot an arrow at Antinous, who was drinking with his throat exposed. Odysseus' arrow hit Antinous in the throat, and dying, Antinous fell from his chair to the floor.

Kill the leaders first, Odysseus thought. *Then it will be easier to kill the followers. One leader is dead; the other leader will be next to die.*

The suitors could not believe what they were seeing. They thought that the old beggar had aimed at another target and had not meant to kill Antinous. They yelled at the old beggar:

"Next it is your turn to die!"

"You killed Antinous!"

"You will not escape your own death!"

Odysseus told them the truth: "You did not think that I would return from Troy! You thought wrong! You have feasted at my palace for over three years, taking and taking and never giving anything in return. You have been sleeping with my female slaves, and you have been trying to marry my wife although I am still alive! You did not fear me, and you did not fear the gods! Now you will pay for your crimes!"

The suitors knew then who the old beggar was, and they also knew that their lives were in danger. People who are guilty sometimes pay for their crimes.

Eurymachus, the other major leader of the suitors, took charge. He tried to talk Odysseus into not killing them: "Odysseus, you're right. The suitors have committed outrages. But you have already killed the leader: Antinous. He wanted to marry Penelope and become King of Ithaca. He is the one who led us astray. You don't need to kill us, too. We will tax the people and repay you for everything we ate and drank. Each of us will give you twenty oxen as well as bronze and gold."

But Odysseus was too wise to be swayed by lying promises.

What if I accept your proposal and don't kill you? he thought. *As soon as I put down my weapons, you will grab them and kill me, kill Telemachus, and kill any servants who are loyal to me. Then one of you will marry Penelope and rule Ithaca. I value my life and the life of my son too much to throw them away foolishly.*

"No, Eurymachus," Odysseus said. "You don't have enough wealth to buy me off. Neither does your father. Now fight or flee! None of you will get away alive if I can prevent it."

Eurymachus then rapidly gave orders to the suitors: "We have no choice. We have to fight Odysseus. Draw your swords. Use tables as shields to block his arrows. Charge him in a pack. We can kill him, or we can drive him away from the doorway and escape."

Eurymachus was the leader of the suitors for a reason. His tactics were sound, and he had the courage to put them in action. He drew his sword and ran toward Odysseus with a battle-cry. Odysseus' arrow hit Eurymachus in the chest, and he fell, dead, to the floor.

Amphinomus, the suitor whom Odysseus had tried to warn, was next to die. With his sword out, he rushed toward Odysseus, but Telemachus speared him. He left the spear in the corpse because he was afraid that the suitors would be able to kill him if, exposed, he tried to pull out the spear.

This is a sign of maturity, Odysseus thought. *Telemachus is fighting well and has killed his first man in battle.*

Telemachus said to his father, "I'll go to the storeroom and get armor and weapons. I'll arm myself and put on armor, and I'll bring you weapons and armor. I'll also bring weapons and armor for the swineherd and the cowherd. We can fight better that way."

"Go, but hurry," Odysseus said. "These arrows won't last forever, and the suitors may force me away from the doorway and then go and get weapons and help."

Telemachus went to the storeroom and got four shields, four helmets, and eight spears and quickly returned without locking the door to the storeroom. He and the two servants armed themselves and put on armor, while suitor after suitor died, cut down by Odysseus' arrows. With the leaders dead, the panicking suitors did not think to rush Odysseus. If dozens of suitors had rushed Odysseus, Telemachus, Eumaeus, and Philoetius, the battle would have ended quickly, and the wrong men would have been victorious.

When Odysseus' arrows ran out, he also put on armor and grabbed two spears. The number of suitors had decreased, but many suitors still lived, and they had their swords, although they lacked helmets and shields.

The Great Hall had a side-door, but the swineherd was guarding it. However, Agelaus asked, "Can anyone climb through the ventilation holes? Can someone reach the courtyard?"

"No one can reach the courtyard," Melanthius the disloyal goatherd said, "but I can climb through the ventilation holes and get you weapons and armor. They must be in the storeroom."

Melanthius did exactly that, returning soon with twelve spears, twelve helmets, and twelve shields.

When Odysseus saw the suitors arming themselves and putting on armor, he knew that it was bad news. He said to Telemachus, "Things just went badly for us. How did the suitors get weapons and armor? Did one of the disloyal serving-women or the goatherd do this?"

"It's my fault, father," Telemachus said. "I did not lock the door to the storeroom, and the suitors have taken advantage of my deadly mistake. Eumaeus, lock the door to the storeroom and see who is taking the weapons and armor to the suitors. Maybe it's one of the women, but my guess is that it's Melanthius."

Odysseus said, "Telemachus and I will fight here. Eumaeus and Philoetius, both of you go to the storeroom. Tie up Melanthius and let him hang from the ceiling in agony until we are done here."

This is a sign of maturity, Odysseus thought. *Telemachus took responsibility for his mistake instead of letting one of the serving-women or Melanthius take the full blame.*

Eumaeus and Philoetius ran to the storeroom and found Melanthius inside gathering more weapons and armor to take to the suitors. He had in his hand a shield once carried by Laertes into battle, but now it was old like Laertes, and it was in poor shape, like Laertes. Eumaeus and Philoetius overpowered Melanthius, tied him up, and let him hang from the ceiling in an agonizing position.

Eumaeus told him, "Stay and guard the storeroom all night, Melanthius. No soft bed for you tonight!" They locked the door to the storeroom and ran to join Odysseus and Telemachus in battle.

The four heroes stood confronting the suitors, and Athena, who had taken the form of Mentor, appeared in the Great Hall. Odysseus was thrilled to see an ally and called, "Mentor, now is the time to fight. We have been friends since we were boys." However, Odysseus knew that this ally was Athena.

One of the suitors, Agelaus, also addressed Athena — with threats: "Don't help Odysseus and Telemachus, or after we kill them we will kill you. Then we will take your property and drive away your wife and sons and daughters."

It is never a good idea to insult a goddess, even one who is disguised as a human. Athena rallied Odysseus with words, "This is the time to fight, Odysseus, just as you fought at Troy. You killed and killed again at Troy; now it is time to kill and kill again to protect your wife and your son."

Athena took the form of a bird and flew to a roof beam. She did not fight for Odysseus with spears and swords — the gods and goddesses can give aid without fighting with weapons.

Agelaus now acted like a leader. He told five suitors, "Now is the time we fight. Mentor is no longer here, so only four heroes stand against us. Let each of us throw our spears together. Six spears thrown against four heroes ought to do some damage. Let's try to kill Odysseus. Once he is dead, it will be easy to kill the others."

All six suitors threw their spears, but Athena made sure that they did no damage.

Odysseus then told his son and two loyal servants, "It is our turn to throw spears now. The suitors would love to kill us and strip the armor from our corpses."

The four heroes threw their spears, and each hero killed a suitor. Next the suitors threw spears — and Athena made sure that they missed. One spear barely nicked Telemachus on the wrist — enough to draw blood, but no more. Again the four heroes threw spears, and again they each killed a suitor. Telemachus killed Amphimedon, whose spear had nicked his wrist. Philoetius the cowherd killed Ctesippus, who had earlier thrown an ox-hoof at the old beggar. Philoetius vaunted, "You're the bad son of a bad father. You once gave Odysseus an ox-hoof as a guest-gift. I hope that you are happy with the guest-gift I just gave you."

Odysseus killed Agelaus, last of the suitors' minor leaders, and Telemachus killed Leocritus, and now the suitors totally panicked, screaming and running around the Great Hall, pursued by heroes dispensing justice, and the floor of the Great Hall was red with blood.

Leodes, the suitor with soft palms who was completely incompetent at stringing Odysseus' bow, fell to the floor, grabbed Odysseus' knees, and supplicated him, "Don't kill me, Odysseus! I never slept with any of your serving-women! I tried to restrain the suitors, keep them from committing outrages! I was only their prophet!"

"You say that you were their prophet," Odysseus said. "As their prophet, you must have prayed that I would never return to Ithaca, that your feasting would go on and on. You must have hoped that you would marry my wife, and that she would give birth to your children. For that, you will not escape your punishment."

Odysseus picked up Agelaus' sword from the floor — Agelaus was dead so he had no use for it — and cut the self-declared prophet's head from his body.

Only one person could now be seen to be alive: Phemius, the bard whom the suitors forced to sing and play music for them. He stood against the wall, staying away from the carnage, with his lyre in his hands. *What should I do?* he thought. *Try to escape from the Great Hall, or beg Odysseus for mercy?*

Supplicating Odysseus seemed the better course, so he fell to the floor and grabbed Odysseus' knees, begging, "Spare my life, Odysseus! Don't kill a bard! I taught myself to be a bard, but the gods have blessed me with talent. I can sing songs for you and play music. I was forced to sing for the suitors — ask Telemachus!"

Telemachus vouched for the bard, "Don't kill him! He's innocent! He was forced to sing for the suitors. The herald Medon is innocent, too. I hope that he's still alive. He may have been killed by one of us in the battle."

The herald was still alive — hiding under one of the chairs. He came out of hiding now and ran to Telemachus, fell to the floor, and grabbed

Telemachus' knees, begging, "Don't kill me, please! And don't let your father kill me!"

Odysseus reassured both Medon and Phemius, "Don't worry — you are safe. Telemachus has saved your lives. Remember this, and tell other people. You have done the right thing, and so Telemachus has saved you. Go to the courtyard. Wait until I call for you."

Medon and Phemius ran to the courtyard and went directly to the altar of Zeus. There they were under the god's protection.

This is a sign of maturity, Odysseus thought. *Telemachus has protected innocent people who needed protection.*

Odysseus walked through the Great Hall, looking to see if any of the suitors were alive. All were dead. He turned to Telemachus and ordered, "Bring Eurycleia, my old nurse, here."

Telemachus brought Eurycleia from the women's quarters. When she saw the dead suitors, she was about to cry out in triumph, but Odysseus stopped her, saying, "Rejoice only in your heart — silently. The suitors have well deserved their deaths. The gods have brought their deaths upon them. They did not respect the gods, they did not respect guests, and they did not observe *xenia*. Tell me — who among the serving-women are loyal, and who are disloyal?"

Eurycleia replied, "Of the serving-women, twelve are disloyal to you, to Telemachus, and to Penelope. Please let me wake up Penelope and tell her that you have returned and killed the suitors."

"For now, let Penelope sleep," Odysseus said, "but bring the twelve disloyal serving-women here."

While Eurycleia went to get the twelve disloyal serving-women, Odysseus told Telemachus and the two loyal herdsmen what needed to be done. The corpses of the suitors had to be carried into the courtyard, and the Great Hall had to be cleaned. The twelve disloyal serving-women would help them do that. Odysseus told Telemachus, "After the Great Hall has been cleaned, take the twelve disloyal serving-women outside and kill them with your sword."

Eurycleia brought the twelve disloyal serving-women to the Great Hall, and the disloyal serving-women carried the bodies of the suitors — their lovers — out of the Great Hall into the courtyard. Crying, they cleaned up the blood of the suitors, and they cleaned up the Great Hall.

After the disloyal serving-women had finished their work, Telemachus took them outside, but instead of killing them with his sword, he told them, "That is too good a death for you." Instead, he hanged them. The nooses went around their necks, they were lifted into the air, and they kicked — but not for long. And so the twelve disloyal serving-women who would have been happy to run to their lovers and tell them to come quickly and kill the old beggar — Odysseus — died.

Next to be punished was Melanthius. He had almost gotten Odysseus and Telemachus killed when he provided weapons and armor to the suitors. He wanted one of the suitors to marry Penelope, and he wanted Odysseus and Telemachus dead. For him, no mercy. The victors cut off Melanthius' nose and ears. And his private parts. And his hands and feet. Once Melanthius had died in agony, they washed off his blood from their bodies and clothing. They did not bury his corpse.

Odysseus burned sulfur and spread its purifying fumes throughout the Great Hall. He had no time to put on fresh clothing — not yet. He also ordered Eurycleia to wake Penelope and bring her to him.

Eurycleia told the loyal serving-women that their master, Odysseus, had returned. They crowded into the Great Hall, happy that their master was home again.

Chapter 23: The Bed of Penelope and Odysseus

Eurycleia went to awaken Penelope. She stood over her and said, "Wake up, queen. What you wished for has happened. Odysseus has returned, and he has killed all of the suitors."

"Eurycleia," Penelope said, "I don't believe you. It can't have happened. Leave me alone."

"I am telling you the truth," Eurycleia said. "The old beggar was Odysseus in disguise. Telemachus knew that the old beggar was his father. Together they have killed the suitors."

Penelope rose from her bed and asked, "How did they kill the suitors? The suitors were so numerous. How could Odysseus and Telemachus kill so many?"

"I don't know," Eurycleia replied. "I didn't see what happened. I did hear the screams of the suitors as they died. The other serving-women and I were in our quarters. We were under orders to stay there. Finally, Telemachus came and ordered me to come into the Great Hall. I saw Odysseus in the midst of bloody corpses strewn around him. That is a sight that you would have loved to see — the man you love splattered with the blood of the suitors who courted you against your will. Now the corpses of the suitors are piled in the courtyard. Odysseus is purifying the Great Hall with the smoke of sulfur. Come into the Great Hall and see him for yourself. He has killed all of the suitors who plagued you!"

"Eurycleia," Penelope said, "can this really be true? Isn't it more likely that a god has killed the suitors? Can one or two people really kill so many? The suitors violated *xenia*. The suitors cared nothing about the gods. Wouldn't the gods want to kill such men? Odysseus must be either dead or gone so long that he has given up hope of ever returning to Ithaca."

"Penelope," Eurycleia replied, "the person who killed the suitors is Odysseus. I have proof. Remember the distinctive scar on his knee — the scar he got while hunting a wild boar? I have seen it for myself. I saw it while I was washing his feet, but he made me stay silent and not tell you — not until he had killed all of the suitors. Come to the Great Hall and see him for yourself."

"I can't believe that Odysseus has returned to Ithaca," Penelope said, "but I would like to see the bodies of the suitors — and whoever killed the suitors."

Be careful, Penelope thought. *The gods can take the shape of men, and they can even replicate distinctive scars. This may not be Odysseus at all, but instead a god who has come down from Olympus. Remember that gods will sometimes take the shape of mortal husbands so that they can sleep with mortal wives. Remember that the father of Heracles is the immortal Zeus, not the mortal Amphitryon. You have guarded your chastity ever since Odysseus went away twenty years ago. You don't want to make a mistake now and sleep with someone who is not Odysseus.*

Penelope went down to the Great Hall and looked at the man whom Eurycleia thought was Odysseus. She sat near, but not beside, him. He looked like Odysseus — at times. But at other times she thought that no, this is not her husband come home again. She could not tell, not for certain.

Telemachus could not believe that his mother was restraining herself. He thought, *Why isn't my mother running up to my father and hugging and kissing him, ecstatic that he is home again? That is what I have wanted to see for many years. Why is she just sitting there?*

"Mother," Telemachus said, "why are you holding back? Why aren't you at least sitting beside your husband, my father? Do you have a hard heart? Would another wife act as you are acting when your husband comes back after twenty years of absence?"

"I can't do anything other than I am doing," Penelope said. "But if this stranger really is Odysseus, I will soon know it. Odysseus and I have secrets that we share — secrets that are not known even by the gods."

Odysseus thought, *This is one of the reasons I married you, Penelope. You have always been intelligent and prudent. By holding back now until you know with absolute certainty that I am Odysseus, you are reassuring me that you have guarded your chastity for the twenty years I have been away. And yes, you and I do have secrets that we share — secrets that are not known even by the gods.*

"Telemachus," Odysseus said. "Leave your mother and me alone. Soon we will know each other.

"Also, think about what our next step will be. We have killed the suitors, but soon their deaths will be known and their relatives will want us dead.

What will we be able to do then to keep them from killing us? When a man kills another man, the family of the dead man will pursue the killer. But we have killed more than one hundred men. All of their families will be after us."

"You are a master strategist," Telemachus said. "Whatever plan you come up with, I will help you to put it into effect."

This is a sign of maturity, Odysseus thought. *Telemachus knows that I have the experience and intelligence needed to come up with good tactics. Therefore, he is asking me what needs to be done and he is willing to help me do it.*

"This is what I think best," Odysseus said. "Go and wash and then return to the Great Hall. You and the servants dance while Phemius plays music. I want passersby to hear music and partying. I don't want them to wonder why the palace is silent. That would make them suspicious. Instead, let them think that a wedding is being held here — that Penelope has a husband. That will buy us a little time. Tomorrow, we will be able to go to one of my farms where loyal servants will fight with us.

"In the meantime, Penelope and I will leave the Great Hall and go into another part of the palace. We can talk there, and I need to rest."

Telemachus and the servants danced in the Great Hall, and passersby thought that Penelope had finally married one of the suitors. They were not pleased:

"Penelope should have stayed faithful to her husband."

"The suitors are worthless. None of them will make a good husband whom a wife can respect."

They did not know that Penelope was still faithful to her husband and still guarding her chastity.

Eurycleia bathed Odysseus, and he dressed in clean clothing. Athena made him taller, stronger, and more handsome. No trace of the wrinkled skin, bleared eyes, and baldness of the old beggar remained.

Odysseus said to Penelope, "Most wives would rush to welcome their husbands home, but not you. Even after I have been gone for twenty years, you hold back from welcoming me. You are a strange woman if you hold back from welcoming me."

Odysseus thought, *Actually, I appreciate your prudence. I know that the gods can make themselves look like a human, right down to a distinctive scar. I want a wife who is completely faithful to me. And I am not going to force you to share my bed, Penelope. I am not that kind of man.*

He then turned to Eurycleia and said, "I am tired, and I need rest. Make up a bed for me to sleep in."

Penelope saw her chance. She said, "You are a strange man if you think I am going to welcome you in my bed without my knowing for sure that you are my husband.

"Eurycleia, take the bed out of my bedroom and bring it here for this man to sleep on."

Odysseus thought, *Way to go, Penelope. Test me. Make sure that I am your husband and not a god in disguise or a mortal imposter. You have been faithful to me for the twenty years that I have been gone. Make sure that you don't make a mistake now.*

"Bring my bed from out of your bedroom?" Odysseus said. "Not likely, I think. I built that bed when I built the palace. I picked a spot for my palace where a wild olive tree was growing. First I built my bedroom over the olive tree, and then I trimmed the olive tree to make a post for our bed. After I built the bed, I finished the rest of my palace. This is our secret sign, Penelope. No one should know about that bed. Not even the gods know about it — they can't see through the walls and roof that I built before I built our bed.

"Penelope, is our bed still deeply rooted, or has a man been in the bedroom to cut the roots of our bed — and our marriage?"

Penelope knew now that the stranger was not an imposter, but was really her husband. He knew the secret sign. She went to Odysseus, hugged and kissed him, both of them rejoicing, and said, "Don't be angry with me, Odysseus. I had to test you. I did not want to make a mistake after twenty years of guarding my chastity. Frauds exist throughout the world. They would love to impersonate a husband so that they can sleep with the husband's wife. Sleeping with the wrong man leads to pain and hardship — look at the pain and hardship that Helen and Paris caused when they had an affair and started the Trojan War. But since you know the secret sign of our bed, which none but you and I know, except for the single trusted servant who makes up the bed, I know that you are my husband, Odysseus, returned at last."

Odysseus cried. He cried as he hugged his wife, feeling as joyful as sailors feel when they see land after Poseidon has sent a storm to sink their ship and many sailors drown and only a few are able to reach shore and live — as joyful as these surviving sailors seeing land was the sight to Penelope of her husband.

They cried together, hugging each other for a very long time. Both thought, *The bed is a perfect symbol of our marriage. Both the bed and our marriage are deeply rooted.*

Having a goddess for a friend has its advantages. Athena made the night last longer. She knew that Odysseus and Penelope needed time to talk together, time to have sex together, and time to sleep. Ordinarily, the night would not have been long enough for them to do all of these things, but Athena held back the dawn.

Odysseus said to Penelope, "Not everything is perfect. I still have another journey to take. I have talked to Tiresias, the Theban prophet, in the Land of the Dead. He told me that I must undertake another journey. But come, Penelope, let us go to bed now."

"If you want the joys of bed, I won't refuse you — ever — now that you have returned home," Penelope said, "but I do want to hear about this journey that you must take."

Just like a woman, Odysseus thought. *She is not especially anxious to jump into bed right away, even with a husband who has been away for twenty years. Instead, she wants to talk first. I can understand that. After all, I have been away for twenty years. She needs time to know me again. And I am not the type of man to force her to go to bed.*

Odysseus said to Penelope, "Tiresias said that I must travel inland while carrying an oar. When I meet a people who have no knowledge of the sea and who call the oar a winnowing fan, I must plant the oar in the ground and make a sacrifice to Poseidon. By carrying knowledge of Poseidon to a people who know nothing of him, I will make peace with Poseidon and the god will no longer be my enemy. At that time, I will return home to Ithaca. I will meet my death here — it will be an easy death. I will die of old age, surrounded by family and friends."

They continued to talk, and Eurycleia and Eurynome made up the bed, and then the two servants went to their own quarters to sleep. After

Odysseus and Penelope had finished talking, they enjoyed the pleasures of bed.

Meanwhile, Telemachus and the servants were dancing in the Great Hall, celebrating the marriage of Penelope, now reunited with her husband.

After Odysseus and Penelope had enjoyed having sex together — Penelope's first time in twenty years — they talked. Penelope told Odysseus the story of how she had been besieged by the suitors, of how she had used her weaving trick to hold off the suitors for three years, of how Odysseus had arrived home just in time. Odysseus then told Penelope the story of his Great Wanderings, leaving nothing out. Penelope marveled at his story, and she was flattered that Odysseus had rejected two goddesses as well as immortality and agelessness because he chose to be with her instead.

Then they slept.

After Athena thought that they had rested enough, she allowed the goddess Dawn to bring morning to the Earth.

Odysseus woke up and told Penelope, "I will be able to recover what we lost to the suitors. I can make raids and take animals to replace those animals the suitors butchered. Also, the Ithacans will replace many of the animals — after all, they owe me.

"But right now I must see my father. He is grieving for me and does not know that I have returned to Ithaca.

"You must stay here. But soon the families of the suitors will know that the suitors have been slaughtered. You and the serving-women must stay in your quarters behind locked doors. Allow no one to enter."

Odysseus then went to Telemachus, Eumaeus, and Philoetius and told them to arm themselves, and then they set out to visit one of Odysseus' farms — the farm where Laertes worked.

Chapter 24: Peace at Last

Hermes, the guide of the dead, went to the ghosts of the suitors and led them down to the Land of the Dead. The ghosts made cries like bats as they mourned the loss of their lives.

In the Land of the Dead, they would meet many heroes: Achilles, the greatest of the warriors of the Trojan War; Patroclus, Achilles' best friend whose death drove Achilles to rout the Trojan Army single-handedly; Antilochus, Nestor's son who was killed during the Trojan War; and Agamemnon, the leader of the Greek armies against Troy.

Achilles said to Agamemnon, "Your fate was not what it should have been. You led the Greek armies against Troy. You fought for ten years to recover Helen for Menelaus, your brother. But when you returned home, your unfaithful wife and her lover slaughtered you. It would have been better if you had died during battle at Troy. Then everyone would have raised a burial-mound for you, and your son would have been proud of the way that you died. But your death is one that no man would want."

"Achilles," Agamemnon replied, "you died well. You died in battle against the Trojans. That is the way that a warrior ought to die. We carried your corpse to our ships, and we gave you a magnificent funeral. We mourned you. Your mother, the immortal goddess Thetis, heard our mourning and rose from the sea with her sea-nymphs. We were afraid, but Nestor told us, 'Don't panic. Be calm. This is Achilles' immortal mother with all of her sea-nymphs. She wants to mourn her son.' Thetis mourned, the sea-nymphs mourned, even the Muses mourned. For seventeen days, we mourned your death, and then we gave you a magnificent funeral that will be remembered throughout the ages. We burned your corpse and then gathered your bones and mixed them with the bones of Patroclus, your best friend, in a gold two-handled urn, made by Hephaestus, that your mother gave us. Over your bones we raised a burial-mound — one that can be seen by sailors far out at sea. Your mother, the goddess Thetis, hosted the funeral-games. She set out magnificent prizes for the winners. You are famous, Achilles. People will remember your name millennia after your death. But as for me, my death was ignoble — I was cut down by my unfaithful wife and her lover."

Hermes led the ghosts of the suitors to the ghosts of the heroes. Agamemnon recognized the ghost of Amphimedon, the son of a man who had hosted him once in Ithaca. Agamemnon asked Amphimedon, "How did you and the others die? All of you are young. All of you are in your prime. Were you shipwrecked and did you drown? Did enemy warriors slaughter you? Do you remember when I came to visit you before I went to Troy? Menelaus went with me, too. We found it difficult to convince Odysseus to join us in the fight against Troy. He knew that the war would be long, and he did not want to leave his home for so many years."

"Agamemnon," Amphimedon replied, "Odysseus was gone for many years, and so we courted Penelope, his wife. She neither rejected us, nor did she accept any of us as her new husband. She fooled all of us with a weaving trick. For three years, she led us on, promising to marry one of us once she finished weaving a shroud for Laertes, Odysseus' father. By day, she would weave the shroud. By night, she would unweave what she had woven. She fooled us for three years. Finally, one of her serving-women told us what she was doing. We caught her in the act of unweaving the shroud. We forced her to finish it."

You say that Penelope neither rejected any of you, nor did she accept any of you as her new husband, Agamemnon thought. *The weaving trick sounds to me like Penelope rejected all of you as a husband for her. You also say you were fooled for* three years *by this weaving trick. It sounds to me as if none of you suitors is intelligent enough to be the husband of a woman like Penelope.*

"Then Odysseus came back to Ithaca," Amphinomus continued. "He did not come openly. He looked like an old beggar. He visited the swineherd, and then Odysseus and Telemachus plotted our deaths. They came to the palace, first Telemachus and then Odysseus and the swineherd. In Odysseus' own palace, we insulted him because we thought he was just an old beggar. He endured it all, but he and Telemachus carried the weapons out of the Great Hall and locked them out of our reach in the storeroom. Then he told Penelope — we guess, he must have — to hold an archery contest in the Great Hall. Whoever would win the archery contest would win Penelope for his wife. None of us suitors could even string his bow. Then the swineherd carried the bow to the old beggar — we ordered him not to do it. But Telemachus ordered the swineherd to carry the bow to the old beggar, and the swineherd obeyed Telemachus' orders, not ours. Odysseus easily strung his bow and easily won the archery contest. Then he killed Antinous. Next he shot us down with arrows, and finally he and Telemachus and his two loyal herdsmen cut us down as we ran screaming in the Great Hall. Our blood flowed across the floor.

"That is how all of us died, Agamemnon," Amphinomus said. "Even now our corpses lie unburied. Our families don't yet know that we are dead."

"Odysseus is fortunate in his choice of wives," Agamemnon said. "Penelope is totally unlike Clytemnestra, my treacherous wife who took a lover and then slaughtered me when I returned from Troy. Penelope's name will be remembered for millennia."

Odysseus, Telemachus, Eumaeus, and Philoetius reached Laertes' farm. The farm was well tended. Laertes had worked hard on it, and now, even in his old age, he was still working hard on it.

Odysseus told Telemachus, Eumaeus, and Philoetius, "Go into the house now. I myself will go and see my father. I would like to see if he is able to recognize me after my twenty years away from home."

Odysseus left his armor in the house and then set off to find his father. He did not see his servant Dolius or Dolius' six strong sons, but he did find his father, working hard despite his old age. Odysseus was overcome with pity when he saw his father. His father looked like a slave, clothed in rags.

What is the best way to proceed? Odysseus thought. *Should I run to my father and tell him who I am and hug and kiss him? Should I speak with him and see if he recognizes me? Should I reproach him because he looks like a slave? My father is working hard, and work is often a good thing, but my father looks like a slave. One can work and still have pride. I won't tell my father who I am right away; instead, I will reproach him for looking like a slave.*

Odysseus went to his father and said, "You are working hard, and the farm shows it. Nothing is out of place here. All is well tended. However, you are old and you look poverty stricken. The plants you look after are in better shape than you. You work hard, so your master should take good care of you. Whose slave are you? And please tell me — I have just arrived — is this island Ithaca? I want to visit Ithaca so that I can tell my news about a friend of mine. This man visited me and became my friend. He said that his father was Laertes of Ithaca. I hosted him, and I gave him glorious guest-gifts. I gave him seven bars of gold, a silver mixing bowl, and twelve cloaks and other clothing, as well as rugs. In addition, I gave him four women, beauties who were skilled in crafts. I let him choose his pick of the women."

"Stranger," Laertes replied, "this is Ithaca, but it is ruled now by uncivilized men without laws. Those gifts you gave him have never reached Ithaca, nor has the man you gave them to. But if he had returned to Ithaca, you would have found him to be a good friend and a generous host. He would have given you guest-gifts to remember.

"Please tell me. When did you host that man? By now, that man must be dead, perhaps drowned and food for fishes. Or if he died on land, then the wild beasts have devoured his corpse. No funeral has ever been held for him on Ithaca. Penelope, his wife, has never been able to properly mourn for him.

"But what is your story? Who are you?"

"I will tell you my story," Odysseus replied, still keeping his identity secret. "I am a wanderer. I have endured many hardships. I know pain all too well. I sailed here from Sicily, and I saw my friend — Odysseus — five years ago. When he left my house, all of the bird-signs were on the right — the lucky side. We hoped to meet again with him as host."

Five years, Laertes thought. *A lot can happen in five years, including death.*

Laertes grieved, and in his grief he scooped up dirt from the ground and poured it over his head.

Odysseus took pity on his father and said, "Father, I am your son, Odysseus. I have returned after twenty years. I have killed all of the suitors."

"Are you really my son, Odysseus?" Laertes asked. "Show me proof."

"Yes, I am your son," Odysseus replied. "Here is the proof. First look at the scar on my knee. No other mortal has a scar exactly like it. I received it when I visited my grandfather on Mount Parnassus.

"Next, let me share a memory with you. I remember when I was a little boy standing at this exact spot with you. You showed me the trees, and you said that I would inherit them. You gave me thirteen pear trees, ten apple trees, and forty fig trees. You also gave me forty rows of vines with grapes for wine."

Laertes knew that his son was standing before him. He hugged his son, and he prayed, "Zeus, thank you for helping to rid the palace of the insolent suitors, but now please protect us as the relatives of the suitors try to kill us."

"All will be well," Odysseus promised. "Let us go to the house. Telemachus is there, as well as the cowherd and the swineherd. Let us eat there."

Talking together, they returned to the house and saw Telemachus, the loyal swineherd, and the loyal cowherd. Laertes took a bath, cleaning off the grime from the fields, and he dressed in clean, fresh clothing — not rags. Athena made him taller, stronger, and more handsome. He looked like a god — not like a slave.

Odysseus complimented his father, who said, "I wish that I were younger. I wish that I had been in the palace helping you to kill the suitors. You would have been proud of me."

As they were sitting down to eat, Dolius and his six strong sons returned from working in the fields. They saw Odysseus and were amazed — they guessed who he was. Odysseus told old Dolius, "Yes, the king has returned. Sit down and eat, old friend."

Amazed and happy, Dolius kissed his master's hand. "Should I tell Penelope that you have returned?"

"That won't be necessary," Odysseus said. "By now, she has heard the news."

I have killed two of Dolius' children: Melanthius and Melantho, Odysseus thought. *I don't want him to know that yet. They were disloyal and they deserved to die, but a father will grieve for the deaths of his children just as sons will grieve the deaths of their siblings, and I want Dolius and his six strong sons to fight for me when the families of the suitors come after Telemachus and me. Soon enough, Dolius and his six strong sons will learn that Melanthius and Melantho are dead.*

As they ate in the farmhouse, rumors swept Ithaca. People heard of the death of the suitors, and their families arrived to take away the corpses for burial. Ships carried some of the corpses to the nearby islands where the families of those suitors lived. The Ithacan families grieved, and the Ithacan elders met together.

Eupithes, the father of Antinous, rose to speak, "Men of Ithaca, Odysseus has been a disaster to us and our families. First, he left to go to Troy, taking ships filled with men with him. But he returned alone. He lost the ships, and every man whom he took with him to Troy is dead. And now look!

He returns home, and he kills more men! Not only did he take many of the Ithacan fathers to Troy and get them killed, but also he returns to Ithaca and kills many of their sons! Let's go after him and kill him before he is able to escape! When someone kills a member of our family, we are honor-bound to avenge the death of our loved one. A death for a death!"

Medon the herald and Phemius the bard arrived at the meeting-ground. Medon told the men of Ithaca, "Odysseus did not act alone when he killed the suitors. A god was helping him! I myself saw this!"

Halitherses, an old and wise man, spoke next, "Men of Ithaca, you let the suitors run wild. You did not restrain them, although Mentor and I warned that the result of letting a generation of young men run wild would be ruinous. Look at what happened! They besieged Penelope, the wife of Odysseus. They courted her against her will! They filled their days with feasts and music and games, and they took and took and gave nothing in return. They disrespected the gods, and they did not observe *xenia*. Don't try to kill Odysseus! We have seen too much death already!"

Half of the men listened to Halitherses and wanted peace, but half of the men listened to Eupithes and wanted revenge. That half ran to get weapons and armor, and they went in a group to find Odysseus and kill him. Eupithes led them.

Athena, watchful, saw them and appealed to her father, Zeus, the king of gods and men, "What will happen now, father? Shall war come to Ithaca? Or shall peace?"

"All has worked out as you wanted," Zeus replied. "Odysseus has returned home and has killed the suitors. You can do what you like now, but I advise that you make peace between the two sides. Make them agree that Odysseus shall be king as long as he lives. We are gods. We can purge their memories of the death of the suitors. We can bring peace between the two sides. We have that power."

Athena flew from Olympus to Ithaca.

Odysseus and the others finished eating, and he asked one of the others to look outside and see if the families of suitors were approaching. One of Dolius' sons looked and reported, "Here they come! They are almost here!"

Everybody, including the old men Laertes and Dolius, put on armor and grabbed weapons. They were ready to fight.

Athena, in the form of Mentor, came into the house. Of course, Odysseus was happy to see her. Odysseus said to Telemachus, "It is time to fight. For generations, our family has fought well."

Telemachus replied, "Don't worry, father. I will fight well. I will not disgrace our family."

Laertes was thrilled to hear his son and his grandson. He said, "This is a great day for me and for all our family! My son and my grandson are both ready to display their courage!"

Athena, disguised as Mentor, advised Laertes, "Pray to Athena, the bright-eyed goddess, and to Zeus. Then prepare to fight."

Laertes did as she wished, and the heroes attacked. Laertes threw his spear — a direct hit! He killed Eupithes, who crashed to the ground. Odysseus, Telemachus, Laertes, and the others ran toward the male relatives of the suitors, and another slaughter by the heroes would have resulted, but Athena ordered them, "Stop, you men of Ithaca! We have seen enough blood! Generations of men of Ithaca have died! We need no more bloodshed!"

Even so, it took more than orders from Athena to stop the slaughter — Odysseus thirsted for blood. Zeus threw a thunderbolt that crashed in front of Athena — that got Odysseus' attention. She told him, "Stop, Odysseus! If you continue to kill, you will make Zeus angry at you. Making a god angry at you is never a good idea."

Odysseus stopped.

Athena kept the shape of wise Mentor, who was respected by all. She made peace between the two sides, and peace came to Ithaca.

Appendix A: Background Information

Roman Gods and Goddesses

The Greek gods and goddesses have Roman equivalents. The Greek name is followed by the Roman name:

Aphrodite: Venus

Apollo: Apollo (same name)

Ares: Mars

Artemis: Diana

Athena: Minerva

Hades: Pluto

Hephaestus: Vulcan

Hera: Juno

Hermes: Mercury

Poseidon: Neptune

Zeus: Jupiter

Note: The Romans referred to Odysseus as Ulysses.

- **What are the *Iliad* and the *Odyssey*?**

The *Iliad* and the *Odyssey* are epic poems that have been created by Homer. Here are two definitions of "epic poem":

- a long narrative poem about the adventures of [a] hero or the gods, presenting an encyclopedic portrait of the culture in which it is composed.

Source: <teacherweb.com/NC/OrangeHighSchool/MrMitchCox/HandyLiteraryandAnglo-SaxonTerms.doc[1]>

- a long narrative poem telling of a hero's deeds.

Source: <wordnet.princeton.edu/perl/webwn[2]>

---

1. http://www.google.com/url?sa=X&start=0&oi=define&q=http://teacherweb.com/NC/OrangeHighSchool/MrMitchCox/HandyLiteraryandAnglo-SaxonTerms.doc&usg=AFQjCNGaBbztLE3YBGtw0kVDdkCOHVVn-Q

The *Iliad* tells the story of one incident that lasted a few weeks during the last year of the Trojan War: a quarrel between Achilles, the mightiest of the Greek (Achaean) warriors, and Agamemnon, leader of the Greek armies against Troy. Both Achilles and Agamemnon are kings of their own lands, but Agamemnon is the leader among the many kings fighting the Trojans and the Trojan allies. The quarrel between Achilles and Agamemnon has devastating consequences.

- **What is the mythic background of the *Iliad* and the *Odyssey*?**

The mythic background of the *Iliad* and the *Odyssey* consists of the Trojan War myth and myths about the Greek gods and goddesses.

- **For what other works did this mythic background provide narrative material?**

The Trojan War myth provided material for many other epic poems, both Greek and Roman, some of which have survived, and for many plays, including both tragedies and comedies, by both Greek and Roman authors. The Trojan War myth is one of the most important myths in the world.

During Roman times, the Trojan War myth provided material for Virgil's great epic poem the *Aeneid*, which tells the story of Aeneas and how he survived the fall of Troy and came to Italy to found (establish) the Roman people. He and his Italian wife, Lavinia, became important ancestors of the Romans. Later, Dante used material from the Trojan War myth and its aftermath in his *Divine Comedy*. Material from the Trojan War myth has appeared in opera and in drama. Of course, James Joyce uses this material in his novel *Ulysses*.

- **Why is it important to understand the Trojan War myth when reading the *Iliad* and the *Odyssey*?**

Homer's audience knew the story of the Trojan War. How did Homer's audience get its understanding of the Trojan War? Partly through stories told by their parents and grandparents. As they were growing up, they heard tales about the myth. Therefore, Homer assumes a lot of knowledge in his audience. Homer does not tell the story of the Trojan Horse; he assumes that his audience already knows the story. Homer does not tell the story of the Trojan War; he assumes that his audience already knows the story. Without

---

2. http://www.google.com/url?sa=X&start=1&oi=define&q=http://wordnet.princeton.edu/perl/

webwn%3Fs%3Depic+poem&usg=AFQjCNEd1O6O1iYkAZOlEWZIuFs9Lf3-5w

a knowledge of the Trojan War, the audience will not be able to appreciate fully the *Iliad* and the *Odyssey*.

• What is the *Iliad* about?

The *Iliad* tells the story of the quarrel between Achilles and Agamemnon. Following the quarrel, Achilles (the mightiest Greek warrior) withdraws from the fighting, which allows the Trojans to be triumphant in battle for a while. The *Iliad* tells about Achilles' anger and how he finally lets go of his anger.

• What is the *Odyssey* about?

The *Odyssey* is about a different Greek hero in the Trojan War: Odysseus, whose Roman name is Ulysses. Following the ten years that the Trojan War lasted, Odysseus returns to his home island of Ithaca, where he is king. It takes him ten years to return home because of his adventures and mishaps. Much of that time he spends in captivity. When he finally returns home, he discovers that suitors are courting his wife, Penelope, who has remained faithful to him and who wants nothing to do with the suitors, who are rude and arrogant and who feast on Odysseus' cattle and drink his wine as they party all day. In addition, Telemachus, Odysseus' son, has found it hard to grow up without a strong father-figure in his life. The *Odyssey* tells the story of how Odysseus returns home to Ithaca and reestablishes himself in his own palace.

• What does *nostos* mean?

Nostos means "Homecoming" or "Return." This is important to know because this is the theme of the *Odyssey*. In this epic poem, we read about the homecoming of Odysseus to Ithaca, the island where he is king. Odysseus has been away from Ithaca for 20 years. He spent ten years fighting in the Trojan War, and it took him an additional ten years to return to Ithaca, after having lost all his ships and men.

The great theme of the *Iliad* is *kleos*, which means imperishable glory or the reputation that lives on after one has died if one has accomplished great deeds during one's battles. The great theme of the *Odyssey* is *nostos*.

The *Iliad* is concerned with the Trojan War, and the *Odyssey* is concerned with the aftermath of the Trojan War.

• What is the *Aeneid* about?

The *Aeneid* is a Roman epic poem by Virgil that tells the story of Aeneas, a Trojan prince who survived the fall of Troy and led other survivors to Italy. His adventures parallel the adventures of Odysseus on his return to Ithaca. In fact, they visit many of the same places, including the island of the Cyclopes. One of Aeneas' most notable characteristics is his *pietas*, his respect for things for which respect is due, including the gods, his family, and his destiny. His destiny is to found the Roman people, which is different from founding Rome, which was founded long after his death. Aeneas journeyed to Carthage, where he had an affair with Dido, the Carthaginian queen. Because of his destiny, he left her and went to Italy. Dido committed suicide, and Aeneas fought a war to establish himself in Italy. After killing Turnus, the leader of the armies facing him, Aeneas married the Italian princess Lavinia, and they became important ancestors of the Roman people.

- **What is the basic story of the Trojan War?**

Paris, Prince of Troy, visits Menelaus, King of Sparta, and then Paris runs off with Menelaus' wife, Helen, who of course becomes known as Helen of Troy. This is a major insult to Menelaus and his family, so he and his elder brother, Agamemnon, lead an army against Troy to get Helen (and reparations) back. The war drags on for ten years, and the greatest Greek warrior is Achilles, while the greatest Trojan warrior is Hector, Paris' eldest brother. Eventually, Hector is killed by Achilles, who is then killed by Paris, who is then killed by Philoctetes. Finally, Odysseus comes up with the idea of the Trojan Horse, which ends the Trojan War.

That is a brief retelling of the Trojan War, but many, many myths grew up around the war, making it a richly detailed myth.

- **Does Homer allude to all of the details of the Trojan War?**

Homer does not allude to all the details of the Trojan War. For example, one myth states that Achilles was invincible except for his heel. According to this myth, his mother, the goddess Thetis, knew that Achilles was fated to die in the Trojan War; therefore, to protect him, she dipped him into a pool of water that was supposed to make him invulnerable. To do that, she held him by his heel. Because she was holding him by his heel, the water did not touch it and so that part of Achilles' body remained vulnerable.

Homer never alludes to this myth; in fact, this myth plays no role whatsoever in Homer's epic poems. Achilles is not invulnerable. If he were, he could fight in battle naked, as long as he wore an iron boot over his vulnerable heel. In Homer, Achilles is vulnerable to weapons, and he knows it. At one point, he would like to join the fighting, but he cannot, because he has no armor. No one who reads the *Iliad* should think that Achilles is invulnerable except for his heel.

Myth changes and develops over time, and it is possible that Homer had no knowledge of this myth because it had not been created yet. Or it is possible that Homer knew of this myth but ignored it because he had his own points to make in his epic poem.

Another myth that may or may not be alluded to is the Judgment of Paris. It may be alluded to in a couple of places in the *Iliad*, but scholars disagree about this.

• **Who is Achilles, and what is unusual about his mother, Thetis?**

Achilles, of course, is the foremost warrior of the Greeks during the Trojan War. His mother, Thetis, is unusual in that she is a goddess. The Greeks' religion was different from many modern religions in that the Greeks were polytheistic (believing in many gods) rather than monotheistic (believing in one god). In addition, the gods and human beings could mate. Achilles is unusual in that he had an immortal goddess as his mother and a mortal man, Peleus, as his father. Achilles, of course, is unusual in many ways. Another way in which he is unusual is that he and Thetis have long talks together. Often, the gods either ignore their mortal offspring or choose not to reveal themselves to them. For example, Aeneas' goddess mother is Aphrodite (Roman name: Venus). Although Aphrodite does save Aeneas' life or help him on occasion, the two do not have long talks together the way that Achilles and Thetis do.

• **What prophecy was made about Thetis' male offspring?**

The prophecy about Thetis' male offspring was that he would be a greater man than his father. This is something that would make most human fathers happy. (One exception would be Pap, in Mark Twain's *Adventures of Huckleberry Finn*. Pap does not want Huck, his son, to learn to read or write or to get an education or to live better than Pap does.)

• **Who is Zeus, and what does he decide to do as a result of this prophecy?**

Zeus is a horny god who sleeps with many goddesses and many human beings. Normally, he would lust after Thetis, but once he hears the prophecy, he does not want to sleep with Thetis. For one thing, the gods are potent, and when they mate they have children. Zeus overthrew his own father, and Zeus does not want Thetis to give birth to a greater man than he is because his son will overthrow him. Therefore, Zeus wants to get Thetis married off to someone else. In this case, a marriage to a human being for Thetis would suit Zeus just fine. A human son may be greater than his father, but he is still not going to be as great as a god, and so Zeus will be safe if Thetis gives birth to a human son.

• Who is Peleus?

Peleus is the human man who marries Thetis and who fathers Achilles. At the time of the *Iliad*, Peleus is an old man and Thetis has not lived with him for a long time.

• Why is Eris, Goddess of Discord, not invited to the wedding feast of Peleus and Thetis?

Obviously, you do not want discord at a wedding, and therefore, Eris, Goddess of Discord, is not invited to the wedding feast of Peleus and Thetis. Even though Eris is not invited to the wedding feast, she shows up anyway.

• Eris, Goddess of Discord, throws an apple on a table at the wedding feast. What is inscribed on the apple?

Inscribed on the apple is the phrase "For the fairest," written in Greek, of course. Because Greek is a language that indicates masculine and feminine in certain words, and since "fairest" has a feminine ending, the apple is really inscribed "for the fairest female."

• Hera, Athena, and Aphrodite each claim the apple. Who are they?

Three goddesses claim the apple, meaning that each of the three goddesses thinks that she is the fairest, or most beautiful.

Hera

Hera is the wife of Zeus, and she is a jealous wife. Zeus has many affairs with both immortal goddesses and mortal women, and Hera is jealous because of these affairs. Zeus would like to keep on her good side.

Athena

Athena is the goddess of wisdom. She becomes the patron goddess of Athens. Athena especially likes Odysseus, as we see especially in the *Odyssey*.

Athena is a favorite of Zeus, her father. Zeus would like to keep on her good side.

Aphrodite

Aphrodite is the goddess of sexual passion. She can make Zeus fall in love against his will. Zeus would like to keep on her good side.

• Why doesn't Zeus want to judge the goddesses' beauty contest?

Zeus is not a fool. He knows that if he judges the goddesses' beauty contest, he will make two enemies. The two goddesses whom Zeus does not choose as the fairest will hate him and likely make trouble for him.

Please note that the Greek gods and goddesses are not omnibenevolent. Frequently, they are quarrelsome and petty.

By the way, Athens, Ohio, lawyer Thomas Hodson once judged a beauty contest featuring 25 cute child contestants. He was running in an election to choose the municipal court judge, and he thought that judging the contest would be a good way to win votes. Very quickly, he decided never to judge a children's beauty contest again. He figured out that he had won two votes — the votes of the parents of the child who won the contest. Unfortunately, he also figured out that he had lost 48 votes — the votes of the parents of the children who lost.

• Who is Paris, and what is the Judgment of Paris?

Paris is a prince of Troy, and Zeus allows him to judge the three goddesses' beauty contest. Paris is not as intelligent as Zeus, or he would try to find a way out of judging the beauty contest.

• Each of the goddesses offers Paris a bribe if he will choose her. What are the bribes?

Hera

Hera offers Paris political power: several cities he can rule.

Athena

Athena offers Paris prowess in battle. Paris can become a mighty and feared warrior.

Aphrodite

Aphrodite offers Paris the most beautiful woman in the world to be his wife.

• Which goddess does Paris choose?

Paris chooses Aphrodite, who offered him the most beautiful woman in the world to be his wife.

This is not what a Homeric warrior would normally choose. A person such as Achilles would choose to be an even greater warrior, if that is possible.

A person such as Agamemnon is likely to choose more cities to rule.

When Paris chooses the most beautiful woman in the world to be his wife, we are not meant to think that he made a good decision. Paris is not a likable character.

- **As a result of Aphrodite's bribe, Paris abducts Helen. Why?**

Aphrodite promised Paris the most beautiful woman to be his wife. As it happens, that woman is Helen. Therefore, Paris abducts Helen, with Aphrodite's approval.

Did Helen go with Paris willingly? The answer to this question is ambiguous, and ancient authorities varied in how they answered this question.

- **To whom is Helen already married?**

Helen is already married to Menelaus, the King of Sparta. Paris visits Menelaus, and when he leaves, he carries off both a lot of Menelaus' treasure and Menelaus' wife, Helen. Obviously, this is not the way that one ought to treat one's host.

- **Who are Agamemnon and Menelaus?**

Agamemnon and Menelaus are the sons of Atreus. They are brothers, and Agamemnon, the king of Mycenae, is the older brother and the brother who rules a greater land, as seen by the number of ships the two kings bring to the Trojan War. Menelaus brings 60 ships. Agamemnon brings 100 ships.

- **Who is responsible for leading the expedition to recover Helen?**

Agamemnon is the older brother, so he is the leader of the Greek troops in the Trojan War.

- **Why do the winds blow against the Greek ships?**

When the Greek ships are gathered together and are ready to set sail against Troy, a wind blows in the wrong direction for them to sail. The goddess Artemis (Roman name: Diana) is angry at the Greeks because she knows that the result of the Trojan War will be lots of death, not just of warriors, but also of women and children. This is true of all wars, and it is a lesson that human beings forget after each war and relearn in the next war.

• Why does Artemis demand a human sacrifice?

Artemis knows that Agamemnon's warriors will cause much death of children, so she makes him sacrifice one of his daughters so that he will suffer what he will make other parents suffer.

• Who does Agamemnon sacrifice?

Agamemnon sacrifices his daughter Iphigeneia. This is a religious sacrifice of a human life to appease the goddess Artemis.

• What do Menelaus and Agamemnon do?

After the sacrifice of Iphigenia, Agamemnon and Menelaus set sail with all the Greek ships for Troy. They land, then they engage in warfare.

• Who are Achilles and Hector?

Achilles is the foremost Greek warrior, while Hector is the foremost Trojan warrior. Both warriors are deserving of great respect.

• Does Homer assume that Achilles is invulnerable?

Absolutely not. Achilles needs armor to go out on the battlefield and fight.

• What happens to Hector and Achilles?

Hector kills Achilles' best friend, Patroclus, in battle. Angry, Achilles kills Hector.

• What is the story of the Trojan Horse?

Odysseus, a great strategist, thought up the idea of the Trojan Horse. Epeus built it.

The Greeks build a giant wooden horse, which is hollow and filled with Greek warriors, and then they pretend to abandon the war and to sail away from Troy. Actually, Agamemnon sails behind an island so that the Trojans cannot see the Greek ships. The Greeks also leave behind a lying Greek named Sinon, who tells the Trojans about a supposed prophecy that if the Trojans take the Trojan Horse inside their city, then Troy will never fall. The Trojans do that, and at night the Greeks come out of the Trojan Horse, make their way to the city gates and open them. Outside the city gates are the Greek troops led by Agamemnon, who have returned to the Trojan plain. The Greek warriors rush inside the city and sack it.

Virgil's *Aeneid* has the fullest surviving ancient account of the Trojan Horse. Of course, he tells the story from the Trojan point of view. If Homer had written the story of the Trojan Horse, he would have told it from the

Greek point of view. For the Greeks, the Trojan War ended in a great victory. For the Trojans, the Trojan War ended in a great disaster.

- **Which outrages do the Greeks commit during the sack of Troy?**

The Greeks committed many outrages during the sack of Troy:

Killing of King Priam

King Priam is killed by Achilles' son, Neoptolemus, aka Pyrrhus, at the altar of Zeus. This is an outrage because anyone who is at the altar of a god is under the protection of that god. When Neoptolemus kills Priam, an old man (and old people are respected in Homeric culture), Neoptolemus disrespects the god Zeus.

Killing of Hector's Young Son

Hector's son is murdered. Hector's son is a very small child who is murdered by being hurled from the top of a high wall of Troy. Even during wartime, children ought not to be murdered, so this is another outrage.

Rape of Cassandra

Cassandra is raped by Little Ajax even though she is under Athena's protection. Cassandra is raped in a temple devoted to Athena. This is showing major disrespect to Athena. Again, the Greeks are doing things that ought not to be done, even during wartime.

Sacrifice of Polyxena

The Greeks sacrificed Priam's young daughter Polyxena. The Trojan War begins and ends with a human sacrifice of the life of a young girl. This is yet another outrage.

- **How do the gods react to these outrages?**

The gods and goddesses make things difficult for the Greeks on their way home to Greece.

- **What happens to the Greeks after the fall of Troy?**

Nestor is a wise, pious, old man who did not commit any outrages. He makes it home quickly.

Apparently, Odysseus' patron goddess, Athena, is angry at all of the Greeks, because she does not help him on his journey home until ten years have passed.

Little Ajax, who raped Cassandra, drowns on his way home.

Agamemnon returns home to a world of trouble. His wife, Clytemnestra, has taken a lover during his ten-year absence, and she murders Agamemnon.

Menelaus is reunited with Helen, but their ship is driven off course, and it takes them years to return home to Sparta.

• **What happens to Aeneas?**

Aeneas fights bravely, and he witnesses such things as the death of Priam, King of Troy; however, when he realizes that Troy is lost, he returns to his family to try to save them. He carries his father on his back, and he leads his young son by the hand, but although he saves them by leading them out of Troy, his wife, who is following behind him, is lost in the battle.

Aeneas becomes the leader of the Trojan survivors, and he leads them to Italy, where they become the founders of the Roman people.

• **Who were the Roman people?**

The Romans had one of the greatest empires of the world.

• **In the Homeric epics, are human beings responsible for their actions?**

Yes, human beings are responsible for their actions in the Homeric epics.

• **Despite Aphrodite, is Paris responsible for his actions?**

Of course, Aphrodite promised Paris the most beautiful woman in the world to be his wife if Paris chose her as the fairest of the three goddesses who wanted the golden apple. However, Paris is responsible for his actions when he runs away with Helen, the lawful wife of Menelaus. Paris could have declined to run away with Helen.

• **Is Agamemnon responsible for his actions?**

Artemis required the sacrifice of Agamemnon's daughter before the winds would blow the Greek ships to Troy, but Agamemnon is still responsible for his actions. He could have declined to sacrifice his daughter, and he could have given up the war.

• **What happens to humans who do impious acts?**

Humans who do impious acts are punished for their impious acts.

• **What is the Greek concept of fate?**

The Greeks believe in fate. We are fated to die at a certain time, although we do not know when we will die.

In addition, people may be fated to do certain things in their lives. For example, Oedipus is fated to kill his father and to marry his mother.

Similarly, certain events are fated to happen. For example, Troy is fated to be conquered in the Trojan War.

• Do the *Iliad* and the *Odyssey* tell the entire story of the Trojan War?

No, they tell only a small part of the story. The *Iliad* tells the story of an event that occurred in a few weeks of the beginning of the final year of the Trojan War. The story of the Trojan War is not fully told in either epic poem. Neither is the story of the Trojan Horse, although knowledge of it is essential for understanding the *Iliad*, and although the Trojan Horse is talked about briefly in the *Odyssey*.

• What happened the first time the author of this retelling read the *Iliad*?

I read the *Iliad* for the first time the summer before I started college. It was my way of preparing myself to be educated. As I got near the end of the *Iliad*, I started wondering, "Where is the Trojan Horse?" When I got to the end of the *Iliad*, I was very surprised that Troy had not yet fallen.

• Did other epics exist?

Yes, other epics did exist, and we do have some Roman epics that were written much later than the *Iliad* and the *Odyssey*, of course. The ancient Greek epics from the time of Homer have not survived. Fortunately, we know from ancient commentators that we have the really good epic poems. The epics that have been lost were not as good as the *Iliad* and the *Odyssey*.

• What do the Homeric epics assume?

The Homeric epics assume that you know the mythic background, which is why I have written about it here.

• What is the society described in the Homeric epics like?

Homeric society is very different from our society; it is patriarchal, slave-holding, monarchical, and polytheistic:

Patriarchal

This is a society in which the men have the power. Of course, the goddesses are a special case and are more powerful than human men. However, even in the world of gods and goddesses, the gods have more power. The king of the gods is Zeus, a male. Often, contemporary USAmerican society is thought of as patriarchal. I won't deny that, but the ancient Greek society was much more patriarchal than contemporary USAmerican society.

Slave-Holding

Slaves exist in the *Iliad* and the *Odyssey*. In the *Iliad*, women are spoils of war, and young, pretty women become sex-slaves to the warriors who have killed their husbands. In the *Odyssey*, slaves are servants in the palace and on the farm. Slavery is taken for granted in the Homeric epics.

Monarchical

Kings exist in the *Iliad* and the *Odyssey*. Agamemnon is a king, Menelaus is a king, Achilles is a king, and Odysseus is a king.

Polytheistic

As we have seen, the ancient Greeks and Romans believed in many gods with a small g. We moderns tend to believe or to disbelieve in one God with a capital G.

- **What do we mean by *theos*?**

The Greek word *theos* (THAY os) is usually translated as "god" with a small g. Yes, this is a good translation of the word, but we modern readers can be misled by it because of our familiarity with the word "God" with a capital G.

- **Are the gods personified forces of nature?**

Originally, the gods seem to have been personified forces of nature. They are more than that in the Homeric epics, but they are still in part personified forces of nature.

One example is that Zeus is the god of the sky and lightning. Of course, in the *Iliad* Zeus is much more than merely the god of the sky and lightning. Maybe that is how belief in Zeus arose, but Zeus became much more than that.

Another example is that Poseidon is the god of the sea.

Another example is that Ares is war. (Here we have an embodiment of human culture rather than an embodiment of a force of nature.) In the *Iliad*, Zeus says that Ares is hated. He is hated because he is war.

Another example is that Aphrodite is sexual passion. She is the personification of sexual passion. We can say that she inflicts sexual passion on other people, but in addition, she is sexual passion. This is not just a way of speaking. Someone may say, "Aphrodite filled me with lust"; in other words,

Aphrodite is a way of explaining human emotion. However, in the Homeric epics, Aphrodite is more than a way of explaining human emotion. In Book 3 of Homer's *Iliad*, Aphrodite forces Helen to go to bed with Paris. She threatens Helen, and she takes Helen to Paris' bedroom.

• **Are the gods anthropomorphic?**

These gods are anthropomorphic. They have human form, with some differences. The gods and goddesses are larger and better looking and stronger than human beings. However, they look like human beings, and they speak the language of human beings. They also eat, drink, and have sex like human beings. They also feel the human emotions of jealousy (Hera is jealous of Zeus' love affairs), passion (Zeus sleeps with many, many females, both mortal and immortal), anger (Ares becomes angry when he is wounded by Diomedes in battle), and grief (Zeus grieves because his son Sarpedon is fated to die).

• **Are the gods omnibenevolent, omniscient, or omnipotent?**

The Homeric gods are not omnibenevolent, omniscient, or omnipotent.

Not Omnibenevolent

Clearly, the gods are not omnibenevolent. They are not all-good; they are not even just. Some of the gods are rapists. Hera is very capable of exacting vengeance on innocent people. The gods are very dangerous, and they can do bad things to human beings. One example is the myth of Actaeon. He was out hunting with his dogs, and he saw the goddess Artemis bathing naked. He did not mean to see her naked, but she exacts vengeance anyway. She turns him into a stag, and he is run down and killed by his own dogs. He suffers horribly because his mind is still human although his body is that of a male deer.

Not Omniscient

In addition, the gods are not omniscient. We see this in the *Odyssey*. Athena has been wanting to help Odysseus, but she does not want to anger Poseidon, who is opposed to Odysseus. Therefore, Athena waits until Poseidon's attention is turned elsewhere, and then she helps Odysseus. Another example is that when Hera seduces Zeus in the *Iliad*, he does not know that she is tricking him. Hera wants to seduce Zeus so that he will go to sleep, and the Achaeans will be triumphant in the battle. If Zeus were omniscient, he would have known that she was tricking him. Of course, the gods do know a lot. For example, they know a human being's fate. In addition, the gods hear prayers addressed to them.

Not Omnipotent

The gods are very powerful, but they are not omnipotent. The gods can change their shape. They can take the shape of a bird or of a particular human being. The gods can travel very quickly. Poseidon can cause earthquakes, and Zeus can cause lightning. The gods cannot go back on their inviolable oaths. For example: When Alcmene was about to give birth to Heracles, Zeus announced that on a certain day a boy would be born who was both a descendant of Perseus, an ancient hero, and who would rule over the city of Mycenae, which later Agamemnon ruled. Unfortunately, this news allowed Hera to interfere. Hera is the goddess of childbirth, and she was able to delay the birth of Heracles. She also was able to speed up the birth of Eurystheus, who was a descendant of Perseus. By doing this, Hera brought it about that Eurystheus, not Heracles, ruled Mycenae. Hera made sure that Eurystheus was born on that day, and not Heracles. After all, Zeus had sworn an inviolable oath that a descendant of Perseus born on that day would rule Mycenae, and the gods, including Zeus, cannot go back on their inviolable oaths.

• How is the *Odyssey* organized?

The narrative structure of the *Odyssey* does not follow a straightforward chronological organization; instead, it is more complex.

Books 1-4: The adventures of Telemachus, Odysseus' son, who undertakes a journey in order to find news of his father. These books are known as the *Telemachy*, so Telemachus stars in his own minor epic poem. In Books 1-2, we see Telemachus on Ithaca. This gives us a glimpse of Ithacan society, and we see Odysseus' palace under siege by the suitors who wish to marry Penelope. In Books 3-4, Telemachus journeys to the mainland to seek news of his father from Nestor and from Menelaus.

Books 5-8: In Books 5-8 we read about Odysseus and his adventures on Calypso's island and following his release from the island. He does not yet land on Ithaca, but he lands on Scheria, the island of the Phaeacians, the kind-hearted people who will return Odysseus to Ithaca.

Books 9-12: These flashback chapters are known as the Great Wanderings. They tell the story of Odysseus' adventures following the Fall of

Troy. We read about Odysseus' adventures in the cave of the Cyclops, and we read about how Odysseus' men died. This is the most famous section of the *Odyssey*, and in it Odysseus narrates his own adventures.

Books 13-24: These books have a straightforward chronology with no flashbacks. In these books Odysseus returns to Ithaca and reestablishes himself as king of the island and as husband to Penelope, father to Telemachus, and son to Laertes.

As you can see, the chronology of the *Odyssey* is not straightforward. If we were to have a straightforward chronological order of the *Odyssey*, we would have to reorder the books like this:

1. Books 9-12: These flashback chapters are known as the Great Wanderings. They tell the story of Odysseus' adventures following the Fall of Troy. We read about Odysseus' adventures in the cave of the Cyclops, and we read about how Odysseus' men died. This is the most famous section of the *Odyssey*, and in it Odysseus narrates his own adventures.

2. Books 1-4: The adventures of Telemachus, Odysseus' son, who undertakes a journey in order to find news of his father. These books are known as the *Telemachy*, so Telemachus stars in his own minor epic poem. In Books 1-2, we see Telemachus on Ithaca. This gives us a glimpse of Ithacan society, and we see Odysseus' palace under siege by the suitors who wish to marry Penelope. In Books 3-4, Telemachus journeys to the mainland to seek news of his father from Nestor and from Menelaus.

And at the same time as Books 1-4:

2. Books 5-8: In Books 5-8 we read about Odysseus and his adventures on Calypso's island and following his release from the island. He does not yet land on Ithaca, but he lands on Scheria, the island of the Phaeacians, the kind-hearted people who will return Odysseus to Ithaca.

Important: The events of Books 1-4, which are about Telemachus, and Books 5-8, which are about Odysseus, occur at the same time.

3. Books 13-24: These books have a straightforward chronology with no flashbacks. In these books Odysseus returns to Ithaca and reestablishes himself as king of the island and as husband to Penelope, father to Telemachus, and son to Laertes.

• **Which problems does Odysseus' absence cause for Penelope, his wife?**

Odysseus' absence for 20 years has caused many problems. Penelope has been without her husband, Telemachus has been without his father, and Ithaca has been without its king. In addition, since Odysseus took the men of Ithaca with him to Troy, Ithaca is a society without fathers.

Odysseus is Missing in Action. This can be harder for a family than knowing that a loved one is dead. If a loved one has died, the family can mourn and then get on with their lives. This is something that all of us do. Or if we have not done it yet, we will do it later because every family knows death. Death is not optional, and we and everybody we love will someday die.

The *Odyssey*, of course, is set in a sexist society. In this society, women are wives and mothers and not much else. Women are expected to be married. In Penelope's case, she doesn't know if she is a wife or a widow. If she is a wife, it is her duty to remain faithful to her husband and to take care of his property. If she is a widow, it is her duty to marry again and to turn the palace over to Telemachus.

In this society, Penelope cannot get on with her life. Today, a woman can get a divorce with her husband not present, or after a few years can have her husband declared legally dead. Penelope does not have those options.

Since Penelope does not know whether she is a wife or a widow, she does not know what she ought to do.

• Which problems does Odysseus' absence cause for Telemachus, his son?

Telemachus also does not know what to do. Should he wait for his father to return, assuming that his father is still alive? Or should he assert himself and throw the suitors out? Because he does not know whether Odysseus, his father, is still alive or not, Telemachus does not know what to do. If Telemachus attempts to throw out the suitors, he may be killed. If Telemachus waits for his father to return, perhaps Odysseus will come back with an army and retake the palace with little problem.

Neither Penelope nor Telemachus knows what they should do because they don't know whether Odysseus is dead or alive.

• Which problems does Odysseus' absence cause for society on Ithaca?

Odysseus' absence has also negatively affected his society. Ithaca, like the other societies in Homer, is a monarchy. Odysseus is the king, and he has not been present for 20 years. Because Odysseus is not present, he is not able to make Ithaca a law-abiding society. Because of this, and because of a lack of fathers to control them, the young men who are the suitors are running wild. They are not behaving with regard for the gods. They are at Odysseus' palace every day, eating his food, drinking his wine, trying to make Penelope marry one of them and plotting to kill Telemachus.

• **What does *xenia* mean?**

Xenia is often defined as the guest-host relationship. English does not have a word like *xenia*, although "hospitality" is sometimes used as a translation of *xenia*. However, "hospitality" is too weak a word for what the ancient Greeks meant. The word *xenia* carries with it an obligation to the gods. Zeus is the god of *xenia*, and when people abuse their sacred duty of *xenia*, they are disrespecting Zeus.

• **In which way is *xenia* a reciprocal relationship?**

Xenia is a reciprocal relationship between guest and host in both the *Odyssey* and the *Iliad*.

Xenia is a reciprocal relationship between two *xenoi*. (*Xenoi* is the plural; *xenos* is the singular.)

Xenos can mean five different things, depending on the context: guest, host, stranger, friend, and foreigner.

• **Which meanings does *xenos* have?**

In ancient Greece, no hotels or motels existed. If you were traveling and you arrived at a town in the evening, you would look for hospitality at a home. In such a case, you and your host would be *xenoi*.

In this case, you would be a guest, a stranger, and a foreigner. You would be a guest in this home. Because your host doesn't know you, you would be a stranger. Because you aren't from this town, you would be a foreigner.

Of course, your host would be a host.

In addition, you and your host would be friends. You would not be friends in the sense that you have known and liked each other for a long time. You would be friends because you have participated in the guest-host relationship.

By the way, *xenia* is a root word of *xenophobia*, or fear of strangers.

In addition, modern Greece has the tradition today of *xenophilia*, or of showing hospitality to tourists.

• Which safeguards protect against the violation of *xenia*?

There can be a lot of danger in such a relationship. What would happen if either the guest or the host were a robber and a killer? Bad things.

Therefore, there needs to be some kind of safeguard in place. The host must not murder his guest. The guest must not murder his host.

Sinbad's Poverty Tour: Early in Sinbad the comedian's career, he knew that he needed to have more experience if he wanted to be a stand-up comedian. Therefore, he went out on what he called his Poverty Tour. He simply loaded up the truck of his car with some tools and clothing, drove to a city, and looked for places where he could do his act. He would tell the owner of the club that he wouldn't charge him or her anything and he would pass the hat around for tips after his act. This was OK with the owners, as it saved them money. Of course, Sinbad didn't make much money that way, and he often slept in his car. To solve that problem, when he did his act for the last time at night, he would ask the audience if someone would let him sleep on their couch. Of course, Sinbad is a big guy and he can take care of himself. He would look over the prospective host, and if he looked OK, he would go home with him and sleep on the couch. If the prospective host looked dangerous, Sinbad would say that he was going to get his car, but he would drive off. Sinbad was a good guest, by the way. In his day job, he had done plumbing and carpentry work. He would unobtrusively look around his host's apartment, find something that needed fixed, and then he would say, "Hey, I've got my tools in my car. Let me fix that for you." Sinbad said that he always left the apartments where he stayed as a guest in better shape than they were when he arrived.

The ancient Greeks did have a safeguard for *xenia*: Zeus *Xenios*, which means Zeus, the god of *xenia*. Anyone who does not follow the rules of *xenia* is not doing the will of Zeus. This offends Zeus, and eventually the offender will pay for his transgression.

• In which way was the cause of the Trojan War a violation of *xenia*?

Of course, the Trojan War began because of a violation of *xenia*. The Trojan Paris was a guest of Menelaus, King of Sparta. When you are a guest, you aren't supposed to run away with your host's wife and much of his treasure. We know what happened to Troy as a result of this transgression of *xenia*: the Greeks conquered Troy. As you can see, *xenia* is important in the *Odyssey*, but it is important also in the *Iliad*.

- **How is *xenia* an important theme in the first four books of the *Odyssey*?**

We see *xenia* throughout the *Odyssey*. Odysseus is often going to have to rely on the kindness of strangers. He hopes that they will show him good *xenia*. Sometimes Odysseus will receive good *xenia*; at other times Odysseus will receive the worst *xenia* possible.

The first four books of the *Odyssey* show us *xenia* in action. In the first two books, we see the bad *xenia* of the suitors. They are violating *xenia*. They are eating up the substance of their host and are giving nothing in return. They are plotting to kill Telemachus, who is their host in the absence of Odysseus. They are trying to force Penelope to marry one of them. Guests are not supposed to act this way.

Books 3 and 4 show us the way that *xenia* is supposed to work. Telemachus visits Nestor and Menelaus on the mainland. They are excellent hosts, and Telemachus is an excellent guest. Of course, this is quite a contrast to the way that the suitors are acting on Ithaca.

The first four books of the *Odyssey* feature Telemachus as the most important character, and so they are known as the *Telemachy*. In Books 1 and 2, we see Telemachus acting as host to the suitors. In Books 3 and 4, we see Telemachus as the guest of Nestor and Menelaus. Therefore, we see *xenia* from both the perspective of the host and from the perspective of a guest.

- **Why is *xenia* important for our understanding of the suitors?**

In order to understand the suitors, we have to understand *xenia* because the suitors are violating *xenia*. The suitors are not acting the way that guests should act. This is something that Telemachus points out in Book 2, when he calls a council on Ithaca. What are the suitors doing? They are eating all of Telemachus' food and drinking all of his wine. They are wasting all of Telemachus' property.

The guests have long outstayed their welcome. They should have left a long time ago. Now, they have been partying in Odysseus' palace for three long years. Each day, more of Odysseus' cows, sheep, goats, and pigs are brought to the palace to be slaughtered and to be cooked as a feast for the suitors.

One of the reasons, by the way, to be a good guest and a good host is because if you are a host this year, you may be a guest next year, or if you are a guest this year you may be a host next year. A host should feel obligated to be a good host because of the times that he has been a guest in the past. We see that with Menelaus in Book 4, who becomes angry when one of his men wants Telemachus to seek hospitality elsewhere. Because Menelaus had received good *xenia* during his travels, he wishes to give good *xenia* now.

The suitors take and take, and they give nothing in return to Telemachus. Telemachus points out that the suitors give nothing in return. They feast and feast, and they give Telemachus nothing in return.

• **An example of bad *xenia*.**

How evil were the people of Sodom? When a stranger arrived in their city, each citizen would give him a piece of gold that had been marked with the name of the giver. The stranger would be grateful, of course, to receive the gold, but he would quickly find that he was unable to spend it. Each time he would attempt to buy food, the shop owners would refuse to sell it to him. In addition, the stranger found that he was unable to leave the city — the guards would not allow him to pass through the gates. Therefore, the stranger — despite his pile of gold coins — would slowly starve to death. When the stranger had starved to death, the citizens would come by the pile of gold coins, pick up the coin with their name marked on it and wait to starve to death another stranger.

Conclusion

Be sure to read a good translation of Homer's *Odyssey* once you have read this retelling.

I recommend that you read the translations by Robert Fagles and by Ian Johnston.

Ian Johnston of Malaspina University-College, Nanaimo, BC has an excellent translation available for a free download at

http://records.viu.ca/~johnstoi/homer/odysseytofc.htm .

I also recommend Elizabeth Vandiver's course on the *Odyssey*, which is available from the Teaching Company. I have used information presented in that course in this section titled "Background Information."

Appendix B: About the Author

It was a dark and stormy night. Suddenly a cry rang out, and on a hot summer night in 1954, Josephine, wife of Carl Bruce, gave birth to a boy — me. Unfortunately, this young married couple allowed Reuben Saturday, Josephine's brother, to name their first-born. Reuben, aka "The Joker," decided that Bruce was a nice name, so he decided to name me Bruce Bruce. I have gone by my middle name — David — ever since.

Being named Bruce David Bruce hasn't been all bad. Bank tellers remember me very quickly, so I don't often have to show an ID. It can be fun in charades, also. When I was a counselor as a teenager at Camp Echoing Hills in Warsaw, Ohio, a fellow counselor gave the signs for "sounds like" and "two words," then she pointed to a bruise on her leg twice. Bruise Bruise? Oh yeah, Bruce Bruce is the answer!

Uncle Reuben, by the way, gave me a haircut when I was in kindergarten. He cut my hair short and shaved a small bald spot on the back of my head. My mother wouldn't let me go to school until the bald spot grew out again.

Of all my brothers and sisters (six in all), I am the only transplant to Athens, Ohio. I was born in Newark, Ohio, and have lived all around Southeastern Ohio. However, I moved to Athens to go to Ohio University and have never left.

At Ohio U, I never could make up my mind whether to major in English or Philosophy, so I got a bachelor's degree with a double major in both areas, then I added a Master of Arts degree in English and a Master of Arts degree in Philosophy. Yes, I have my MAMA degree.

Currently, and for a long time to come (I eat fruits and veggies), I am spending my retirement writing books such as *Nadia Comaneci: Perfect 10*, *The Funniest People in Comedy*, *Homer's* Iliad: *A Retelling in Prose*, and *William Shakespeare's* Hamlet: *A Retelling in Prose.*

If all goes well, I will publish one or two books a year for the rest of my life. (On the other hand, a good way to make God laugh is to tell Her your plans.)

By the way, my sister Brenda Kennedy writes romances such as *A New Beginning* and *Shattered Dreams.*

Appendix C: Some Books by David Bruce

Retellings of a Classic Work of Literature

Arden of Faversham: *A Retelling*

Ben Jonson's The Alchemist: *A Retelling*

Ben Jonson's The Arraignment, or Poetaster: *A Retelling*

Ben Jonson's Bartholomew Fair: *A Retelling*

Ben Jonson's The Case is Altered: *A Retelling*

Ben Jonson's Catiline's Conspiracy: *A Retelling*

Ben Jonson's The Devil is an Ass: *A Retelling*

Ben Jonson's Epicene: *A Retelling*

Ben Jonson's Every Man in His Humor: *A Retelling*

Ben Jonson's Every Man Out of His Humor: *A Retelling*

Ben Jonson's The Fountain of Self-Love, or Cynthia's Revels: *A Retelling*

Ben Jonson's The Magnetic Lady, or Humors Reconciled: *A Retelling*

Ben Jonson's The New Inn, or The Light Heart: *A Retelling*

Ben Jonson's Sejanus' Fall: *A Retelling*

Ben Jonson's The Staple of News: *A Retelling*

Ben Jonson's A Tale of a Tub: *A Retelling*

Ben Jonson's Volpone, or the Fox: *A Retelling*

Christopher Marlowe's Complete Plays: Retellings

Christopher Marlowe's Dido, Queen of Carthage: *A Retelling*

Christopher Marlowe's Doctor Faustus: *Retellings of the 1604 A-Text and of the 1616 B-Text*

Christopher Marlowe's Edward II: *A Retelling*

Christopher Marlowe's The Massacre at Paris: *A Retelling*

Christopher Marlowe's The Rich Jew of Malta: *A Retelling*

Christopher Marlowe's Tamburlaine, Parts 1 and 2: *Retellings*

Dante's Divine Comedy: *A Retelling in Prose*

Dante's Inferno: *A Retelling in Prose*

Dante's Purgatory: *A Retelling in Prose*

Dante's Paradise: *A Retelling in Prose*

The Famous Victories of Henry V: *A Retelling*

From the Iliad *to the* Odyssey: *A Retelling in Prose of Quintus of Smyrna's* Posthomerica

George Chapman, Ben Jonson, and John Marston's Eastward Ho! *A Retelling*

George Peele's The Arraignment of Paris: *A Retelling*

George Peele's The Battle of Alcazar: *A Retelling*

George's Peele's David and Bathsheba, and the Tragedy of Absalom: *A Retelling*

George Peele's Edward I: *A Retelling*

George Peele's The Old Wives' Tale: *A Retelling*

HOMER'S ODYSSEY: A RETELLING IN PROSE

George-a-Greene: *A Retelling*

The History of King Leir: *A Retelling*

Homer's Iliad: *A Retelling in Prose*

Homer's Odyssey: *A Retelling in Prose*

J.W. Gent.'s The Valiant Scot: *A Retelling*

Jason and the Argonauts: A Retelling in Prose of Apollonius of Rhodes' Argonautica

John Ford: Eight Plays Translated into Modern English

John Ford's The Broken Heart: *A Retelling*

John Ford's The Fancies, Chaste and Noble: *A Retelling*

John Ford's The Lady's Trial: *A Retelling*

John Ford's The Lover's Melancholy: *A Retelling*

John Ford's Love's Sacrifice: *A Retelling*

John Ford's Perkin Warbeck: *A Retelling*

John Ford's The Queen: *A Retelling*

John Ford's 'Tis Pity She's a Whore: *A Retelling*

John Lyly's Campaspe: *A Retelling*

John Lyly's Endymion, The Man in the Moon: *A Retelling*

John Lyly's Galatea: *A Retelling*

John Lyly's Love's Metamorphosis: *A Retelling*

John Lyly's Midas: *A Retelling*

John Lyly's Mother Bombie: *A Retelling*

John Lyly's Sappho and Phao: *A Retelling*

John Lyly's The Woman in the Moon: *A Retelling*

John Webster's The White Devil: *A Retelling*

King Edward III: *A Retelling*

Mankind: *A Medieval Morality Play* (A Retelling)

Margaret Cavendish's The Unnatural Tragedy: *A Retelling*

The Merry Devil of Edmonton: *A Retelling*

The Summoning of Everyman: *A Medieval Morality Play* (A Retelling)

Robert Greene's Friar Bacon and Friar Bungay: *A Retelling*

The Taming of a Shrew: *A Retelling*

Tarlton's Jests: A Retelling

Thomas Middleton's A Chaste Maid in Cheapside: *A Retelling*

Thomas Middleton's Women Beware Women: *A Retelling*

Thomas Middleton and Thomas Dekker's The Roaring Girl: *A Retelling*

Thomas Middleton and William Rowley's The Changeling: *A Retelling*

The Trojan War and Its Aftermath: Four Ancient Epic Poems

Virgil's Aeneid: *A Retelling in Prose*

William Shakespeare's 5 Late Romances: Retellings in Prose

William Shakespeare's 10 Histories: Retellings in Prose

William Shakespeare's 11 Tragedies: Retellings in Prose

William Shakespeare's 12 Comedies: Retellings in Prose

DAVID BRUCE

William Shakespeare's 38 Plays: Retellings in Prose
William Shakespeare's 1 Henry IV, aka Henry IV, Part 1: A Retelling in Prose
William Shakespeare's 2 Henry IV, aka Henry IV, Part 2: A Retelling in Prose
William Shakespeare's 1 Henry VI, aka Henry VI, Part 1: A Retelling in Prose
William Shakespeare's 2 Henry VI, aka Henry VI, Part 2: A Retelling in Prose
William Shakespeare's 3 Henry VI, aka Henry VI, Part 3: A Retelling in Prose
William Shakespeare's All's Well that Ends Well: A Retelling in Prose
William Shakespeare's Antony and Cleopatra: A Retelling in Prose
William Shakespeare's As You Like It: A Retelling in Prose
William Shakespeare's The Comedy of Errors: A Retelling in Prose
William Shakespeare's Coriolanus: A Retelling in Prose
William Shakespeare's Cymbeline: A Retelling in Prose
William Shakespeare's Hamlet: A Retelling in Prose
William Shakespeare's Henry V: A Retelling in Prose
William Shakespeare's Henry VIII: A Retelling in Prose
William Shakespeare's Julius Caesar: A Retelling in Prose
William Shakespeare's King John: A Retelling in Prose
William Shakespeare's King Lear: A Retelling in Prose
William Shakespeare's Love's Labor's Lost: A Retelling in Prose
William Shakespeare's Macbeth: A Retelling in Prose
William Shakespeare's Measure for Measure: A Retelling in Prose
William Shakespeare's The Merchant of Venice: A Retelling in Prose
William Shakespeare's The Merry Wives of Windsor: A Retelling in Prose
William Shakespeare's A Midsummer Night's Dream: A Retelling in Prose
William Shakespeare's Much Ado About Nothing: A Retelling in Prose
William Shakespeare's Othello: A Retelling in Prose
William Shakespeare's Pericles, Prince of Tyre: A Retelling in Prose
William Shakespeare's Richard II: A Retelling in Prose
William Shakespeare's Richard III: A Retelling in Prose
William Shakespeare's Romeo and Juliet: A Retelling in Prose
William Shakespeare's The Taming of the Shrew: A Retelling in Prose
William Shakespeare's The Tempest: A Retelling in Prose
William Shakespeare's Timon of Athens: A Retelling in Prose
William Shakespeare's Titus Andronicus: A Retelling in Prose
William Shakespeare's Troilus and Cressida: A Retelling in Prose
William Shakespeare's Twelfth Night: A Retelling in Prose
William Shakespeare's The Two Gentlemen of Verona: A Retelling in Prose
William Shakespeare's The Two Noble Kinsmen: A Retelling in Prose
William Shakespeare's The Winter's Tale: A Retelling in Prose